THE SYMBICATE 2

ATTACK OF THE LIGHT WIZARDS

SEAN M. T. SHANAHAN

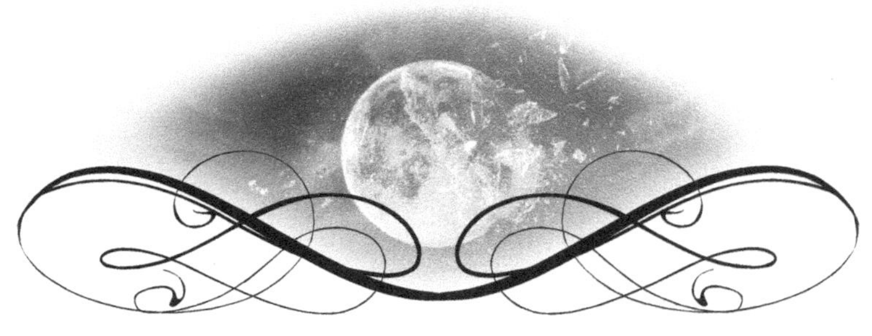

CHAPTER 1

The New Symbicate

Weznin's astronomers were worried.

The shattered moon cast itself across the night sky with wisps of trailing green luminescence—but this was old news. Everyone's eyes now turned to the streak of fractal light that tore through the ether, sliding between the broken pieces of the celestial body. To the unassisted eye, the approaching comet looked like a ball of burning white and gold light, a tail of polychromatic space dust in its wake. The colourful appendage pulsed and wavered as it dissipated into the black void behind.

No one knew what the comet was, or where it came from. What they did know, though, was that it was getting closer, close enough to pass between the broken segments of the pale green moon that the people of the world had grown so accustomed to.

Thomas had no time for such heavenly matters; he had to focus on what was going on beneath his feet ... a hundred paces beneath his feet.

"Deep breath." Thomas blinked into existence.

The sinewy tendrils of his symbioid split along with his body and wove back together in an instant atop the victory arch, the huge stone structure in the central district in Quartrant. He stumbled, and the solid concrete stop-fall—otherwise known as the ground—wavered in his vision.

The last one to wield the Blink symbioid did so against its will. It resisted, causing dizziness and wheezing. But the Blink was loyal to Thomas Marrow, and it caused no such distress. The heights on the other hand ... they were a different story.

He took a breath and tried to focus on other things. *Lovely night for a mission, at least*, he told himself.

The warm breeze caressed his dark olive skin, gently billowing his maroon cloak while the rest of him was rooted in place, weighed down by his swords and the brass armour plates woven into his leather waistcoat. The shattered moon cast a sickly green glow about the neat streets of Quartrant's Upper District even as the warm light of the street lanterns tried to defy its foreboding lustre.

"Okay, okay." Thomas steeled himself to look back down to the square. "I've got this."

His target—a smartly dressed magistrate—strode across the plaza. *Is he a magistrate or a councilman?* Thomas struggled to remember; he supposed it didn't really matter. What did matter was that the municipality of Quartrant had discovered inconsistencies with the cubes to rebuild the banking quarter after it was ravaged by a baulsaw many weeks ago.

Thomas ignored the bile that rose in his throat when he remembered it was Viscount Eric Futruble who had stopped that attack.

The crux of the matter was that workers were underpaid, corners were cut, buildings collapsed, and innocents suffered while someone got rich with red and amber cubes. A sergeant of the constables, having noticed the detectives were too fearful to investigate due to illicit reprisals, turned to someone else ...

The New Symbicate, a collection of skilled agents taking on the mantle of a crumbled crime ring to face the evils of the world. They had met some success so far, despite painting quite the target on their backs.

"That just means we're doing a good job," Tara had said. "The other crime syndicates are getting desperate. Innocent people are starting to push back against them, and they think we're the figurehead of this newfound backbone—the criminals need to take us out."

She had also done most of the legwork in tracking this magistrate ... councilman ... This *aristocrat* who would be the weakest link in the chain of corruption.

The aristocrat strode with arrogant purpose across the plaza and up a set of marble steps belonging to a fancy establishment, aptly named the Establishment. Two large bouncers checked him off a list and gestured him inside. The opening door shed orange light onto the grey ground outside, and hints of dainty music frolicked across the clear night and up to Thomas.

Above the Establishment, Tara slinked through the shadows, almost imperceptible unless one knew she was there. Thomas knew that Billie was somewhere close by too, but she wouldn't let him see her unless she wanted him to.

A shifting shadow caught his eye as Tara scaled down the alley side of the building. She was a lithe figure, slight and deadly, with a long brown leather coat with a hood sewn haphazardly into its shoulders. In place of her red scarf, she now wore a yellow one, a gift from a now gone friend. She slipped through a window and disappeared from sight.

Thomas bit back a hint of sorrow at the thought of the scarf, and the man it once belonged to.

Focus. "Okay, time for some solid ground." Thomas blinked and was met by the strange sensation of his body splitting into hundreds of sinewy fibres that wove through the air and reassembled a way off from the Establishment. "Let's hope this pays off."

As he made his way towards the bouncers, a woman approached from the other side of the street. She was tall with dark brown skin and wore a powder-blue dress that complemented her athletic form. It had strategic slits within the skirt to allow for freedom of motion should she require— the slits also doubled as a distraction for dumb thugs, and she wore silk gloves with a smattering of jewellery. The back of her dress had wrapping wound around a long, ornate device that spanned from her neck to her calves. A strange decorative piece until you looked closer.

The bouncers eyed each other as she approached and produced an invitation; then they allowed her to enter.

Thomas followed up the step a moment after her and was halted by one of the meatheads. He was taller than Thomas as much as he was wider, with a chunky fist obscuring most of Thomas's chest as he held him back. The second bouncer was bigger and meaner looking. They wore dark frock coats that barely closed around their barrel chests and had sabres at their sides that looked like toothpicks in comparison to their bulk.

"Invitation?" the smaller of the two grunted.

"I don't have one; my name is Thomas Marrow. I ..."

"You ar'n'n th' list," the bigger one mumbled.

Thomas got most of the gist.

"I know, you moonrock moron, I'm a Hired Hero. My client is attending this event and believes someone is after him. I'm just his personal security," Thomas said.

"Name?" the smaller one said.

"He would like to be discreet." Thomas coughed. "He did put me at liberty to say that the one after him might be a Baul Islander woman."

The two bouncers eyed each other.

"Has ..." Thomas summoned all of the dread his lack of acting skill could muster, "has a Baul woman entered?"

"She had an invitation," the smaller bouncer said.

"Of course she would! She pilfered it from my client's correspondence just a day ago! If she's trying to get to my client, she'll infiltrate this place for sure!"

"Ca'm d'n," the bigger bouncer said. "D'you h'v pr'f?"

"Is he having a stroke?" Thomas asked.

"Calm down," the smaller bouncer clarified. "Do you have proof, identification?"

"Oh." Thomas fumbled around his coat and produced a leather wallet, offering it to the smaller bouncer.

"I can't read," he said.

The bigger bouncer grunted, snatched the identification from the smaller one, and scrutinised it. Thomas hoped the big guy wouldn't scrutinise so much that he realised his mercenary licence hadn't been renewed in a month.

"Alr't," he mumbled, "No f'n'ee bis'n's."

Thomas looked at the smaller bouncer and made a baffled gesture.

"No funny business. If you see your target, bring her outside."

"Thank you," Thomas said. "I'll do what I can."

The bouncers parted and Thomas was let into the Establishment. He was immediately assailed by overly polite violin tunes and shuddered. *Give me a jaunty jig any day.* He walked through smartly dressed waiters and past a cloakroom into the main event in the grand ballroom.

Richly adorned bigwigs danced upon a large, smooth oaken floor. A grand staircase on the far side ended in a single landing which branched into two flights of stairs running along the wall to an all-encircling balcony around the hall. There was an enormous chandelier hanging from the centre of the ceiling which cast dazzling lights across the colours, sequins, and trimmings of the guests.

"Nobles," Thomas murmured.

He saw the Baul Islander woman in her blue dress turning down an offer to dance while she homed in on Thomas's target. She caught him staring out of the corner of her eye, and smiled. Thomas blushed and looked away, making his way down the other side of the ballroom. There were some Estakan decorations about the place, including rice paper sliding doors leading off to another room where people sat on cushioned floors and drank tea from intricate pots. The room smelled richly of herbs and sounded of bubbling water.

One of the waiters saw him looking and offered him a tray of fortune cookies.

"Weren't these actually made here in Weznin?" Thomas asked as he crumbled open the cookie and ate it while unfurling the message inside.

The waiter smiled. "It's all marketing here. The owner has some tea deal going down with a magnate from the east and is trying to drum up interest in the culture. You aren't a guest?"

"I'm working," Thomas said through a mouthful of dry biscuit. "That tea smells good though."

"I'll get you a sample. Any good fortune?"

Thomas read the little slip of paper. "Your true love is close by."

The waiter laughed. "Mysterious."

Thomas gazed at the Baul Islander as she positioned herself by the exit and signalled to Thomas that she was ready. "Very." He turned back to the waiter, who smirked mischievously. "Don't jam my gears!" Thomas laughed. "But cheers, mate, duty calls."

The waiter bowed and stepped away. Thomas moved up to the aristocrat who was conversing merrily with some poor waitress trying to pull away from him.

"Excuse me, councilman," Thomas said.

The target turned around with a confused expression on his face. "I think you might have me mistaken for someone else, kind ..." he looked Thomas up and down, "... sir. I am a magistrate."

Thomas rolled his eyes. *Who cares?* "My organisation has an offer for you," he said.

The magistrate released the anxious waitress, who scurried off, and he looked around like a squirrel sensing prey. "Are you sure this place is discreet enough for this kind of business?"

"Not really," Thomas answered truthfully. "It would be better if we were to go somewhere private."

Thomas's ears prickled, a lifetime of training and instinct instructing him that the house security was cluing on to him, but he felt other eyes watching as well. His team's eyes, well, he hoped they were their eyes, at least.

"Before I saunter off into lonely places with you, sir, may I inquire as to the nature of this offer and the name of your organisation?" the magistrate said.

Thomas cocked his head. "We would like to offer you a deal, a chance to share information in regard to the cube embezzlement from the Banking Quarter rebuild." The nearby partygoers shuffled away as the magistrate's eyes bulged and the colour drained from his face. "And my organisation is called the New Symbicate."

The violins stifled with a spine-shuddering scrape as the musicians halted their song and the guests turned to stare at the disturbance. The gobsmacked magistrate stuttered as he took a hesitant step back.

Yep, Thomas thought, *that's a guilty bloke.*

Thomas drew his sabre, eliciting a shocked gasp from the partygoers, and pointed it at his target—who threw something down at Thomas's feet. A splooge of yellow gloop squelched out of the magistrate's hand and plopped onto the edge of Thomas's boot.

"Huh?" Thomas tried to stamp out of the gloop, but it hardened and stuck him to the floor. "Cogrust!" he cried as the magistrate barged through the dancers to the alley side exit. "He's woven with some kind of excreting symbioid!" Thomas warned as Eleanor—the Baul Islander woman—

stepped before the exit, drawing her sword-shield from the back folds of her dress.

The magistrate skidded to a halt and lobbed gloop at her.

With a flourish she expanded her blade with the symbioid woven into the mechanism, and it fanned out into an all-encompassing tower shield which took the gloop impact.

"Help!" the magistrate cried as he made for the stairs. "Guards!"

The guests cleared out with a panicked hubbub as Thomas tore his foot from the gloop and Eleanor made after the target. Thomas strode forward, each step with his glooped boot halting his momentum. He struggled to keep ripping the thing from the ground each time it stuck, until a hand grabbed his shoulder, a big, meaty hand. With a sigh he turned to face the smaller of the two bouncers glaring down at him.

"We said no funny business," the bouncer said, with a tinge of hurt feeling.

"Well, to be fair," Thomas's eyes darted frantically between the bouncer and the guards armed with blunderbusses filing into the encircling balcony up above, "no one seems to be laughing."

Knowing the bouncer's next move, and fully aware that his foot was still stuck to the floor, he closed his eyes and waited for the first hit.

It walloped him against the nearby wall and knocked the wind out of him.

* * *

"Ooft!" Tara pushed through the clustered onlookers on the above balcony just in time to see Thomas slam into the wall.

Eleanor was at the base of the stairs and crouched behind her shield as the guards around the room levelled their blunderbusses at her.

The volley was marked by ridiculous trumpeted explosions as the flanged barrels launched shots pretty much anywhere near Eleanor except for her shield. Tara guessed it was *probably* safe for Eleanor to move around under a blunderbuss volley at that distance, but she also knew she couldn't *really* judge her for seeking cover, seeing as she wasn't in their sights herself.

She decided to take out some of the shooters as they reloaded. She pulled her brown leather hood in place, pushed some stray light brown hair aside, secured her yellow scarf across her pale face, and drew her two long knives. *Time to work.*

She sped from the onlookers and moved around the encircling balcony, clobbering with the pommels of her knives and fly kicking the guards from the side before they even knew she was there. One poor man—endowed with *just* considerable enough reflexes—was unfortunate enough to sense her presence, and turned in time to cop a full boot to the face.

There was a yelp from the stairs as Eleanor grabbed the magistrate by the collar on the first landing; he spun and glooped her hand to the wall with a squelch. He turned to continue his escape up the next flight of stairs only to find the final member of the New Symbicate—Billie, who had appeared out of thin air.

She had traded in her black assassin's robes for a long, navy-blue cloak and hood that obscured her face. A single brass goggle with a blue lens jutted out from the sinister darkness. Before the magistrate could react to her presence, she kicked him down the stairs.

Then the wall behind her exploded.

The bigger bouncer emerged from the new hole in the wall with even more enormous muscles bulging from his jacket. The brawn was sinewy and throbbing, threatening to pop the buttons that were already struggling to contain his bulk. He caught Billie off guard and tackled her through the banister and onto the dance floor with such a deafening crash that the chandelier bucked and swayed.

"Whistling steam!" Tara swore in awe.

She took stock of the situation from her rampage upon the balcony. Thomas was dealing with a large but manageable brute, Billie was smooshed against the floor by a muscled monstrosity who was growing more massive by the second, and Eleanor was pinned against the landing wall with gloop, shielding herself from blunderbuss fire—albeit unnecessarily as those weapons were hilariously inaccurate—from new henchmen entering from below.

"I have to do everything around here!" She wove deftly through the henchmen above and flung a throwing knife at the chandelier.

A rather large chunk of crystal broke off and lodged itself into the muscle-y mass of the monster bouncer pinning Billie. He reared and screamed in a pained rage, allowing Billie to slink out from under him.

Tara continued around the balcony until she reached the stairs—the flight with the banister that Billie had *not* been crash-tackled through. She slid down the intact banister and onto the landing. She dropped a smoke bomb to obscure herself, the stunned magistrate, and Eleanor ... at least, that's what she envisioned doing.

In reality—the moment she hit the chandelier with her throwing knife, the gunmen below were drawn to her presence. Something tingled down her spine—a regular occurrence since Masonville—as the trumpeting explosions followed her around the balcony; she hit the banister at the wrong angle and tumbled down the stairs as the wall erupted into splinters behind her. She landed awkwardly on top of the magistrate, and her smoke bomb went off in her face.

She coughed and hacked her lungs clear—as did her target—but at least they were obscured for the time being. She slapped the magistrate unconscious and ignored her coughing fit to feel through the smoke for Eleanor.

* * *

While Tara was stumbling around, Thomas slashed at the smaller bouncer's knee with his blade and kicked at the other knee simultaneously. The bouncer cried and stumbled back as Thomas leaped up and kneed him in the face, knocking him down.

For good measure Thomas stomped on his head—and immediately regretted it as the remaining gloop on his boot stuck to his opponent's jaw. With a swear, Thomas half hopped, half fell onto the ground.

"This is getting annoying!" he said.

The bigger bouncer was lumbering up with a scream that caused the swaying chandelier to tremble. Tendril upon tendril of sinewy symbioid muscle burst through his shredding frock coat. He filled the room and loomed ever more dangerously over Thomas and Billie.

"Do we have a plan for the big one?" Thomas cried.

Billie launched the grapple mounted on her forearm in brass gauntlets and swung around the room in a low arch. As she sailed around the growing bouncer, she launched the grapple gauntlet on her free arm to lace around the muscled monstrosity's legs. With a flex of the symbioid woven into the tethers and latching mechanisms, her grapple unlatched from the ceiling—allowing her to drop to the ground—and the tether tightened around the bouncer's legs. With a confused grunt his legs snapped together, and he wavered unsteadily.

"Hit him high!" Billie screamed, straining on the tether to pull the monstrous bouncer's legs towards her.

As one, Tara and Eleanor leaped from the smoke on the stair landing and slammed into the bouncer from the back. He toppled like a felled tree, and the women sprung over him into action against the advancing gunmen.

Eleanor fanned her blade into a shield, and Tara hugged closely behind her. The sword-shield blocked several more shots as they charged and then Eleanor snapped it shut into a sword again. She swung it around to cut a blunderbuss in half and followed up by skewering the gunman. She fanned the blade into a shield which tore the man in half, and his nearby companions fled in terror.

Tara lashed out with knives to distract and confound the henchmen but ultimately ended up resorting to kicks and punches to subdue them more humanely.

Billie had grappled upstairs to deal with more henchmen rushing in to fire from above, and Thomas had just wrenched his foot from the smaller bouncer's face. He turned, hopping on his unaffected foot to survey the battle. The growing, sinewy bouncer was getting up slowly, so Thomas readied himself to fight him.

A buzzing whirring drew his attention, but he was too slow to turn.

A guard blindsided him.

The guard wielded a small brass fork with a large crank at its base. The guard worked the crank, which caused the whirring sound and generated sparks that leaped between the prongs.

"What is tha …" Thomas went into rigid convulsions as the guard jammed it into his side. The power coursed through him, and the Blink convulsed too. He was vaguely aware of being flung across the room and blinking right into the middle of one of the rice paper walls. It crumbled under his weight, and he found himself in the cushioned tea section.

He shook himself off and stood. "Cogrust, what was that?" he said to no one in particular.

"That thing is called a taser, sir," the waiter from earlier said. He was hiding behind a tea cart and peeked over it meekly.

"Oh …" Thomas said.

The buzzed whirring approached from the din in the main room, and Thomas readied to face the taser again. The guard lunged through the hole in the rice paper and jabbed the weapon at him. Thomas sidestepped and grabbed the man by the wrist; he struck him in the groin with his knee and manhandled the now groaning enemy by the arm to turn the taser against him. The guard convulsed and flew back through the hole in the wall.

Thomas kept hold of the taser and flourished it. "This could come in handy."

"Wait!" Thomas was halted from returning to the fray when the waiter approached him with a small paper parcel held with shaking, feeble hands. "Your tea sample."

"Oh, thanks." Thomas took the parcel of tea with a grin and pocketed it. Then he pulled out a small green cube, tossing it to the waiter. "Buy yourself something nice."

"We're being overwhelmed!" Eleanor cried from the ballroom.

"Oh, right." Thomas made haste through the hole in the wall.

He was greeted by dozens of men entering the room as the giant muscle-symbioid bouncer rose to his feet and roared.

"We need an advantage!" Tara cried.

"On it!" Billie grappled out from the balcony where she had been running interference with the gunmen and pulled herself out onto the chandelier. She fired another grapple at the gas lamp control dial on the lower wall and flexed the latch on the grapple to turn it off. She cut the chandelier cable with her blade, and it fell onto the massive bouncer with a titanic crash, showering the room with crystalline shards and blanketing it in darkness.

Thomas dove behind the bar to avoid the shards while Tara and Eleanor ducked behind the sword-shield.

The henchmen were assailed with hundreds of tiny cuts.

The monstrous bouncer was down, for now.

"Cogrust, Billie!" Thomas yelled. "You're the only one who can see in the dark!" He ducked back behind the bar as a henchmen fired in the direction of his voice.

The room was lit with the sudden flash of light from the powder ignition, and Tara flung a knife an instant later. A cry signalled that the henchman regretted his hasty action.

Billie smiled to herself from her vantage point, gripping the chandelier cable and hanging above the room. She adjusted her goggles, the symbioid within them utilising different wavelengths of light to paint her a picture in the dimness. The trembling henchmen were bright colours in her sight, as were her companions, who were tentatively peeking from behind their cover and peering into the gloom. The massive bouncer writhed under the shattering chandelier with shifting heat signatures—the symbioid was bundling sinews to add to his mass. He would be up again soon.

"Best make quick work," she said to herself.

Thomas, Tara, and Eleanor waited patiently as violent sounds rang out in the dark room. There were punch impacts, there was the wet ringing of blade through flesh, and cries of pain and terror as Billie went to work cutting down the blinded men. After a few brief moments and a few cracks and crashes, Billie found the dial and turned up the gas in the wall lights.

The room shone in dull luminescence. The henchmen were either dead or unconscious—except for the monstrous bouncer, who was stirring, causing a cascade of crystalline shattering as the chandelier shifted.

Thomas hopped over to him on his unimpeded foot while cranking the taser and jammed it into the bouncer's neck. The sinewy muscle fibres of the symbioid trembled and receded as the man convulsed, shifting broken glass while he shook, and finally left an unconscious, regular-sized strongman beneath the shards.

"That was harder than we thought it would be," Eleanor sighed.

"We knew the Establishment wouldn't take to uninvited guests kindly," Billie said, standing from a fallen man and cleaning blood from her rapier. She let her hood down, revealing a young woman with pale olive skin and dark hair, bearing resemblance to Thomas.

Her goggles only had the one lens, as her other eye was covered by a brass patch fitted onto the goggle's leather bindings. She lifted the goggles from her face via a hinge with a flick of her head—beneath the bronze eye patch was an eye scarred white and protected with a monocle set in place with a separate strap around her head. The edges of the monocle whirred with copper gears as they readjusted the lens to compensate for her injury. She smiled. "Besides, that was good exercise."

"Let's just get the judge and get him to Matchins," Thomas said, eyeing Tara.

She was standing over the man who copped her throwing knife in the dark. She was trained from a young age to be an assassin, like Billie, and took life when she needed to, but it never sat well with her.

She pulled the knife from her victim and turned, pulling her brown hood lower over her face. "Magistrate," she corrected Thomas without her usual mirth. "Can we be gone?"

"Sure," Thomas said, hauling the unconscious magistrate over his shoulder and making for the exit with a half hopping motion, making sure to walk only on the heel of his glooped boot. His companions followed, leaving the silent, wrecked ballroom in their wake.

He noticed Eleanor's glooped hand had no issues, but she was missing one of her silken gloves. It was still stuck to the wall on the stairs. The glove was no real loss; she only donned them for the night.

They heard the commotion before they even got to the door; Tara, Billie, and Eleanor took the magistrate and slinked away to other exits. Thomas sighed and entered the circus. He was immediately assaulted by the flashes of box cameras and a barrage of questions as the reporters of Quartrant rushed to the latest site of the New Symbicate's campaign.

"Mister Marrow, Mister Marrow, can you comment on your group's actions here tonight."

"No." Thomas pushed through the crowds to where Sergeant Matchins stood stoically with a team of constables in their navy-blue uniforms.

"Can you comment on why you're the only one who is seen at these sites?" a reporter asked.

"I'm the only one of my team who doesn't give a crumbled moon rock about you lot," Thomas said as they crowded in. "Sergeant," he greeted Matchins as his constables moved in to separate the reporters from Thomas.

Matchins nodded his greetings, his thick brown moustache obscuring any small smile he might have given.

"Can you comment on the rumours that the New Symbicate was involved in Eric Futruble's death?" another reporter asked.

Matchins's stoic demeanour broke, and he barked at the rabble. "That is out of line!" he roared. "Now clear off and leave this do-gooder in peace before I have you all done for disturbance!"

The rabble backed away and the constables moved to enforce Matchins's threat. Many retreated to the far side of the plaza while still snapping pictures.

"Evening, Thomas," Matchins said. "My lead paid off?"

"Not yet, Sergeant, the target was … not cooperative. Some bodies in there for you and maybe a few street ruffians on your lists. We can question the magistrate safely at the usual place," Thomas said.

"Very well," Matchins sighed. "It sickens me our own detectives are too fearful to touch this."

"Their fear is well placed. This guy was backed up by serious muscle … woven muscle."

"If you say so," Matchins said. "I'll be there to discuss the new intelligence with you tomorrow, with a team to transport the magistrate to a very long incarceration."

"Only bring men you trust, Sergeant," Thomas said. "Keep your lumps of wet coal here. Our hideout is kinda nice, and I'd hate to see it wrecked by a reprisal."

"I trust my men with my life," Matchins said. "The only reason I don't send them on these missions is because they also trust me with their lives. You and your team are the only ones willing *and* able to engage in this level of crime fighting."

"It's what Eric would have wanted," Thomas said.

"Indeed." Matchins looked at the ground. "If you would excuse me, I have a long night ahead of me." Matchins moved past Thomas and led his constables into the Establishment.

"Evening, Sergeant," Thomas said in his wake as he gazed up at the pale green celestial night.

CHAPTER 2

The New Symbicate

"So are you going to apologise?" Thomas asked.

"For what?" The magistrate sat handcuffed to the table with a straight back and drooped head.

"My boot! I had to throw it away, and even then it stuck to my hand!" Thomas slammed his palm against the table, rising to stand over the trembling aristocrat. "They were brand-new! Best adventuring boots I ever owned!" The magistrate whimpered under Thomas's onslaught. "Imported from Lathridge—do you know how expensive their crafts are?"

"Pl-Please!" the magistrate stammered.

Thomas's fury paused as the door creaked open, and Eleanor stepped in. "Thomas, can we stay focused please?"

"But my boots," Thomas fumed and crossed his arms.

"Take a break, I'll handle this one." Eleanor smiled and Thomas huffed, storming out the door.

The door slammed shut behind him, and he marched down the corridor to the next room, where Tara, Billie, and Matchins turned to him with bemused looks. They were watching from the double-sided mirror set into the interrogation room.

"You sounded genuine," Billie joked. "Must have been some boots."

"Imported from Lathridge?" Tara raised an eyebrow.

"Well, that's what the merchant said." Thomas gave a sly wink and leaned against the wall.

"I must say," Matchins said, "I didn't realise the good cop bad cop routine was actually a real thing." He stroked his moustache thoughtfully. "I always got the impression that Eleanor would be the bad cop."

"What are you talking about?" Thomas said, pushing off from the wall and taking a spot beside Billie. "I was just venting about my boots. Eleanor is all business."

"I hope this 'business' is legal," Matchins said. "I'm copping the Perversities from my superiors over letting an unofficial organisation take point on this."

"Consider us private contractors." Tara leaned in, cocking her ear towards the mirror. "Now quiet, she's just cracked him."

"Already?" Matchins and Thomas said as one.

They all leaned in. The magistrate was practically spluttering actionable intelligence while Eleanor watched on with a steely-eyed gaze.

"See? All business." Thomas grinned. "In ya pop, Sergeant." Thomas clapped Matchins on the shoulder and ushered him into the room with his notepad.

* * *

Billie sighed as she strode out onto the balcony of their hideout. Formerly a concealed smuggler's bunker, back when it was formerly an over fortified constable station, back when it was formerly a military outpost built into the side of the coastal cliff.

It had changed many hands and was marred by a hodgepodge of tastes both practical and not. It was set into the head of the cliff by a beach that Billie now looked out over. The sand was the colour of shale and was littered with strewn boulders which spread out along the whole beach where Matchins's men had set up camp on the bleak, coastal expanse.

The constant waves broke on the cliff side bunker, sending salty spray to kiss at her neck. Dawn was breaking, but it was dulled silver grey as the morning mists drifted lazily over land and out to sea. Tinrod—the derelict fishing town that lined the upper edge of the beach—was silent.

The cliff bunker fortification and the lack of nearby innocents made this place ideal for the New Symbicate to set up shop. The villagers had vacated the area recently when the coast was plagued by attacks from symbioid woven giant squids—or SWiGS as Tara and other younger people liked to call them. Smugglers moved into the derelict fort after the local constables moved out, and then the New Symbicate took them down, finding a nice new base in the process.

She removed the goggles from her face, rubbing salt and grit from the mechanisms set around the lens and cleaning her geared monocle sitting over her injured eye with a silk cloth.

"That salt will get into your grapple mechanisms too," Thomas said, exiting the doors behind her. "It was always a battle to keep them maintained living along the coast."

"I know how to take care of my equipment!" Billie snapped. Thomas hesitated, and Billie sighed again. "I'm sorry, it's just, I was trained as an assassin my whole life," she explained. "I can take care of my equipment."

"Fair enough." Thomas leaned against the balustrade. "I just … we missed out on a lot of time. I was supposed to be there to look out for you."

"That wasn't your fault, Thomas. The Symbicate took that from us. And we got them back for it; we found each other."

"Have we though?" Thomas looked hard at her. "I still have nightmares about when they killed Dad, about you screaming as they carted you off while I drifted out of consciousness … and about everything that I had to do since. Killing Eric … he's been there in my nightmares too. And here you bite back at me when I try and make up for lost time?"

"You think you're the only one with nightmares?" Billie spun on Thomas with venom. "You think the things you had to do as a Hired Hero would do anything but pale in comparison to what I had to endure growing up as an enslaved assassin!" She shoved him. "Damn you! How dare you blame me for being distant?"

"So because I was a child mercenary and not a child murderer, I'm less justified in my trauma?" Thomas squared up against her.

"Guys!" Tara appeared over the balustrade out of nowhere. "Guys! You've both had bad lives, okay?" She leaped between them and raised her hands in a placating manner. "It's gonna be hard but you can move past that, okay?"

"Where did you come from?" Thomas asked.

"She's a Night Assassin, trained from childhood like me," Billie said flatly. "She came from wherever she wanted to."

"We aren't Night Assassins anymore," Tara grunted. "We left that life. Now we're a brand-new family." She gave Billie a hard stare.

Billie crossed her arms. "Sorry, Thomas."

Tara turned her stare onto Thomas.

Thomas also crossed his arms and turned away. "I'm sorry too, Sybilla," he muttered. "It's just hard, going from guarded to ... not guarded."

"I agree. But don't call me Sybilla, I'm Billie ... Sybilla Marrow is a name that still eludes me."

"It was a name that was taken from you. I will support you until you can embrace it on your own again," Thomas said with a sad smile.

"Speaking of guarded," Billie changed the topic, "don't think you caught me off guard, Tara."

Tara had a distant look. "Huh? Oh? You should have seen the look on your face, Miss Master Assassin!" she chided.

Billie lashed out at Tara playfully, and Tara lashed back. Before Thomas could react one of them had dropped a smoke bomb—one coughing fit later and they had vanished from the balcony. No doubt embroiled in epic, unseen combat throughout the compound.

He shook his head as he wiped the smoke-induced tears from his eyes. "Gear jammed ninjas."

"Mister Marrow?" One of Matchins's constables was in the doorway. "We have deciphered the intelligence into something useable."

"Ah, excellent." Thomas strode into the office from the balcony.

The interior of the cliff bunker was chilly, a lighter shade of grey than the beach outside as it was constructed from reinforced concrete. It had heavy iron doors on bronze fixtures, and steam-driven gear mechanisms powered from a boiler in the basement. It was sparsely decorated save for the eclectic assortment of trophies the smugglers had the time to fill it with.

Thomas sat behind the desk and swung his feet onto it. Eleanor was sitting against the wall, sharpening her sword-shield, and Matchins was consulting his notepad.

"So what do we have to work with?" Thomas asked, leaning back in his chair with his arms behind his head.

"We ..." Matchins was cut off by a pained roar and the sound of some kafuffle moving around the room. "... what's that?"

"Tara and Billie are *bantering*," Eleanor said without looking up. "Sounds like they are fighting throughout the ventilation system this time. It could go on for some while; just carry on."

"Ah." Matchins looked at Thomas uncertainly.

"Ninjas." Thomas shrugged.

"Right, well. The magistrate offered up his contacts of where the cubes were going after they went through his administration's accounts. It seems he was a middleman coerced to funnel illegal profits elsewhere," Matchins said.

"To who?" Thomas asked.

"Slavers."

Eleanor's whetstone slid off her sword-shield with a shriek, and she snapped her gaze over to Matchins. "Where?" Her voice cut through the sudden silence like a bolt through the heart.

Matchins did not react to the change in her tone. "Not too far south actually, a small trade town just on the edge of the Weznin Coast. He also talked about how some of their profits were moving around as a direct result of ... well ... you guys. The New Symbicate has taken down a few crime rings since it formed, and they're getting nervous. There are rumours of people trying to set up shop in Crankod in the moors between the highlands. You know, forcing out little players and getting in with the big cubes there, but they aren't enough of a presence for my superiors to bother warning their municipality about. So far your group hasn't done work there, so perhaps they're running. We also have word about big moves being made by certain organisations you may have had contact with. The Night Assassins have been forcing out the other assassin dens in the region ... I know some of your members have a dubious history with them ..."

"I don't know what you're talking about," Thomas said.

"Of course." Matchins scratched his chin. "Just be careful, these kinds of organisations don't forgive easily. And the New Symbicate is on their list."

"And they're on ours," Thomas said.

Matchins nodded. "I'll be back in a few days with some constables, and we can trade intelligence again."

* * *

As bleak grey morning progressed into bleak grey day, Matchins and his constables loaded the magistrate into the steam engine paddy wagon. It was a two-carriage transport with copper-hued caterpillar tracks—opting to use the shoddy road rather than the rickety, rundown train track that terminated in Tinrod, with big rotting stoppers standing guard on the ridge of the rocky beach.

Thomas and Eleanor watched from the balcony as the engine spewed steam and churned itself to life, chugging off through the abandoned town on its way inland to Quartrant.

"Would be more reliable to take the boat by river rather than brave that rundown road," Thomas said.

"Less eyes on an abandoned road; people would be watching the waterways for strange constable activity," Eleanor said.

"I guess. It's a shame they let the train tracks run down," Thomas said.

"They were maintained by my people in generations past, unwillingly." Eleanor's voice hardened. "Perhaps it is a good thing the tracks fell into disrepair."

"Hmm," Thomas hummed, "I have much more to understand about the world than I realised. Now that I am not solely focused on hunting down my family's enemies, struggling from contract to contract to keep me going, it's like there is so much out there I once neglected."

"What else have you been neglecting, Thomas?"

He tried not to meet her eyes, but their dark warmth drew him in despite his best efforts.

"Much."

The silence stretched between them, a moment that each tried to draw out into eternity. Finally, Eleanor broke away from it. "So we've got our work cut out for us, eh?"

"I guess so," Thomas replied.

"So what's the news?" Billie swung down from the upper balcony with her grapple, and Tara appeared at their side.

They were both ruffled and sweaty but seemed in good spirits.

"We have preventative and reactive plans," Thomas said, settling down from being startled by Tara. "The Night Assassins are making big moves in the world. I should go to Bronstone Port and contact the Hired Heroes, warn them about potential trouble. Bronstone is right near the Night Assassin headquarters at Copper Cobble."

"I'll go," Billie said. "If the Night Assassins are active in that area then you'd stick out like a sore thumb. I can contact your old pals discreetly."

"Fine," Thomas said. "Just be careful."

"We also have potential criminal activity at Crankod," Eleanor said. "Tara, you relish building networks—wanna set one up so when we move in we can combat the threats in a more targeted fashion?"

"Sounds like that's right up my alley," Tara said. "I'll get on it."

"That just leaves the slave activity in a small port called Drifton," Eleanor said coldly. "I'm heading there immediately."

"Why don't I take you?" Thomas said.

Tara and Billie eyed each other.

"We have that steamboat in the dock here," Thomas said nervously as Eleanor's intense gaze turned to him. "We can leave tomorrow when the fogs clear up and be there in half a day."

Eleanor's gaze softened and she smiled. "I'd like that. I'm going to get my things together." She turned from them and left the three on the balcony.

"It's settled then," Tara chirped. "The ninjas will go do the real work."

"And the lovebirds will have a pleasant cruise," Billie finished.

"What?" Thomas felt his cheeks going red. "You guys are crazy. She's … I'm … You … do you think she's interested?"

Tara rolled her eyes and leaped onto the balustrade. "I'll let you sort this one, Billie. I'm off to Crankod. I hear they have a new Mason-style eatery along the Barcos. Can't wait to eat me some more of that!" She leaped off the balustrade and out of sight.

Billie leaped up after her and shot her grapple up the cliff. "Don't fret, dear brother," she said with a smirk. "And don't be afraid to let those walls down either." With a click she shot up the cliff face.

Thomas stood there sweating despite the cold, pondering on the alone time he now had with Eleanor. "Well, they didn't tell me anything." He twiddled his thumbs. "I hope she's interested," he mumbled.

CHAPTER 3

Tara Night

It was a surprisingly speedy journey to Crankod. Tara was in the mind she would have to travel by foot before she realised she had more than enough cubes and autonomy to travel a bit more easily. No need to slip under the radar on this trip, so she could be much more direct.

Travelling north from Tinrod she exited the central highlands and descended onto the slopes of the moors. She met Thomas and Eric in a place like this, much farther north on the Dread Coast. She stopped and looked over the bleak, crater-pockmarked and moon-rock-scattered plains. The dull green grasses had grown plentifully, but chilly winds and grey skies kept the mood damp.

It was a frightful place, those moors, full of banditry and the like in the distant stretches between towns and herdsmen.

That made Tara a trifle terrified—not of being attacked, of course, but of her ability to retaliate.

She pulled Eric's yellow scarf up around her neck, pulled her brown leather calf-length military coat in close, and pulled her hood low against her head, leaving the warming springtime of the highlands to descend into the windswept desolation.

The rainbow comet streaking through the celestial dust tendrils of the shattered moon was more prominent today, even through the grey curtain over the world. It had lost its length and seemed to be barrelling straight towards Tara. It was a beautiful sight that had Weznin's astronomers scratching their heads, but Tara watched it with awe.

After a day's sodden travel by foot, she reached the inlet to the river Barcos, which led inland to Crankod. Her spine started tingling again, a strange sensation she could not describe, but it prompted her to pick up her pace.

Ever since Masonville, that tingling ... she wondered.

She expected another day of walking upstream until she found a town with a boat to take her right to Crankod, rather than dare the paths of the moors. But to her delight, a fleet of barges was setting off from the jetty by the water's edge at the inlet.

"Ho there, bargeman!" Tara called, racing over the hill along the coast and down to the workers who were moments from casting off. "Which way do you head?"

"Which way do you want to go, young missy?" the captain of the closest barge replied.

"Crankod."

"Well, you're a lucky lass there. We were delayed here for a day given the fog; it's a good thing you caught us when you did."

"Luck isn't how I would describe my life, dear captain." Tara smiled. "How much for passage?"

The captain was torn from the conversation by the shouts of other bargemen heading farther along the water, the burning coals and steam from their boats adding dark smog to the grey skies above.

"We're in a hurry, lass. Why not just hop on and pay us a darker blue cube?"

Without a word Tara leaped across the jetty and onto the barge as it pulled away. She turned for one last glance back at the blue-grey ocean as she was taken deeper into the moors.

By barge, it was a cold and damp, day and night journey up the river Barcos, but the weather cleared, and hints of blue sky and golden sun won over the next morning. The dull colour of the grass on the moors turned into vibrant green, and the strewn moon rocks that littered the place took on a lustrous effect. The towns they passed were quaint, with a water mill here, a fishing pontoon there, rustic with brown lumber walls and maroon tiled roofs.

Tara found the time pleasant, no bandits, no need to fight or kill or to use her deadly talents.

But she was blown away once they came within sight of Crankod.

She had heard the stories. "The city run by the dead!" they would say ... and then add sheepishly, "... dead symbioids ..." and it always sparked debate between anyone who had an opinion on whether it was right to call that class of symbioid "dead" or "mechanical," so mostly no one talked about it out of fear of becoming embroiled.

The city was built across a high weir as the moors inexplicably formed a shelf at this junction, creating an imposing cliff that loomed over Tara's approaching barge. Golden-hued buildings with red tops glinted in the morning sunlight on either side of the river, the structures clustered over the two different levels of land, and a curtain waterfall dissected the city at the weir.

The barges entered into the outskirts, and Tara's senses were assailed by rich-smelling food boats, the scents and colours of hanging gardens along the riverbanks, and the majesty of intricate, moving, clockwork buildings. The transforming infrastructure was propelled by mechanical gadgets and gears that were cranked endlessly by the symbioids woven into them.

It was a city of moving sculptures, a hub of trade and exotic foods and culture from beyond the sea and from the lands to the north which were funnelled into the dullness of Weznin.

But that was not the best part.

"Lass," the captain asked, "would you like to disembark here or do you wanna be taken up the boat lift?"

Tara's heart lit up, but she kept her expression stoic. She raised an eyebrow at the captain. "I didn't come all this way to take the stairs, Captain." She allowed the faintest hint of a smirk to grace the corner of her mouth.

"Right you are there, lass, cool yer boiler!" He laughed. "I ain't a moon rock moron for asking. I just needed to make sure." The captain felt no need to be stoic; his smile beamed as brightly as the golden-hued buildings.

The current intensified against them as they progressed deeper into the city and towards the weir-wide waterfall. The river leading into the shelf above was as wide as the one below, but as it entered the city on the top shelf, it split into an artificial delta. It was divided and filtered through clever aqueducts and canals for gardens and water features and plumbing, all before falling over the edge in a mass, citywide curtain of water to be filtered back into the river through another clever series of lower-city-spanning aqueducts and canals. It was so beautiful; the roaring of the water was constant amidst the gentle twisting of thousands of gears and birds and the sounds of busy townspeople.

They finally reached the weir, its shadow looming over them with a damp chill, and they entered into a confined rectangle to the side, out of the current and under the spraying waterfall. It was big enough to fit ten barges twice the size of the ones Tara travelled with. It felt cavernous; she felt exposed and involuntarily crossed her arms.

"Stand by!" the boat lift operator shouted down to them as he toggled switches and levers within his station.

"What's taking so long?" the captain of Tara's barge bellowed up the echoing space.

"Some cogrusted idiot jammed some gears the other day … been dealing with the Three Perversities ever since," the operator roared. "Just stand by, it'll take a moment!"

The minutes passed by, and Tara's anxiety grew, but she couldn't put a finger on why. Eventually a gate slowly lurched up from the depths behind them to seal them into the large space … which now felt claustrophobic. *Stupid girl,* she chastised herself. *You've squeezed through vents smaller than you are. You aren't closed in; in fact you're too exposed. Just relax and this will all be over soon.*

The operator struggled with more levers, and part of the waterfall from the weir was redirected into their chamber, the barges rose with the water level, and they were slowly raised up the sheer surface of the weir. It was half an hour of fretting for Tara, exposed and boxed in at the same time. So much for something she thought she would enjoy.

They finally emerged onto the upper level of the weir, and the barges drifted out of the cavernous tomb and into the river again. They were protected from being drawn over the edge by an iron grate constructed on the edge, upon which was built a popular pedestrian thoroughfare. Tara breathed a sigh of relief as the barges drifted towards the pontoons jutting out from the impeccably maintained river's edge and alighted. Out over the highlands over the drop, the path of the Barcos wound its way through the bleak heath and finally ended at the edge of the blue-grey ocean on the horizon.

The sight took her breath away.

Her first point of call was to find street urchins and pickpockets, and befriend them.

She started by walking around the town, marvelling at the mechanical statues and the wares and street foods with a false sense of obliviousness, waiting for the first bite to nip at her.

It wasn't long before a child pickpocket tried their luck.

* * *

It had been some hours since she alighted in Crankod, and Tara was squinting past her own bloodied nose and down her arm which pinned the ringleader to the wall by the neck.

"Okay," he yelped. "You're in charge! I'll do whatever you say!"

Tara tightened her grip around his neck as the ring of child thieves looked on in bewilderment from the dank shadows of the alley.

"You're damn right I'm in charge, you damp coal! Now you'll take care of these kids a damn sight better than you have been, and you'll report to me, or I'm going to come back and break every bone in your hand. I'll work through all of your other extremities from there." She leaned in and whispered in his ear, "And I do mean *all* of them."

He uttered something that was lost in his trembling voice and slid down against the wall as she released him—defeated.

"Boss?" One of the pickpockets tentatively emerged from the shadows. "He'll take it out on us as soon as you leave."

"Oh, I don't think he will." She shot the ringleader a glance over her shoulder, her cowled gaze causing him to wince as if she had struck him. She turned back to the kid and leaned over, speaking in a hushed whisper, "But if he does, you contact me. I look after my family." She ruffled the child's hair. "When you're old enough I'll put you in charge; until then I need an adult with a bit of muscle to help protect you guys."

"Yes mu'm," the urchin replied before slinking back into the shadows, which erupted in whispers.

"Now here are my instructions until I return: continue to work the streets, beg and thieve only upon the unscrupulous types, and keep your ears open. I will send cubes to the ringleader here to ensure you're all properly fed and sheltered. And I will hear of it if the cubes are used poorly, because you will all be reporting directly to me via the address I gave you. I am on the lookout for other people weaselling their way into your town, taking it on from the top. Keep an eye on the magistrates, constables, and officials. I have built a stronger base than they have, and I have the strength of you wonderful miscreants to rely on. Do me proud." She turned to the snivelling ringleader, who was pulling himself onto his feet. "Now you'll feed them all a hearty meal today and move out of that damp warehouse that I found you in. I purchased an old boarding house on the outskirts of the upper level. Do you know it?"

"Yes mu'm," the ringleader answered.

"Move them there and have them all fed well."

"I don't have the cubes for such a feast tonight, mu'm. Your new network numbers in the hundreds!"

Tara sighed and felt the cube in her pocket. She pulled it out, and the children gasped as they saw the bright orange hue. She was glad they had not seen her purchase the boarding house, when the cube was a dark shade of amber. She slid the cube apart, drawing a yellow cube from the bright orange, as if they were made entirely of light. The initial cube devalued, fading instantly as the yellow was pulled from it. It morphed from orange to yellow to green until it settled on dark blue.

She tossed the yellow cube to the ringleader. "That should keep them warm and fat until I return. Don't disappoint me, worm," she said. "Hop to!"

"Yes, mu'm, I'll get right to it, mu'm." The ringleader bowed profusely and shuffled away.

"Cogrust," Tara swore, as the scuttling of the child pickpockets and urchins dissipated through the nooks and crevices in the shadows of the alley. "Now I won't have enough to try that new Mason restaurant!"

Her stomach rumbled in vexation, and she grabbed at it in angst, ignoring the tingling sensation travelling down her spine. "Fine," she answered her stomach's call. "But we can only afford an entree!" She stalked out of the alleyway and into the crisply lit and smoothly paved roads of Crankod, heading for the Barcos, where she sighted her target earlier.

She smelled it out soon enough and approached the red canvassed shop front with the lethargic gait of one woozy with hunger and travel. Her mouth was salivating at the taste of spice on the air, and she was hoping that her meagre blue cube would be enough to buy at least some delicious morsels.

Her spine's tingling intensified, giving her pause, but she pushed the sensation aside and carried on.

She stepped up the polished lumber steps and slipped, falling face first before the bustling restaurant. A fancily dressed couple laughed as they walked over her to the usher by the door.

"Watch your step," the lady dressed in an elegantly laced gown sneered. "Honestly, the city is now crowded with bumbling oafs. We need to round them up, I tell you!"

"Quite right." The gentleman in coattails with a top hat laughed.

Tara clenched her fist against the cold, unforgiving ground and forced herself up with a sigh. The couple were ushered in by the usher, and Tara ambled to the door, waiting to be seated.

The usher returned an agonising moment of hunger later. "That was a nasty fall there, mu'm. Are you all right?"

"I could have used your help actually; I'm a bit angry you helped those wet coals to a table before helping me up!" Tara snapped. "I'm sorry," she said, "I'm just irritable when I'm hungry."

"Yes." The usher smiled. "I helped them in first because it made you our one thousandth customer!" He beamed.

Tara halted mid-sigh and raised an eyebrow. "What?"

"We have a promotion where our thousandth customer gets a free three-course Mason meal." He leaned in conspiratorially. "On the house!"

Two Mason-born waiters emerged carrying tambourines and performed a jig and dance. "Congratulations!"

"I'm ..." Tara tried to speak in bafflement as the waiters escorted her to a private booth, much to the seething eyes of the pompous couple who had scorned her earlier.

"I'm ..."

The usher handed her a menu. "Now you peruse this while I attend to some other customers, and I'll be back to take your complimentary order."

"I'm ..." was all Tara could manage; perhaps her luck was starting to change after all.

* * *

An hour later the full to bursting Tara emerged from the restaurant with a satisfied belch, thanking the waitstaff and waving goodbye to the pompous couple. As she stepped onto the street, the tingling intensified—then she promptly slipped on a scrap of paper and fell flat on her face, again.

"Why I oughta!" She mumbled incoherent threats as she rose and snatched at the object that tripped her, planning to induce some hideous punishment onto the slip of paper.

But she stopped cold.

She was looking at a vague sketch of herself, hood and scarf up, but with a likeness enough for people to recognise her by her garb. There were also sketches of Thomas, Eleanor, and Billie.

It was a bounty notice.

"Wanted," it read, "by concerned Copper Cobble party — The New Symbicate — each member, DEAD, one amber cube per head."

"Well, crap." Tara scrunched the poster and stumbled up onto her feet, holding her swollen belly as her eyes darted around hurriedly. "Stupid girl!"

Her assassin training had warned her to always check the notice boards when entering a new town, find the bounties to pay your way, and stay a step ahead of competition or disgruntled relatives of past targets.

The New Symbicate had been making waves, and in retaliation the Night Assassins had placed an enormous bounty on their heads. Now any shadow could hide a knife, any passer-by could be a murderous killer, any ... she froze ... any group of armed mercenaries could be a group of armed mercenaries ...

A group of them had just alighted from a barge down the way from her, and she slinked into the shadows between the buildings. The group was mismatched, four mercs, three with copper plate armour under their coats and an assortment of cutlasses and blunderbusses.

One was indigenous Weznin with tan olive skin, another was either new Weznin or Soth with his paler skin, and the girl was probably Mason judging by her dark umber skin.

The fourth she couldn't make out, but he was tall and lagged behind them, uninvolved in their conversation. He wore a long grey robe which concealed all but the protrusion of a blade hilt, and the hood was so enormous that it must have been concealing some giant headpiece.

Tara strained her ears to catch their conversation as they passed her little hideout.

"... here too late, the Needle Gang already turned up this morning by the looks of that bar. The place is crawling with competition, I tell ya!"

"What is the Needle Gang going to do against the likes of us? They're nothing but a thorn in our side."

Needle Gang. Tara racked her brain. *A group of marksmen bounty hunters who don't use gunpowder weapons.*

"That is entirely what I'm worried about."

"It doesn't matter; we've got our own symbioids to level the playing field, against them *and* the New Symbicate lass who was sighted here. And don't forget we've got him now!" The apparent ringleader jerked his finger at the tall, hooded figure. "He's got a score to settle. We wouldn't even be here unless I crossed paths with him down in Oiltol."

Tara tried to place the names. Oiltol was one of the minor towns she passed up the Barcos. *Stupid GIRL!* She was too exposed on that barge—of course someone sighted her. That tall one had obviously been tracking her for a while. *Stupid, stupid, stupid! Who even are these people?*

"I still don't trust him," the Mason woman said. "He says nothing."

"Ah, don't listen to them, Regen!" the leader said. "She's always a bit jumpy."

Tara's heart quickened. It was so forceful, the torrents of blood coursing through her ears were so loud, she was surprised they couldn't hear it.

Regen, the legendary bounty hunter from Estaka. Named after his symbioid, which repaired all injuries he sustained with sinewy tissue. The last time she saw him she left him beside a canal in Masonville, with most of his blood *outside* of his body. He lost so much blood, he couldn't even speak. He must have a grudge, and seemed the type to tailor his training to Tara's tactic and come after her for revenge.

"COGRUST!" she would have cried if her jaw wasn't locked rigid.

I've got to get out of here and warn the others!

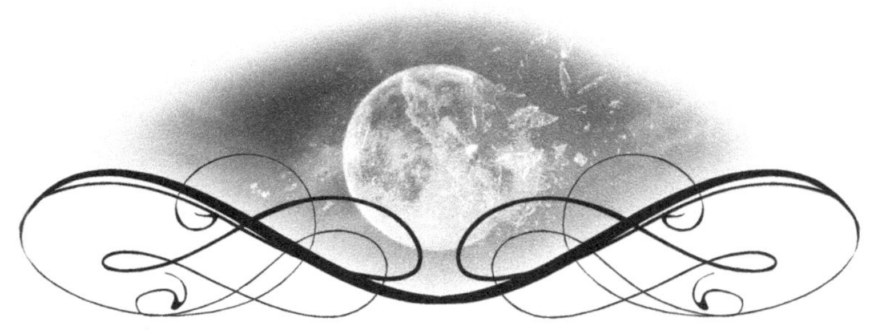

CHAPTER 4

Thomas Marrow

Thomas struggled against the knife inching closer to his heart. He struggled with all of the strength that propelled him through years of revenge seeking. But it amounted to nothing. He was only a boy, weak and coughing in the smoke of his dead father's workshop as they hauled his sister away.

His haste for vengeance was so great that he did not stop as he would normally to deescalate the situation.

And in his haste, he did something terrible.

The knife slipped through the ether of the dream world and plunged into Eric's heart. His friend's heart.

Eric's eyes bulged, full of grief, full of betrayal.

"Why?" He uttered amidst blood and bile.

"He tore my family to bits," Thomas blubbered.

"He's my uncle." Eric sank to the cold, hard ground and dragged Thomas with him in his death grip. "You kill your friend because he is protecting his family, like you tried when you were but a weak child. And that's all you are, all you'll ever be. A weak, selfish child, hell-bent on petty revenge. That's the real why."

Eric's body faded from the world, and Thomas was left alone for a time in that empty quadrangle. It was overflowing with mist which shone green under the shattered moon. And something emerged from that mist with a shambling gait.

"You do not deserve the life you crave!" it rasped. "Let your folly take it from you!"

The corpse lunged at Thomas, exploding with the insidious tendrils of the rampant symbioid infection, Rella.

Thomas awoke in a dark room, screaming bloody murder. A woman's hands held his face trying to usher some calm.

"Thomas, be still."

He battled cold sweat and numb limbs, attempting to swat away some attacker, which he realised were his own numb limbs. The tendrils of death that were encircling him were just his hands, and the hands of Eleanor, in her nightgown. She broke away for a moment to turn up her oil lamp, and the room was illuminated in a warm, friendly glow.

"Thomas, are you all right?"

"Eleanor?"

"Yes, you're back with us now, be still," she cooed, stroking his hair.

"I'm sorry, I didn't mean to wake you. I must have been screaming so loudly for you to bolt in here like that."

She smirked. "You are in my room, hero."

Thomas looked around, noting the sword-shield racked on the wall above the bed. The bedposts were decorated with frilled adornments and cross-stitched patterns. He noticed Eleanor's clothes dumped in a heap on her desk chair and the scent of subtle perfumes.

"I sleep-walked ... I mean, slept-walked ... in here?" Thomas asked.

"No, you fool." She laughed. "I keep my door bolted at all times. You blinked in here. I nearly gutted you." She tapped the blade of her curved dagger against his leg. "Luckily I was only just to bed; my mind is fraught with toil lately ... as it seems yours is too."

"I blinked in here?"

"Yes." She paused. "It was quite terrifying actually. Your eyes were open, but you weren't there."

"But I can't blink through solid objects," Thomas wondered, his breath returning to normal.

"You were quite distraught. Perhaps that drove your symbioid to take drastic action?"

Thomas remembered how the electronic prodder—the taser—had sent him blinking through a paper wall not a day ago; he assumed he just barged through it, but apparently not. "Not an action I'd like to take again. I wouldn't want to end up inside a wall."

"What troubles you, Thomas?" She caressed his hair again.

His heartbeat eased, and tingles ran down his skin. "Just nightmares from my journey of vengeance."

"About putting Constantine away?" she asked. Thomas looked away. "About your friend Eric? I was there, Thomas. It was a clean kill."

"What is that? I've killed many people in my years. I don't think I could ever really say any of them were clean."

"You were trying to incapacitate him, and he was trying to kill you!"

"Because I was trying to kill his uncle. I would have done the exact same thing even if he had committed atrocities!" Thomas batted her hand away and pushed off the bed to pace the room. "I am destined for a life of retribution."

"So you won't allow any goodness into your life, even though you helped pull Tara and your sister from the depths of the Night, even though you presented me an opportunity to avoid the same vengeful path you yourself had set out upon?"

"Tara saved Billie. I just happened to turn up. You decided to break from your mother's crusade on your own." Thomas leaned against her desk, looking at her. "Is that what's jammed your gears?"

Eleanor glanced away. "Yes, that and," she glanced back at him and then away again, "that and other things of a more trivial nature."

"We can put it behind us on the morrow," Thomas said. "The fog should be cleared, and I'll take us down to Drifton within a day. More than enough time to intercept those slavers." He waited for her to reply, but found only half-committed glances. His heart quickened again. "Well, good night then." Thomas unbolted the door and was halfway out when Eleanor called out to him.

"Do you need any company?"

Thomas hesitated. He yearned for her company, but the words of his dreams rang clearly through his mind as if someone had spoken them out loud. *You do not deserve the life you crave.*

"No thank you," Thomas said. "We should try and rest. Good night, Miss Brune."

"Good night," Eleanor said as Thomas stormed away. She rose to relock the door and sighed. "Mister Marrow."

* * *

As the bright, late morning sun steamed away the last remnants of fog, Thomas was busy at work. He tinkered with some contraption by the workbench in the cave dock under the cliff. The sea lapped gently about the pontoon, causing the moored boat to sway lullingly within the secret cove. The air was still, salty, and cool, lit amber by brass gas lamps lining the damp walls.

Despite the chill, Thomas was sweating.

He had spent the morning shovelling coal into the boat's furnace. It burned fiercely, which drove the sea chill from the cave, and the steam hissing from the mechanisms onboard increased the humidity. But that wasn't why he was sweating.

"Are you well rested, Mister Marrow?" Eleanor said as she gracefully descended the stairs into the cave.

"As rested as I'll ever be. About last night ..."

"It's quite all right." She smiled. "It's been some time since a man has entered my room so enthusiastically and then left so shortly afterwards."

Thomas raised an eyebrow, and they shared a bemused gaze. The silence grew between them. Thomas laughed first.

"What are you tinkering with over there?" she asked.

"Just going through the backlog of equipment we inherited from the bandits who once lived here. Four dozen aerobreaks." Thomas hit the rack with his ratchet, ringing a tone that echoed throughout the cave. "Who would have thought those bastards were capable of such a ploy, cliff jumping onto unsuspecting merchant tugs hugging the coast—ingenious really." He shook his head in wonder.

"Will we need them?" Eleanor asked.

"Not at all." Thomas pocketed the ratchet and moved to the gangway, ushering Eleanor onto the small tugboat. "I just like to tinker around."

"That isn't what you were tinkering with though." She strode over to the workbench, sliding her hand over the warm copper bulbs Thomas was trying to distract her from. They billowed steam happily, like the boat. "Is this a teapot?"

"Ah." Thomas hesitated. "I was brewing some of that tea the waiter gave me from the Establishment."

"But with this ... contraption?" Eleanor gestured at the intricate mechanical display which twisted and bobbed as the heat eddied throughout the different devices.

"I was toying around with an idea, that maybe, maybe after ... it's stupid really."

"Not at all," Eleanor said as she reached for the teapot with a cosy on it and poured the dark liquid into two terracotta mugs. She took them both and sat with her feet over the edge of the pontoon. "Join me for one?"

Thomas shrugged and sat with her, taking the tea. "Thanks."

"You made it." She took a drawn-out slurp of the steaming substance. "You made it quite well."

"You drink tea horribly." Thomas nudged her, sipping from his own.

She nudged him back. "So what idea were you toying around with?"

Thomas took a longer draught and lowered the mug; he looked hard at Eleanor, and decided to trust her. "I had this vision when I first tried this tea. Maybe I could order a shipment and have my own tea shop somewhere. Imagine it, full of novelty tinkered kettles and intricate brewing mechanisms. A shop of oaken shelves and brass and glass devices brimming with steam and the lovely, bitter smell of different herbs ... When I envisioned that, it was like, it was like I could imagine a life other than this, other than the path I was set on." He finished rambling, looking down at the dark, lapping waters as he waited for her to laugh at him.

Instead of laughing, she rested her head on his shoulder. "That sounds wonderful. I've often wondered what I would do if my crusade were to end. It never seemed likely though."

"Tell me about it."

"But something homely, like your shop, something warm and pleasant ... Cogrust!" The cool sea water splashed her foot, and she dropped her mug with a yelp. It plopped into the body of dark water and sunk into the depths. "Moon rock moron!" she yelped again as she shot up onto her feet. "Let's just get on with this!" She stalked down the gangway towards the boat.

Thomas downed his tea quickly and placed the mug to the side, a sad smirk on his lips as he boarded the boat. "I let those thoughts of another life swirl in, and the cosmos itself cuts it short," he muttered to himself and made for the control panel on the tug. "Guess I really don't deserve what I crave," he said, even quieter still.

"Is this going to be safe?" Eleanor asked from the bow.

"I should be able to see the rocks now that the fog is gone and the sky is clear," he replied as the small boat chugged out of the cave and turned down the coast. "Whistling steam, that rainbow comet has gotten closer."

Eleanor scanned the heavens, squinting to see between the drifting shards of moon, ghostly pale in the daylight and ensnared in pale, luminous green tendrils of cosmic dust.

"I can't see it too well," she said. "But I was more worried about giant squid attacks."

"You're more likely to be struck by lightning than encounter one of those," Thomas said. "Except for ..." He went quiet.

"Except for what?" Eleanor asked.

"Except for, well, I've totally come across one, and it sank the ship I was on." Thomas paled. "Maybe we should walk." He half smirked again. "Then again, maybe we should have an adventure!" He spun the wheel, taking the boat farther out from the black jagged rocks that rose from the blue-grey sea.

Eleanor shuffled back from the railing and crossed her arms. "You enjoy this too much!" she cried.

Thomas laughed, the sound cut short by the cries from seagulls and the grunts of the seals amassing on the grey sands of the beach. He waved them goodbye as the little steam tug carried them to their destination.

* * *

The journey passed with minor pleasantries and comfortable silences. As the sun rose it faded the rest of the crumbled moon and approaching rainbow comet from view. It cast golden lances across the breaking waves of the sea, and by the time they reached the midpoint of their journey, it was soaring overhead. This was when they crossed south of Arrow Point—the obtuse, jutting piece of land that marked the centre of the Weznin coast. The sun then dipped farther inland with the afternoon, as they came within sight of their destination, Drifton.

It was a dingy town—more a glorified fishing village than a port of wares—constructed mostly over a shallow bay with damp wooden structures, thatched with hay roofs and supported by thin stilts. The lumber was gnarled and may have been mostly rot at this point, but it was the only thing keeping the town above water.

Thomas slipped a greening blue cube to the dockmaster as they offloaded onto the rickety pontoons, who shoved it under his oversized tricorne hat and noted the arrival of two nameless prospecting traders from Soth. Thomas and Eleanor exchanged looks at this marking on the manifest. Soth were ginger-haired people from across the south sea with skin brighter than the beam of a lighthouse. Thomas's dark hair and tanned olive skin with Eleanor's brown Baul Islander complexion did not suit this cover one bit.

But the town was dead, save for a tall mast ship in dock and a smattering of fishing vessels—no one would look too closely at their minor vessel.

"Shall we find the Jaunt Saloon?" Eleanor asked.

"No need, I think we've found an ally." Thomas gestured to the end of the docks, where a Baul Islander man with green robes and a sword-shield strapped to his back waited.

Eleanor's eyes widened. "Alexander?" She charged down the pontoon and threw her arms around the Baul Islander, who stood stoically.

"Hello, sweet sister," he said through strain. "I am so glad and so sorry to see you here."

Eleanor leaned back. "Why are you saddened, Alexander?"

"Because you left the family, Eleanor, and Mother can't have that."

Several Islanders sprung from the stalls and crates with weapons drawn. Thomas blinked forward in an instant, his own sword flourished from his cloak and into his hand.

Eleanor laughed. "Please, Alexander," she flicked her brother on the nose, "even if you wanted to kill me, these warriors aren't enough to handle me alone, let alone with my friend here backing me up."

Alexander glanced at Thomas. Thomas glanced back and nodded. "Hi, ah, Eleanor has told me a lot about you."

"I know nothing about you." Alexander narrowed his eyes. "But you made enough of an impression on my sister to justify her abandoning our purpose. I also heard about a mercenary who teleports as you do. Are you the viscount?"

Thomas stiffened. "That man is dead."

"Alexander," Eleanor cut in. "Where is she?"

"Mother is watching from over yonder."

Eleanor and Thomas followed Alexander's gesture; he pointed past his armed comrades to a two-storied salon across the gravelly path where the stilted town latched onto land. A familiar piano jig spilled from the swinging windows and over the drunken debauchery that was taking place around it. The jig was jaded, as if the player piano had not been maintained, as if the salty air had gotten into the strings and gears.

"Great." Eleanor smiled. "I can tell her to un-jam her gears to her face."

Alexander blanched. "You wouldn't disrespect Mother like that!"

"I won't use those words," Eleanor said bitterly. "But this kind of response is infuriating. I left the family because I didn't want to be a mindless butcher anymore. I'm still fighting for our people, Alexander, just differently."

"How are you fighting for our people?" Alexander asked, his eyes hardening.

"I'm here, aren't I?" Eleanor responded. "Evidently you're here because you got the same information I did about a slave ring operating from this port. Only I suspect my methods only involved the one scrap and an interrogation rather than the family's usual bloody methods."

Alexander stared her down. Thomas flitted his eyes between the potential assailants, all eying him with the same hate they threw at any of the Weznin people. And Thomas didn't blame them one bit. The things his country did to their people was a dark stain on Weznin's history.

"Excuse me?" The band of fighters turned to the dockmaster, who had limped over without a care for their menacing looks. "I'm sure this is all quite important, but if you could clear the docks? We have a shipment due out soon, and you're impeding the workers."

The band turned to the dockworkers smoking across the street, who watched the altercation with boredom. This kind of thing must happen often around here.

"We'll clear right off," Thomas said and flourished and sheathed his blade. "Let's go meet this mother of yours, Eleanor. I could use a drink."

Thomas, Eleanor, and her brother trundled along the creaking, stilted path until they reached the gravelly land and headed for the jaunt saloon—an information broker of sorts that always presented itself as a sagging, wooden slat building which, for once, matched the aesthetic of the surrounding town. They pushed through the swinging slat doors; the other Islanders stayed out on the patio with the belligerent drunks. The trio was immediately assailed by the scents of alcohol and bad odour, and their ears rang with the sound of hearty banter, as well as the sounds of fists colliding with faces, and the ever-present jig on the failing player piano.

Eleanor scrunched her face. Thomas smirked. As much as he hated debauchery, this was a familiar scene.

"She's upstairs, Eleanor," Alexander said, gesturing to the stairs on the far side of the bar.

Eleanor glanced up and took a deep breath before leading the way.

Upon climbing the rickety staircase, they found a balcony looking over the chaos below, with hallways shooting off towards the barely liveable rooms that the saloon offered. Sitting on an empty table, smoking a gnarled pipe, was the head of the Brune family.

"Hello, Mother," Eleanor said reverently. "I'm glad to see that you are well."

Thomas cocked his head.

Madam Brune was a frail-looking woman, dark-skinned and wrinkled with greying hair. But there was something to the way she sat, something to her posture that set alarm bells ringing in his head. They gave up their warnings, stunned silent when she turned the might of her withering gaze onto him. The malice in those eyes, the sheer predatory anger, it almost shook him to bits.

But he remained stoic, not from any sense of bravado—he was used to battling the terrible and dangerous folk of the world.

"So this is the boy who has spirited you away?" she said, her voice hard.

"Yes, Mother ... no, Mother ... this is Thomas Marrow."

"Pleasure to meet you," Thomas said with a small bow.

"Oh?" Her wrinkled brows creaked into an arch, and she puffed foul smoke across the table. "Full of false charm this one."

"False charm, Madam Brune?"

In a blink of an eye she had risen, cutting through her pipe smoke to have a curved blade at Thomas's gut. The smoke held the shape of her passing form for an instant before billowing away.

"You will speak when spoken to!"

Thomas glanced at Eleanor and blinked. The sinewy form of his symbioid broke him down into tendrils of matter which passed around the matriarch and reassembled where she was originally sitting. As sharp as a tack, she had already turned to face him by the time he blinked back into existence. He casually picked up her discarded pipe and took a draught.

"By all means then ..." He coughed horribly, holding up a finger—asking for a moment—as he beat his chest with his fist. "Sorry, shouldn't have tried to look casual. I hate this stuff." He coughed even harder. He gained control of his fit and looked at his aggressor with watering eyes. "By all means," he attempted again, "deal with your daughter then. I'll wait."

"You upstart little ..." She made her way around the table, but Eleanor caught her arm.

"Mother, enough! He is an ally to our cause!"

"An ally, is he? Would an ally steal your daughter away? Take her from the one fight that's been her focus her whole life, strip your people of one of their greatest defenders? Hmm?"

"I can't keep fighting like you do, Mother. It's tearing my soul apart!"

"Like the souls of our ancestors? Chained and bought for, shipped across the seas, and made to perform back-breaking labours until death?" She flipped the knife around her calloused fingers.

"There is such a shipment arriving today," Thomas said with a gravelly voice, his eyes still watering. "Eleanor and I were here to liberate the slaves and probe the slavers for information on their network."

Madam Brune glared daggers at Thomas, but Eleanor took her attention again.

"He is right, Mother, I am still fighting for our cause. We are here to fight it, but with the New Symbicate, we are also taking down the web of crime rings that help prop up the slave trade. Mother, he is an ally, and I will fight you to defend him!"

Madam Brune glanced at her daughter. *With contempt, with pride?* Thomas had already given up trying to read her.

"You have grown much in your absence, daughter," she finally said, sitting at the table. "My pipe, boy." Thomas handed her the smoking pipe. "Perhaps it has been good for you to get away for a bit. You did seem … shaky, once we slaughtered the smugglers in the Den at Shanty Towers … not enough to waver your conviction, but enough for me to see that you are paying a toll that should have resided solely with me."

"It is my duty to share that toll, Mother. I am just paying it a different way now." Eleanor sat and embraced her. "It is good to see you."

Madam Brune acquiesced and hugged her back. "You too, daughter, you too."

"So," Thomas said, "may I speak now?"

"You may speak, boy, but know that your shipment has been delayed. Our recent actions on the Baul Islands halted their ship. It eventually broke away and fled north, I assume it knows we were waiting for it here."

"Then where will it go?" Thomas asked. "We have to help those people."

"There is a town farther north; it'll take some two days to sail there. My son was chartering a ship when he saw you."

"I can transport us. We can rest after the first day at our stronghold," Thomas said. "So long as we *are* allies?" He smiled mischievously.

"So long as we are," the matriarch said, taking another drag on her pipe and billowing smoke into Thomas's face again.

His vision was obscured, but not before he saw Eleanor's half-hidden smile.

CHAPTER 5

Billie Night

illie stalked into Bronstone under a twilight of fast-moving clouds. Streaks of golden sun cut through the shifting grey sky like bright, diced ribbon, and the wet cobblestone road danced like a surface of flat flame. In the waning light her robed form blended into the sides of the road, beneath rocky overhangs and half-ruined brick structures as she made her way into the port town.

The gulls cried on the salty wind, and the smell of fish rose to meet her. Billie grimaced; the air was always too heavy by the coast. She longed for the clear mountain air. But the high peaks in the distance nested the den of predators she was trying to avoid.

She entered the town proper and made for the central plaza by the docks, melding into the small crowds of business owners heading home for the night, in groups of fishermen on their way to debauchery, and among the lackadaisical Hired Heroes who wandered around, off duty.

She did not fit in, a silent shadow among the casual mouth-breathers of the port. But she could go unnoticed nonetheless.

Making her way to the notice boards, she perused the lay of the land. The damp and mottled papers pinned to the poorly covered display surfaces revealed a wealth of knowledge. They provided information on anything a travelling assassin could need for the local area. Reading through the boards, she took note of the petty thieves stupid enough to gain warrants and bounties this close to a merc town, and of far-flung criminals who had managed to spread the municipal nets too thin, and of the odd side mission to pay for a night and meal in a respectable establishment ... but mostly, it warned her of danger.

"Cogrust ..." She stopped perusing, drawn to the newest addition to the board.

It had tacked-up sketches of the faces of her companions, and her brother. The posts were titled "Wanted, New Symbicate, offshoot of former criminal organisation. One amber cube each, DEAD."

"That's troubling," she whispered, ensuring that her goggles were clicked up in place beneath her baggy hood as she regarded the crisscrossed sketch of herself; hooded, lenses protruding, with a rough estimation of her pointed jawline and thin lips. *Will the Heroes take this up?* she pondered. *Will they believe we are criminals?*

She paused over Thomas's portrait; it had bold red writing scrawled over the description. "YEAH, RIGHT. *He's* a hardened criminal? Then I'm the Duke of Weznin."

She smiled. "Perhaps not."

She swept her gaze around the damp square, finding disenfranchised eyes belonging to worn-out locals who stared into the distance, expecting another cold night ahead. No one seemed to be watching her, which caused some alarm. *If you can't detect anyone watching you, assume that someone of greater skill is stalking you.* The Night Mother's trainings echoed through her mind. She would follow this lesson with a swift slap to the face, *and that is for not detecting them!*

Billie instinctively felt her cheek. Even after all these years, she could still feel the residual burn from her many punishments.

She shook off the memory and made for a side street. The Hired Heroes' headquarters were located in a revamped ironworks by the marina. After half an hour of slinking between buildings and through crowds, she found it.

The wooden sign swung meekly from two chains in the cool breeze, sporting faded green paint on a cracked surface. Warm golden light oozed from frosted windows lined black with wrought-iron bars. It was a stark and garish building, like many in this town from the industrial boom which died out years ago. It was an awkward brick block with large chimneys that spewed warming smoke, and it had extra rooms tacked on in a haphazard fashion as the need had arisen.

This is the home of the greatest merc force in the country? She grimaced at the thought.

She strode up the entrance steps as the last of the twilight dimmed into night; faint hints of moon debris replaced ribbons of yellow-red sun through the gaps in the clouds.

A pleasant enough sight, but one she could not linger to enjoy.

As she pushed through the door, a bell beyond the threshold rang, and the receptionist sitting behind the cramped desk in the tiny entrance room roused herself from her dozing. She was petite, blonde, with round spectacles and a thick coat and scarf. Billie took a moment to control her instantaneous infatuation as the clerk woke.

"Welcome to Hired Heroes." She yawned. "How may I help you?"

Billie glanced away from the receptionist's enchanting, dopey expression and towards the crammed notice boards filling the four small walls. "I'm here to meet with Boss."

"Boss is busy meeting with potential clients at the moment." The receptionist pushed her spectacles up her face, and her eyes widened as she took Billie in. She sat up more alert and spoke enthusiastically. "Oh, they didn't tell me a straggler was coming; your associates are already inside."

Billie glanced at the receptionist as she gestured through the small door which led into the rest of the compound. "Associates?"

"You're part of the Dark Guild from Copper Cobble, are you not? You have a similar robe."

Billie thought of several expletives. The Dark Guild was the Night Assassins' front organisation of muscle hire. "I just have dark tastes," Billie said more calmly than her inner monologue sounded. "When would Boss be free?"

"I don't know, I'm afraid. The clients have been meeting with him and several of our Heroes for some time—seems to be a tense negotiation. Some of our Heroes left on edge about twenty minutes ago."

"You seem to be comfortable?" Billie inquired.

The receptionist shrugged and glanced at Billie up and down. "This is my job. Negotiating with dangerous folk, that's Boss's job, and if he stuffs up, this place is full of ample Heroes to lay down the law. It's boring for me really; I need to find other things to keep me ... excited." A sly smirk graced her lips. "You seem to be into excitement." She pulled the scarf from her neck, tugging at her collar as if she was overheating. "Care to *excite* me while you wait?"

Billie blushed and tried to sink back into her hood. "Maybe later. I have other business to attend to in the meantime."

The receptionist's shoulders sagged, but her smile beamed more brightly. "Well, once you've taken care of business ... you can come and take care of me?"

Billie looked away to avoid the receptionist's intense gaze, trying to push down her own blushing smile. "Until then," she said and turned to leave.

"The name's Sally, by the way."

"... Billie." Billie pushed through the door.

"Take care!" Sally called after her.

Billie stole away into the lamplit street—pushing down the warm, fuzzy feelings that were stirring in her chest—and darted around the corner of the building, keeping her eyes sharp on the rooftops and any apparent beggar for danger. The Night Assassins were out here too, she knew it in her bones; she had to be focused on the danger and not think on Sally's pretty smile ...

It *was* dangerous out here, but she needed to risk that to get ears on the meeting between the Heroes and the Assassin representatives.

She sidled behind a dumpster bin under a garbage chute protruding from the Hired Heroes building. Holding her breath, she leaped up into the chute, using her symbioid-powered grappling hooks for purchase. She dropped down into a hallway by the mess hall reeking of garbage, but she took solace in the fact that in here it was dark and quiet. The floors were hard concrete and covered with wall-to-wall, dusty red carpet, and the walls were thin wooden partitions, added after the place had been converted from an ironworks.

Keeping to the recesses and alcoves of darkened doorways and windows, Billie scuttled along until she reached a prominent door. It had a frosted glass window on the top half, which was lit gold from the light within, with black lettering spelling "Hired Heroes — Boss." Blurry silhouettes moved within. She snuck closer and placed her ear against the door. There were muffled voices beyond, but she could tell they were agitated.

Billie reached up to her goggles and pulled down a small earphone component over her ear. She retrieved a tiny cord which spooled from the earphone and connected to a small, conical receiver pulled from her robes, which she pressed up to the keyhole.

The sounds on the other side of the door—filtered through the conscious symbioid woven into her goggles—jumped into her ear as if she was standing in the centre of the room. And the voice she heard chilled her bones.

"This is disappointing, Boss." The Night Mother's sinister, cool voice froze her in place. "I was under the impression that the Hired Heroes would relish such a bounty for such a criminal organisation."

"The Symbicate is a criminal organisation," a gruff voice replied. "Or it was, before The *New* Symbicate took it out. For a group of not-assassins, you sure are misinformed." There was a tone of mirth behind that gruffness. *A man trying to antagonise the Night Mother is a man not long to live*, Billie thought.

"Not-assassins?" the Night Mother whispered. "You are too bold, Boss."

"Making fun of a bald man now, eh?" Boss countered.

"You are trying our patience!" another voice cut in. Billie recognised this one too, Nicholas Night, her old partner before she started training new recruits, of whom Tara was the first. Last she saw of him was when the Night Mother threatened her in the Den back at Copper Cobble.

She grimaced. This town was becoming too crowded.

"If you take one more step forward in anger," a laidback voice cut in, one with a rounded accent; it sounded Soth, "I'll shoot those throbbing veins right off your forehead."

"You might not know David here by his appearance," Boss said. "But you'd know him by his alias, Snipes. And I guarantee you that it is not one of those ironic nicknames. So be a good lad there, and sit back down."

"I could kill you both with a flick of my wrist!" Nicholas said.

"Indubitably," Boss replied. "But you'd still be outnumbered five to one. Even if those are favourable odds for you, the two scores of Heroes in the building will take offence to you killing off the man who distributes the cubes." Boss chuckled, his voice carrying echoes of his Mason accent.

"There will be no need for offence," the Night Mother said. "We offered a simple proposition and you declined. All that means is we have more cubes to pay out the mercenaries who do accept our contract." There was the sound of someone rising from a chair.

"There will be much more to share around once you action that contract," Snipes said. "Our lad Hooks is no pushover, and neither is the company he keeps. There will be plenty of cubes left over."

"Heh." Boss laughed. "And that's from the man here who hates Thomas the most!"

"It's a risk we'll take. I must advise you not to warn them though," the Night Mother said. "That could be unfortunate for you."

"I have no idea where they are to even warn them," Boss replied, his agitation returning in full force. "But threaten me or mine like that again, and I'll tear your throat out."

"Is not Thomas one of your own?" Nicholas cut in.

"He left months ago," Boss said. "And like I said, I couldn't help him even if I wanted to. You've outstayed your welcome here, *Dark Guild*." He laughed. "Get out of my house!"

"Good day then, Boss, stay safe," the Night Mother replied.

There was a bustling commotion as people started leaving. Billie spirited down the hallway and around the corner while the Night Assassins left. Once the shuffling receded and the office door was shut, Billie slinked back down the corridor to listen in on the Heroes.

A new voice was speaking. "Anybody else get the creeps from those guys?"

"You have sound instincts," Snipes said. "The old lady alone would almost be too much for us to handle." Billie nodded. *Smart man.* "Boss," Snipes said. "We have to warn Thomas."

"Of course we do! I'm just surprised you agree. After your last encounter with him, I figured you'd want him dead."

"We do have a score to settle, Boss, but not like that. He had every right to kill me, but he let me live. I owe him one."

"Are there any objections?" Boss asked.

There was a resounding sound of nays from the others in the room.

"Then we have just one problem," Boss said. "We need to find dear Thomas before they do. What are you all standing around looking at me for?" His voice rose to a roar within an instant. "GET TO WORK, YOU RUSTED COGS!"

There was another bustling commotion, more hurried than the last, from those in the room and the sound of several footsteps heading her way. Billie hurriedly withdrew from the door and darted down the dark hallway again. She made for the mess hall and dived headfirst down the garbage chute, landing within the heap of food waste.

She breathed out a sigh of relief, and immediately regretted it when she caught a lungful of refuse.

"Cogrust!" She gagged and pulled herself out of the dumpster, slamming onto the wet cobblestone alleyway.

She rolled onto her back, looking up at the clearing sky. Green luminescence and crumbled moon bits with trailing celestial dust spanned the narrow gap between the dark buildings above her. She tilted her head, seeing the rainbow streak appear to move in front of one of the moon chunks.

That's odd.

But the thought was struck from her mind as two silhouettes leaped across the gap and onto the Hired Heroes' rooftop.

Billie sighed. "Never a dull moment."

She raised her left grapple and triggered the symbioid to launch. It silently whipped from her brass gauntlet and latched onto the edge of the building. She flexed again and the symbioid woven between her and the mechanism began to spool, pulling her up the building, as quiet as a mouse.

When Thomas gifted the grapples to her, she was shocked, absolutely shocked at how loud the mechanisms were. But with some tinkering she adjusted them to her purposes nicely.

She reached the gutter of the building and pulled herself over easily, keeping low, as a part of the structure as the vent stacks and chimneys. The robes of her quarry disappeared from view as they scrambled stealthily over the next roof, and she followed. She flipped down her goggles and flexed the symbioid woven into it. The dark rooftop—barely illuminated by the broken moon above—became as bright as day. The faint impressions of her passing prey in the dampness shone out like pulsating red foot and handprints. Judging by the scrambling nature of one of the tracks, she assumed an apprentice and a teacher.

That told her their course of action.

She reached the top of the slant in the roof and peeked over it to see the two Night Assassins crouched over a vent; they had removed the roof cap. The younger one had spooled some thread through the vent and had a vial with a dropper. They cautiously added drops to the thread, which dripped downward into whatever vessel they deemed to poison.

It was a classic initiation killing for the Night Assassins. It was one thing to kill a fellow human, to rip the bandage off and be done with it. But it was a whole other test of resolve to leave poison, to have the knowledge that you still have time to warn your target, to back out of the life of killing.

It was a favourite trial of the Night Mother's, who said it weeded the chaff from the wheat.

"You don't have to do this, you know?" Billie said, sliding over the roof and down the slant to the flat, vented area.

The two assassins started and rounded on Billie. The apprentice was just a boy, his eyes wide with fear. His teacher's eyes went wide with malice.

"So, the traitor is here," she said.

"If you say so," Billie replied and turned her attention to the boy. "I said you don't have to do this. There's another life for you, if you have the courage to choose it."

The boy's gaze flickered between the two women; his teacher moved between them. "You won't sway another child of the Night," she spat.

"We shall see," Billie said.

The two women faced each other intently.

The assassin was the first to strike. With a twitch of her hand, a throwing knife was launched at Billie's neck. Billie flung her own, which clanged with its opponent mid-air. Before the assassin could react, Billie launched her grapple. The sinewy symbioid woven into the tether wrapped around her neck and wrenched her across the roof to Billie, who had a knife waiting to ram into her heart.

The assassin's cry was cut short when Billie tightened the tether around her throat. "It didn't have to be this way," she whispered into her ear. "Damn you."

She wrenched her knife out and let her enemy droop to her knees and topple over. The blood from her wound seeped out in a dark puddle which pooled in the flat space before finding a drain and being carried down towards a gutter.

The apprentice stood frozen, vial in one hand, thread in another. Billie Night would have killed him without a second thought ... but what would Sybilla Marrow do?

"What's your name?" Billie asked.

"F-Francis," he said.

"Francis, how old are you?"

"S-sixteen."

Billie sighed. "Would you like to fight me, Francis?"

He shook his head, but said, "But I don't have a choice!"

"You do—run, run far away, and once this has all died down, I will come and find you," he stiffened, "and show you a better way." He cocked his head. "But you must leave now." She brandished her knife.

With a yelp, Francis turned and scrambled over the rooftops, dropping the vial and thread.

Billie smiled. "Good lad." She knelt to inspect the vial, sniffing it cautiously. "Ibane." She grimaced.

She picked up the thread and traced it through the vents; peeking down she could see an open bottle of whiskey, one that had been left out perhaps due to some subterfuge from the meeting beforehand. It was a cramped office below, dark, with a small furnace and wrought-iron works around the place. Two men were down there talking. Billie recognised them from their voices as Boss and Snipes.

Suddenly the bottle was moved and poured into two glasses, which Boss shared between them.

"Cogrust!" Billie ripped the vent open and heaved the body of the assassin with her grapples. With a rushed spool she dragged it to the open vent and dumped it into the office below.

"What in the ever-loving Perversities?" Boss cried as Billie dropped down on top of the body which had wrecked the cramped office, her impact splattering blood about the tiny room.

Snipes had his rifle shouldered and aimed, his finger squeezing on the trigger.

"Hold!" Billie yelled, raising her hands. "I mean you no harm!"

"Stand down, Snipes, stand down!" Boss cried. "There is more afoot here than the obvious."

"She has Hooks's gear," Snipes said, his aim not wavering.

"And a dead assassin who dripped poison into your drink," Billie countered. "Hooks, Thomas, is my brother."

"Baulsaw shit," Snipes said, eyeing the whiskey. "His sister's dead—that's why he was such a mopey arsehole!"

Billie eyed down the barrel of the strange rifle with scepticism. "Weren't you two enemies?"

"I can respect someone as a fellow professional and an enemy," Snipes replied, "and I can still hate them at the same time."

"Cool your boiler, Snipes," Boss said, waving off the Heroes who barged through the small door and stared wide-eyed at the scene. He calmly placed his monocle on his eye to regard Billie. "But, ma'am, he is right. Thomas was always questing on the side to find the people who killed his father and carted his sister away to die. What is his sister's name?"

"Sybilla," Billie said sternly.

Snipes eyed Boss, who nodded. "So you are Sybilla then. Thomas's sister survived?"

"Yes, but call me Billie Ni ..." She caught herself, feeling the sickeningly soft dead body beneath her, a former sister of the Night, knowing that young Francis was scrambling away terrified for his life and not bleeding out on a rooftop because she was no longer what she was. She was not Billie Night anymore, but neither could she be Sybilla Marrow. She was now something different from each of them. "I now go by Billie ... Billie Marrow."

"Well, Billie," Boss said, sitting down, tipping out his glass of whiskey, and lighting a cigar. "Judging by the fact you have his gear, I assume Thomas is already dead?"

"He gave them to me. We work together with two other agents as the New Symbicate."

"About time he gave those hooks up," Snipes said, slumping back against the wall. "He was always moaning about heights."

"He still does," Billie laughed, "but he is also in danger. If the Night Assassins have gathered bounty hunters and mercenaries against us, they must also know where our base is. The New Symbicate is in danger. Will you help me?"

Boss took a drag on his cigar. "We turned down a great deal of cubes to stick by our code, young ma'am. Normally I would just let the respective parties duke it out. But normally our contracts are taken out against the organisations arrayed against you and your brother. If the New Symbicate is taken out, Hired Heroes may be next. It isn't just good morals to protect a former Hero; it's good business."

Billie smiled. "Then I shall take you, and any Hero willing, to our hideout." She gazed at Snipes. "Care to repay your life debt to my brother?"

Snipes glowered at her, but Boss laughed.

"Snipes, get this girl an army!"

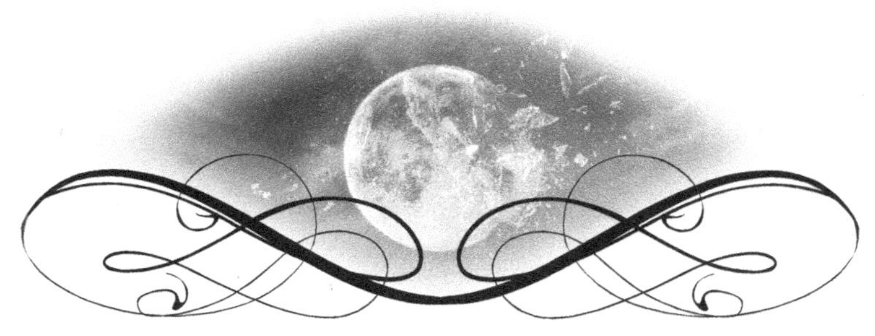

CHAPTER 6

Tara Night

Running around rooftops and alleys is hard work when you're full to bursting with Mason cuisine. It's even harder when you are being chased by several symbioid-woven thugs. A tingling distracted Tara, causing her to slip on litter and skid to the ground as a dart whistled overhead.

"Cogrust!" she swore, scrambling up and heading down a side alley.

I should count my blessings, she thought. *At least the bounty hunters chasing me right now aren't the group Regen was with.* She rounded a corner and tumbled straight into Regen. She knew it was him because of the curved Estakan blade he had half drawn before she inadvertently tackled him. As he fell over, his baggy cloak and hood fell from his head and shoulders, revealing his steel-plated conical hat and his banded armour. The group he was with all jolted in surprise.

"That's her!" the Mason woman cried, raising her blunderbuss over Regen's sprawled form.

This last shot of adrenaline was too much for Tara's poor full stomach; it emptied itself—violently—into the blunderbuss's barrel. The Mason woman, flecked with vomit, blinked and pulled the trigger. There was a wet spark and the sorry sound of the gun not doing its job ... on account of being clogged with Tara's half-digested dinner.

"I'm so sorry!" Tara mumbled through the acid burning her throat, before remembering with a tingling sensation that she was being chased by an entirely separate group of killers.

Her eyes widened and she ducked when another dart flew over her shoulder and imbedded in the copper plate armour of the Mason woman.

"It's the Needle Gang!" The leader of Regen's group stepped forward, eyeing down the group of four Soth bounty hunters who rounded the corner, armed with bow, crossbow, blow dart pipe, and one unarmed woman.

"It's the cogrusted Body Changers!" The leader of the Needle Gang stepped forward; like his companions he wore drab brown clothes with a white undershirt and a tricorne hat. "This is our bounty ... we found her first!"

Tara's eyes flickered with recognition—the Body Changers were a group of symbioid-woven bounty hunters; they all had their own aliases. The Mason woman covered in vomit was called "Puddle," the paler member of their team "Cocoon," and the indigenous Weznin's name was "Stretch." She didn't remember what abilities their symbioids gave them, but she could imagine.

"She seems to like us better," the leader of the Body Changers—Cocoon—said, crossing his arms.

"Enough of this." The unarmed woman with the Needle Gang stepped forward and held out her palm. A sinewy spike emerged from her flesh and launched at Cocoon.

Cocoon's own symbioid sprung forth in defence, and sinews tore from his flesh to envelop his exposed skin in a hardened shell. It was useless as the barb was halted by his copper breastplate before it could sink into the hardened, cocooned skin anyway.

Still an impressive display, Tara thought.

The next shot—a crossbow bolt—sailed right into Regen's neck. He choked and fell back. Tara knew—unfortunately— that he would be fine. The two groups lunged into combat over her, and she dropped her smoke bomb. With that added confusion she slinked past their embroiled ankles and leaped up onto a dumpster, onto a bronze fire escape, and scrambled several stories out of her smoke cloud and onto a roof.

"She's heading up!"

Two darts, a symbioid barb, an arrow, and a blunderbuss shot pursued her, all fired blindly. She scrambled up over the lip of the building and rolled panting onto the flat reddish surface. Then a hand reached up and gripped the lip. She stopped mid-pant and cocked her head.

None of them were that hot on my heels, she panicked.

She looked over the lip to see that the hand was attached to an incredibly elongated arm, which was sourced from the smoke below. Someone—the one called Stretch—shot up from the smoke as it cleared, held onto by his companions, Puddle and Cocoon. Regen remained below distracting the Needle Gang.

"Body Changers indeed!" Tara flung a knife down, turning to run before she saw if it struck true or not.

Knowing her luck, probably not.

She hopped the gap between the adjacent buildings but turned at the sound of footsteps landing behind her. Instinctively she slashed out with her blade to find Puddle had disembarked from Stretch first and was pursuing her closely.

As Tara's blade cut through the air towards Puddle's exposed neck, she melted. By the time Tara's swing had reached where her enemy's neck should have been, she had liquefied into a stream of water which shot between Tara's legs.

The water form rose rapidly behind Tara and solidified into the mercenary Puddle.

Tara didn't even look before she instinctively kicked back, clobbering Puddle in the gut while she solidified. There was a shuddering impact and a wet grunt as she collapsed, but Tara's attention was caught by the hand shooting towards her from a lengthening arm across the gap in the buildings. It gripped her throat and pulled her back towards the edge.

She lashed out with her blade in a desperate motion, lopping the sinewy arm off in one, clean strike.

Stretch cried out and recoiled as Cocoon sprinted forward to make the leap. Tara threw her knife at his eyes, which seemed unprotected enough. She had a split second of dismay when the blade hit his brow ... it then ricocheted off his hardened skin downwards, landing under his foot as he was about to jump the gap. He skidded off the knife, committed by his momentum, and sailed headfirst across the gap, slamming into the lip of the building. There was a wet, rolling crack as his neck—along with his jaw and face—shattered. Cocoon collapsed in a heap onto the street below, falling between the clotheslines across each building, full of drying laundry.

"Cocoon!" Stretch's face contorted with fury, and his sinewy hand re-wove itself into existence and launched after her.

Tara turned in terror to flee, making to run over the winded Puddle. Only to falter in dismay as the Needle Gang mounted the opposite side of the roof and took aim. Puddle instinctively melted to liquid when Tara ran over her, causing her to slip and land on her back as the bolts, darts, arrows, and barbs sailed overhead and embedded themselves in Stretch. He cried out and fell back on the other rooftop, looking like a pin cushion with comically long arms.

Before Tara could wonder what just happened, Puddle solidified beneath her and held her in a chokehold. Tara struggled to free herself to no avail, and the Needle Gang advanced on her while reloading their various weapons.

The lady with the barb symbioid raised her hand. Tara frantically elbowed her captor in the ribs and spun in a grappling motion, carrying Puddle onto her back as the barb thrower shot a dart from her hand. It struck Puddle in the back of the head.

She grunted and melted into water as she died, allowing Tara to leap up and spin to face her new enemy.

"Just give me a gear jammed break!" she choked.

The dart blower laughed, speaking with a thick Soth accent. "We'll break every bone in your body, little girl."

"But once we have subdued you, of course," the bowman added.

"Yes," the crossbowman said as he trained his sights on Tara. "Surrender, hon, it's all over."

"You moon rock moron," Tara said. "Why would I surrender if you're just going to break all of my bones? You're a stupid, swollen ignoramus! I'll gut you all before you lay a finger on me!"

The barb thrower cocked her head, and red locks of hair fell from her tricorne hat. "Then we shan't lay a finger on you at all. Take aim."

The Needle Gang followed her command—the dart blower brought the blowgun to his lips, and the bowman drew an arrow alongside the aiming crossbowman and the barb thrower.

Tara grimaced and raised her blade, rage and tingles spurred within her along with a growing stubbornness that surprised even her. "You'll shoot, and I'll still be alive, and then you'll have to contend with a pissed-off assassin without any ammunition in your weapons!"

"You're just as tough as that Estakan man," the barb thrower said. "But we made short work of him nonetheless."

Tara smiled. "I hope I live long enough to see you choke on your ignorance."

The barb thrower smiled back. "Shoot."

Tara had a split moment to take a breath.

The arrow twanged loose first, and Tara stepped back as she slashed it away. The bolt launched after it, and she dodged to the side in an instant. Then the symbioid barb caught her in the shoulder; she dropped her blade and spun in pain, stumbling onto the edge of the building and looking down the dizzying height into the dark alley below. She contemplated the broken cocooned man down there through the clotheslines full of laundry, knowing she would join him shortly.

The darts from the blowpipe hit her then, three of them in quick succession across her back.

Tara toppled down into the dark alleyway like a sack of scrap.

She was gripped by the pull of gravity, that sudden lurch in her stomach as the air rushed past her face, blowing back her leather hood and billowing Eric's yellow scarf with her pale brown hair. She closed her eyes, waiting for the hard, inevitable impact.

She hit the first clothesline with her gut, jolting her with a startled grunt. The line snapped and it swung down into the next, which caught in her armpit and yanked her like a fishing line before it, too, snapped.

At this point she had the wherewithal to grab on and swing down relatively safely within the alley. Though she came in at a high speed and slammed into the now soft body of Cocoon. She tumbled over his corpse with a string of curses and cries of pain, winding up on her back looking up at the bright sky, regarding the growing rainbow comet as it passed between the pieces of the broken moon.

"Whistling steam, what is going on out there?" Disgruntled tenants with disturbed laundry poked their heads out of apartments on either side of the narrow lane. Upon seeing Tara and Cocoon, they thought that it was better to protect their ruined garments at a later time. They retreated, locked their windows, and drew the curtains closed as the Needle Gang descended the building via a rickety fire escape.

Tara's vision was swimming from the pain, but she still noticed something odd out of the corner of her eye. From the lingering haze around the corner of the alley—where she had dropped a smoke bomb earlier—a pin-cushioned figure was staggering around and coming towards them. The pins sticking out from it quivered like bristling reeds with each pained movement it made. Despite her curiosity and slow-building dread, Tara could not focus on the strange figure anymore; she was distracted by the closer threat.

Tara gritted her teeth and tried to stand, but she was woozy—those darts must have dosed her with something. Not to mention she was pretty sure that if every bone in her body wasn't broken from the fall, they at least felt just as bad. The barb thrower landed first as Tara pushed herself up into a seated position, and the rest of the gang followed shortly after.

"Well, you are a girl of grit, aren't you?" Barb said. Tara had decided to just think of her as Barb.

Tara laughed. "Not gritty enough it seems. I'm done."

"At least you know when you're beaten. I'm happy that it is us that have beaten you."

"You haven't beaten me." Tara looked past Barb at the human pin cushion that had started sprinting.

The Needle Gang turned to face the new threat, but they weren't fast enough for Regen. He was incensed, full of barbs, arrows, darts, and bolts that rattled against each other while he sprinted with a battle cry. He cut through the bowman's bow, his blade passing through his enemy's heart in the same motion. He rolled under the bolt from the crossbowman—splintering his pin-cushioned projectiles against the cobblestone—and slashed at his knees. The crossbowman cried out and dropped as Regen followed with an upper swipe that cleaved his face in two. The blow-dart man turned to flee but was skewered where he stood. Barb was frozen in shock.

"We killed you," she said.

"I don't die," Regen spat, before ending her in a swift strike.

Tara watched in morbid fascination as her soon-to-be killer dispatched her attempted killers.

"I guess I should thank you?" she said. "Before cursing you." She looked down with a sigh. "It isn't fair."

"Life not fair, little warrior." Regen righted himself from his last swipe and started wrenching arrows and barbs from his flesh.

Each wrenching was followed by a spurt of blood which was quickly shored up by his regenerative symbioid, leaving sinewy white scar tissue. He strolled up to her, standing over her defeated, slumped form, and she looked up to meet his gaze.

"I'm very aware that life is not fair," she spat. "So how is this going to go?"

"Last time we fight, you beat me, first to beat me since I was a boy. Since then, I train. I train against death by a thousand cuts, which is how you beat me. Now I can withstand more blood loss; now I can protect from little cuts as well as big. I did this for one purpose. To track you down, and give you this honour." He hefted his sword.

"Then do it already. I'm getting cold," Tara said through tears, through the lump rising in her throat—*this was it*.

Regen flourished his blade; Tara shut her eyes tight, waiting for the end.

The end didn't come.

She risked peeling one eye open, and gasped.

Regen was on his knees, offering her the handle of his blade.

"What's ... this?"

"My sword."

"Yes, I can see that, but ..."

"I offer you my sword, one who is worthy of my skill and abilities. One who shows mercy, one who shows skill," Regen said. "I have worked on my weaknesses, and am worthy of this role to you. I shall serve you. I shall die for you."

Tara stared at Regen's submissive form. "... Oh" was all she could say.

After a time Regen looked up, inquisitive. "What say you?"

Tara gazed about the battle-strewn alleyway. "Are you hungry?"

* * *

Twenty minutes later they were munching on barbeque skewers while leaning on a railing by the weir. They overlooked the lower city and the spreading highlands. They could see all the way out to sea and the glistening green water reflecting the ethereal moon shards.

"So why did you become a bounty hunter, Regen? Why did you travel from Estaka?"

Regen was silent for a while as he munched thoughtfully. He swallowed and took a deep breath. "My brother and his wife raised me, were good people. He had Regen symbioid. It help him fight for the good. Then one day, we were trapped, in a carriage; his enemies set it alight ...” He paused, and Tara gripped his hand. “He transferred his symbioid to me, told me to do good, and he and wife threw themselves over me to protect me from the flames. They died, I survived.”

“I’m so sorry,” Tara said.

“Once I recovered, I tracked down the criminals. I make them pay. Then I travel, finding only the bad to stop. Can make cubes doing so at times. Now I find you, know you fight the bad. Now I can do this with someone else. I tire of being alone. I do not like most other people. They are bad. You are not—you fight with honour, clean. You are good. I can put in the effort for someone good.”

“I am not one of your good people, Regen. I am bad also, and you should hunt me down as much as the rest.”

“This not true.”

“I’m a born killer.”

“So am I.”

Tara gazed out over the dark vista. “I don’t think you understand. I have had a hard life, just like you, but I turned to the arms of assassins. I have a friend. She was an assassin too; we both shared the name ‘Night.’ But now that we’re free, she has a name to fall back on, and I don’t. All I’ve got is Night, Tara Night, the killer, the monster.”

“You only young,” Regen replied. “Now you out on your own, you can make a new name. Life may be hard, but you do not need to let it make you hard. It makes me hard, sometimes.”

Tara smirked. “Now you’re just making silly jokes.”

“Worth it, to make you smile.” Regen grinned. “How is your food?”

"A far cry from the Mason meal I had earlier, but it will do." They were distracted by shouts from the weir. "I was going to be on that boat," she said, gesturing to the barge pressed up against the outer wall of the boat lift. "It's a good thing the Needle Gang spotted me before I got onto it, or the boat lift would have broken again, and I would have been a sitting duck out on that river."

"You are lucky." Regen's eyes narrowed. "More so than seems normal."

Tara cocked her head. "I killed a man in Masonville, after you and I had our duel. He had a symbioid that generated luck. It didn't do him any good, and I did not deserve the gifts it could bestow upon me. I told the symbioid to crawl away and find someone worthy of it. I often wonder how things would have progressed there if I did let it weave with me."

"Did it?" Regen asked, watching her intently.

Tara chuckled. "I think I would have noticed if I wove with a cogrusted luck symb ..." She was cut off by a flash of blinding multicoloured light, a beam of rainbow which streaked from the sky and materialised into a massive object hovering over the city. "What in the Perversities is that?" Tara cried along with the startled expletives all around her.

It was a ship. The rainbow comet had shot down from the sky and solidified into a giant, chrome-hulled ship, with a shape not unlike a mast ship, with an enclosed top and tall sails the colour of rust but pulsating with crimson power.

Shocked cries rose from the busy streets, and the symbioid-powered buildings of Crankod went to work with mechanical groaning. Steel shutters rose over windows, balconies retracted into the superstructure of buildings, and cannons rose out of the official structures, all pointing towards the floating ship.

"Mmm," Regen said, "I thought this some new contraption of Crankod. Their reaction proves otherwise."

"It's not from the city," Tara said. "It came from that rainbow comet—that thing has been travelling towards us from the heavens for months … it's from another world!"

"That is not possible," Regen said.

"Why? The evidence is there!" She gestured towards the sheer hull hovering before them over the lip of the weir.

Its sides and lower hull changed, and hatches retracted, leaving square openings and the hissing of escaping air. Large tubes extended from the hull, strange objects with crystalline lights pulsating along their lengths with a prism set into their ends.

"I don't like this," Tara said.

A voice broke out over a megaphone. One of the constables was on a railing with the comically large conical device amplifying his voice. "You have entered a ship into the municipality of Crankod without a permit. Disembark immediately or be fired upon!"

"I don't think that's going to work," Tara said, grabbing Regen's arm, the sudden tingling sensation in her spine settling into dread. "Come on, let's get away from here."

The prisms set into the ends of the tubes extending from the ship's hull lit up with sinister red beams of light which strafed over the city. There were dozens emanating from the ship, dozens of beams of red light which homed in on structures or people.

"What are they?" Tara said as one of the lights crossed the street and halted over a symbioid-woven mechanical statue.

"They are aiming," Regen said, "targeting. Those things are cannons! Let's go, now!"

"This is your last warning!" the constable boomed.

The prism cannons hummed with a growing pitch, then exploded. Blinding white light shot out from the prisms at their ends, completely vaporising whatever was in their red-beamed sights. The statue before Tara and Regen disintegrated, people cried out as they dissolved in other targeted beams of white light, and the targeted buildings crumpled.

"Symbioids!" Tara cried in terror. "They're aiming for symbioids! We have to get you out of here!"

"This whole city is woven with symbioids!" Regen said. "Head for the Barcos!"

The two took off between the streets as the flying ship continued its assault on Crankod. The cannons upon the rooftops returned fire. The cacophonic exchange rippled across the highlands, piercing Tara's eardrums, and she clutched them in pain, leaping over collapsing debris and strewn bodies in the mad dash from the crowds to find shelter or flee.

Tara tripped over a child and stumbled onto the ground. She was further driven into the ground by stampeding feet as she tried to crawl towards the child and cover her with her own body.

She rose up onto her knees. "Are you okay?" she yelled at the frightened youngster.

The world went red as they were saturated in targeting light. Tara looked up. The ship drifted farther over the upper city, and one of the cannons had sighted her and the kid. The high-pitched hum rumbled, and Tara braced for the end.

Just as it fired Regen grabbed her by the shoulder and yanked her. She lost her grip on the girl and then lost sight of her as the ground erupted in white light.

"The girl!" Tara screamed over the roaring inferno as Regen dragged her along. "We have to save her!"

"We can barely save ourselves!" Regen roared.

The streets were chaos, soaked in the smell of smoke and ash, of the fires, and of burning flesh. When she could hear over the cannons and the light blasts, she could discern only screams of fear and pain.

This was hell.

The building in front of them was targeted at the base, and after a white blast it crumbled, causing a landslide of debris which smothered the crowd at a chokepoint. Regen surged up the landslide ruins and Tara followed. They emerged onto the roof as the fierce battle raged. The city's cannons were still firing; blast after blast glanced harmlessly off the ship's chrome hull as it slowly laid waste to Crankod's defences, along with the rest of the city. Tara and Regen reached the other edge of the building and found the Barcos below it. Crowds were streaming into the water, onto boats, into the surrounding streets, anywhere to find cover.

"It's no use if the weir is blocked," Tara said.

They jolted and the nearby crowds shrieked as the barge Tara had travelled up on was targeted and incinerated.

Then her world went red again. The targeting beam from a smaller cannon on the enemy ship lit her up. As the high-pitched chime sounded from the charging cannon, Regen was in front of her. The world went bright white, and even over the deafening blast Tara could hear Regen scream in agony; her nostrils flared with the scent of his sizzling flesh.

The world dimmed and she was holding his seared form, eviscerated and mashed save for sinews from his symbioid working to reassemble his broken form.

"Come on, Regen, we can make it, you can survive!"

The world went red yet again, a larger cannon from the marauding ship targeting their location. Regen used the last of his strength to shove her. She tripped over the edge of the roof as Regen was consumed in white fire. This time, he did not scream. As she fell over the edge, she caught the fleeting moment of his entire body—silhouetted by the white fire—dissolve completely into ash and oblivion, before the lip of the building rushed past her as she fell and impacted the water.

The world went quiet when the cold waters of the Barcos filled her ears, the embroiled surface above her lit strobically by the flashes of the conflict. The cries were muffled, and the splashing from others in the water reverberated strangely as she sunk, white water ripples above that signalled people tearing through the water. There was a repressed boom as the weir was targeted, and the waters rushed over the shelf edge like the breaking of a dam. Tara bit back the urge to scream as she was carried down the racing current and jettisoned off the upper shelf of Crankod and fell into the lower river.

She hit the broken churning waters and sank further while the torrent carried her away. She was a crazy, tumbling mess, and her head throbbed with the strain of holding her breath as her body was thrown around like a rag doll.

She hit something, stray debris, or stone, or another body, and the wind was knocked out from her. Instinctively she drew in a breath only for the cold Barcos waters to flood her lungs. She went into spasms and her world began to go dark. The bright flashes through the water were losing their luminosity, the pain ebbed, the ringing in her ears died out, and the only sensation was the tingling down her spine ...

Something grabbed her; something dragged her to the surface and towards shore. She had the vague memory of someone pounding on her chest until she coughed and spluttered cold water everywhere, and that same someone dragged her behind a ridge of boulders.

"Who are you?" She choked the words out to the masked figure.

"You can call me Frogman," her saviour said.

She looked up the river to Crankod as her vision returned from blurriness in order to survey the horror. The weir was shattered, and the once stymied water was flooding in torrents, flooding the lower city while the upper city went up in smoke. The screams were distant now. The Barcos that Frogman had dragged her out of was a coursing flood, full with flotsam and the dead. Her head throbbed and her ears rang and the tingling spiked and ... and ... *Regen*. She threw up again, taking in the destruction and gore that flowed down the now raging river.

"Why did you save me?" she asked, panting and wiping the vomit from her mouth.

"I could only save one, and you were the first person I grabbed," he said, removing his breathing mask.

"Do I know you?" Tara asked.

"I know many people," he said. "Do you know them?" He gestured at the chrome ship that was still laying waste to the city.

She shook her head. "They are like wizards, the way they transformed from a rainbow into that battleship, the way they turn light into a weapon."

"Light Wizards?" Frogman said, frowning up at the destruction. "Sounds too whimsical for such devastation."

The ship turned, floating downriver as it mopped up straggling parts of the city.

"We best be gone; it is coming this way ... errr."

"Tara."

"Tara, come, let's go." He took her hand, and together they stole into the dark highlands.

CHAPTER 7

Billie and Snipes

There was a brisk breeze weaving between the lower mountain ranges, whistling in gusts about the ridges and outcroppings where two figures lay prone. They observed the adjacent peak through their respective looking glasses, one in the form of symbioid-woven goggles, one in the form of a sniper's scope. Billie and Snipes had perched in their little lookout for most of the morning—the bright sun beaming directly into the little valley between the mountains—watching the dormant signalling station across the way.

The signalling mechanisms always freaked Billie out. They were like giant windmills at great heights with sailed arms that bent at odd hinges to form symbols. The next relay station leagues away would observe the symbols through a scope and mimic them, sending the message down the line.

Their hinged, awkward movements were what unnerved her. But she put up with them as they were generally always moving with the many messages of import shared between city states and their satellite population centres.

This one was still, and that unnerved her more.

"What was the message again? An assault train?" she asked, adjusting the zoom on her eyepiece to home in on the open door of the tall silo-like superstructure. "We can't just march or use a boat?"

"Yeah, an assault train," Snipes answered. "Tinrod has an abandoned train line. Boats are hard to charter at the moment with more SWiGS sightings, and a lot of our Heroes are out on contracts. They couldn't get there fast enough by other means." Snipes twisted a dial on his scope as he talked. "We can hustle to a small waystation north of here via steam wagon and board the train on the way to Tinrod. The waystation is more central for where most of our Heroes are at the moment, so it'll be faster to meet there rather than Bronstone. Also, if we're going into battle, it could be useful; 'assault train' isn't an ironic name. They were how the Weznin nobles kept their city states autonomous during the Great Migration. They're armoured, with quick offloading platforms built into the walls, and harnesses to survive derailing attempts." He adjusted another dial and scribbled on a notepad propped up by his rifle. "Five hundred yards," he murmured.

"Five fifteen," Billie corrected. "Wind from the north, about thirteen knots based off the flapping of the canvas on the arms. Take that with a grain of salt though; there are a lot of gusts."

"Hmm." Snipes seemed appreciative. "I've never had a spotter before. It's nice."

"Aren't many weapons like yours around, and there aren't many goggles like mine to match." She smiled at him. "It's an interesting device, the honing barrel at the end of your blunderbuss."

"Don't tell your brother, but he gave me the idea."

"Did he make it?"

"No, I hired another tinkerer for it."

"Ah, yeah, didn't seem like Thomas's work; he's more forward thinking than that," Billie said.

"What do you mean?"

"Your barrels burn out after several shots, don't they, hence your bag of spares?"

"Every two-and-a-bit magazines. How did you know?"

Billie nodded. "A tempered alloy would solve that; your tinkerer was not worth his salt."

"And that bastard Thomas would have known all along?" Snipes asked.

"Yep." She laughed.

Snipes swore under his breath. "I guess I couldn't expect him to offer me too much help."

"I take it you two weren't close?" Billie said.

Snipes was silent, taking great care to twist another dial on his scope. "No," he finally said.

"Why? You don't seem all that bad. He can be a little stubborn at times, but ..."

"It was a job that went bad at Foundton," Snipes cut in. When she waited for him to speak, he continued. "We were hired to run interference for an information broker who sold intelligence to a bounty hunter who was an informant for the royal guard ... the gang whose intel was sold wasn't too happy about that, and we had to smuggle him out of the city. Hooks ... Thomas, he was close protection detail. The road out of Foundton goes through a sparse wood, lots of places to set up ambushes, but there was a stretch of road under a ridge that gave me ample sight of most of the route.

"We got the broker out easily. I was just there as a failsafe, in case any gang members pursued them past the city limits ..." Snipes sighed again.

"Then what happened?" Billie prompted.

"Thomas and the broker made the road on the ridge, I was perched above, and they passed out of sight under an overhang—but they didn't come back into sight after that. I relocated. Turned out a bunch of bandits on the road had surprised them, but Thomas seemed to be talking them down. He was holding a stand down signal with his fingers." Snipes made a gesture using his index and thumb. "But while I was relocating, the ground shifted, I stumbled, and the bandits attacked. Thomas was going to be overwhelmed, so I started shooting. I killed them all before they reached Thomas, or the client."

"... So?" Billie ventured.

"They were just kids, displaced, hungry kids. Thomas was furious, told me he could have incapacitated them without killing them ... I didn't know, the situation was developing too fast ... I don't think he ever really forgave me."

"Did you forgive yourself?"

Snipes was silent for another moment. "Every time I pull the trigger now, I am afraid I'll hesitate. I never do, it's just a lingering fear; sometimes being so far away from the action makes me doubt whether I actually know what's going on, you know?"

Billie nodded. "But you soldier on?"

"I ground myself," Snipes corrected. "Those kids died because I moved to unstable ground. As long as I have solid ground beneath my feet, I know everything will be all right."

"It is a shame," Billie said. "The death of those children must weigh on you heavily."

"It keeps me up most nights."

"Hmm," Billie hummed. "I don't sleep much either. Not until I took control of my own life has that begun to heal. Maybe you need to find a way to take control—after losing it with your footing, that is—and atone to the universe for what you did?"

"Maybe," Snipes said, "but until I find out what that might be, we have a job to do. The runner Boss sent hasn't returned from sending our message out all morning, and a still signal house means only one thing."

"Subterfuge." Billie nodded and toggled her goggles. The valley turned into a dull blue, and the station was painted as a black shape upon grey peaks, with a line of wavering red dots on the bottom floor. "Looks like the signal crew have been captured. And there are strange readings I can't quite make out, like they're withholding their heat signatures from me."

"Heat signatures?" Snipes asked.

Billie flipped up her goggles with a flick of her head. "Never mind. I'm going to waltz up there—you cover me?"

"Sure." He slid the bolt down on his rifle as Billie slinked back from their hiding position to make for the road.

"Stay rock solid," she called as she trudged down the ridge.

* * *

Snipes battled the growing cramps in his sides from holding his position so long and tried to ignore the urgent call to pee, but after about half an hour, Billie emerged on the road on the far side, ascending to the flat of the next peak that the station was built into.

"Finally," Snipes breathed.

* * *

Billie huffed and puffed, a little ashamed of herself. These peaks were lower than Copper Cobble, but she had still spent too much time in the lowlands. She wasn't used to the elevation as much as she'd like to be.

But still, she liked these peaks; they were low enough to balance the best of both worlds if she thought about it. The air was light and breezy, and it was not as cold as it was farther up the ranges at her former home. Wild mountain grass grew in dense thickets over the slopes, and the river from the Copper Cobble mountain range was visible up valley beyond the signalling tower.

She looked back to give Snipes a nod. Somewhere behind the peak he was set up, the ocean was lapping against the shores. She could almost hear it, if she imagined hard enough, but the salty tang on the air was unmistakable, and when mingled with the pristine gusts, this sweet spot was almost perfect. Save for the danger zone she was entering in front of the signalling tower.

Billie cautiously made her way to the half ajar door to the superstructure, not bothering to conceal herself.

She trudged into a circle of strange depressions in the ground—where she had noted the anomalies earlier—and waited, slowly turning to count them off. "... three, four, five," she nodded, then turned to the station, "... six. Six assassins to kill the likes of me?"

An object rolled out from the darkened door, a severed head, bloodied, with a pained expression.

Billie suppressed a gasp—Francis—the assassin apprentice she had spared the night before upon the Hired Hero headquarters.

"If you don't want your Hero messenger in here and the poor signal crew to suffer the same fate as that, weakling, you'll drop your weapons and goggles now."

"Terri?" Billie responded, unsheathing and dropping her weapons with an absent mind. "I must say it's a first that someone has me remove my goggles." She tore them off—symbioid tendrils peeling painlessly from her skin—and let them drop to the ground, along with her swords, half a dozen knives, a belt of smoke and flash bombs, and numerous sharp throwing implements.

An assassin in black robes emerged from the doorway, a young woman with fiery red hair and a sinister smile. "Mother would be so disappointed," she sneered.

The mounds of earth around Billie erupted as the other assassins clawed their way free and stood in a circle around her. Billie shot Terri a look and shrugged. "Was that supposed to intimidate me?" She brandished her grapple gauntlets. "I'm hardly unarmed."

"Even you couldn't take all of us!" one of them mocked from her rear.

"Not half blind," another chided.

"I guess you're right." Billie resisted the urge to touch the monocle over her scarred eye; without her goggles it was effectively blind. "I'd be hard pressed to kill most of you." She gave Terri another pointed look. "Most." She raised her hand and gave a thumbs-up.

A crack rang out about the valley, echoing up and down the mountain range, and the assassin on Billie's right collapsed without a head.

The other assassins scrambled as Snipes fired again, downing an assassin who stupidly dove for Billie. Then Terri dropped a smoke bomb, and the others followed suit.

The assassins were enshrouded in a growing cloud of grey smoke which blinded Snipe's shots. From his little sniper's roost across the valley, he cursed, "Cogrust."

Within the smoke cloud, Billie recognised her disadvantage immediately.

A shape rushed at her from the side and slashed at her leg, then two from the rear who struck for her shoulders. Billie shifted and parried with her grapple gauntlets as the onslaught continued. She defended herself from some attacks, but not all. The wounds were not designed to kill, but to bleed. Death by a thousand cuts.

"You see now why I had you remove your goggles?" Terri said as she leaped high and kicked Billie into the ground. "Novice assassins aren't so good with smoke bombs. They haven't had the experience to fight using senses other than sight." Billie struggled to her feet and copped a slash to the leg, collapsing to one knee with a suppressed grunt. "However, the more experienced we are, the more we rely on sound, anticipation, and pure muscle reflex to minute stimuli. You have relied on your goggles too long."

Billie gazed heavenwards. The top of the smokescreen was blown to wisps already by the mountain breeze, now thin enough for her to see the windmill arms locked in place up above. The smokescreen was also dissipating enough for her to make out figures in the cloud, but not enough to allow Snipes a confident shot.

Billie raised her grapple and aimed for the closest windmill-like arm. "You always talked too much, Terri," and launched her grapple.

It shot out of the cloud and knocked free a locking mechanism at the hinge of the lowest arm, and her grapple went limp as it fell to the ground.

"You fool. Those arms would never support your weight!" Terri boasted, stepping forward to finish Billie off.

"Nor your stupidity," Billie said.

The arm swung low—the locking mechanism at the hinge knocked free by Billie's grapple—and buffed the smoke away, clearing the air like a fan.

Terri's eyes went wide, and she looked to Snipe's roost as her shoulder exploded in a wet blast of blood and bone. She fell back—quite separate from her decapitated arm. With rapid shots the rest of the now exposed assassins were downed.

Billie took a deep breath and rose, collecting her weapons as the signalling arm swung back and forth, fanning away more of the choking smoke. She finally donned her goggles and turned to give Snipes another thumbs-up, and with her zoomed lens she could see him salute with two fingers in response.

The signalling arm swung back once more as it slowed to a halt, settling on a hanging position. The wind woke Terri and she coughed and spluttered awake from her shock, reaching for her crimson gushing stump, pushing with her legs to get away.

"You'll never escape our wrath!" she coughed. "The New Symbicate is doomed!"

"Yeah." Billie threw a knife at Terri, silencing her suffering. "I'm sure."

She limped into the signalling station, much to the relieved cries of the hostages within.

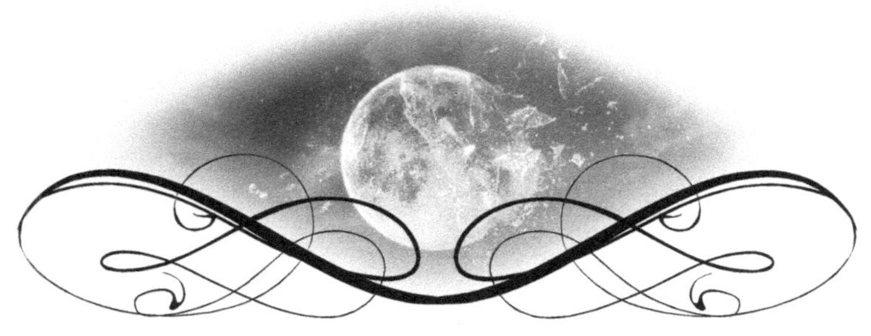

CHAPTER 8

Thomas Marrow

It was an awkward trip, a really awkward trip.

The whole time Madam Brune scowled at Thomas from the bow of the ship as he manoeuvred it along the sketchy coast of Weznin. Alexander was no better, leaning cross armed against the port rail, staring, but at least with a blank expression.

Eleanor interacted with them and the other Baul Islander freedom fighters, a whole dozen of them who were crammed onto the tiny steam tug. They also stared at Thomas, but it was more out of amusement at his apparent discomfort, or so he hoped. Thomas could not blame them for their hostility. These people had led hard lives, as a direct result of what the Weznin people had done to their Islands. They regarded him with hate, blame, and Thomas was pretty sure that Eleanor's mother and brother caught him glancing at her when she wasn't watching, which added another layer of distaste he was sure.

Thomas also realised that their gazes of distrust, hate, and malice had been their experiences from the people of Weznin, so he put up with it for now. As warriors they bore the odd blunderbuss, long, curved knives, and shoddy tin plate armour beneath their traditional frilly Baul Islander robes.

It was after twilight now; the sky was laced with the last rays of the sun, which rested well below the horizon. The shattered moon—although fantastically radiant—was impeded by low-lying clouds moving in from the ocean, and the rainbow comet was nowhere to be seen.

"We should be there soon," Eleanor said over his shoulder.

The sudden friendly voice was so out of place among the glares of bubbling rage, he jolted.

"You still jumpy, Hero?" she teased with a nudge.

"I feel like your family might want to kill me," Thomas said with a wry smirk, nodding at Madam Brune.

"Thomas, if a Brune doesn't try and kill you upon a first meeting then they aren't being polite." She laughed.

Thomas laughed back. "Well, I guess that's comforting. There's our beach." Their grey, desolate expanse of home by a derelict town came into view; the cliff bunker was on the north side of the beach from them.

It was quiet, no seals, no gulls.

"Thank heavens," she said. "I'm getting seasick."

"You don't look too bad ..." Thomas felt as if a pressure gauge was rising—something was wrong. He could tell from the lack of movement on the beach, from looking out to the ocean where something rippled. "Did you see that?"

"See what?" Eleanor followed his gaze.

Her body language must have communicated some unease at Thomas's question, because the other Baul Islanders reacted, readying weapons and scanning the dark waters with her.

"What is it, my dear?" Madam Brune said without stirring. "What does the Weznin mercenary see?"

"I saw ..." Thomas said. "It must have been an oddly lit wave. It seemed to ripple like ... like ..."

"GIANT SQUID!" A Baul Islander readied his blunderbuss to fire into the depths right before a tentacle exploded from the lapping waters and dragged him under without so much as a cry for help.

"Cogrust!" Thomas hit the throttle and steered the tug towards the rocky beach. The boat whined in protest but ultimately chugged away obediently. "Stay away from the sides!"

The tug exploded with the sound of blunderbuss shots as the Islanders defended themselves from the emerging tentacles on either side.

"It's right beneath us!" Alexander sprinted to the other side and produced his sword-shield, lopping off the end of a tentative, slimy appendage that crept over the railing.

There was a high-pitched rumbling sound, and the boat rocked violently. A pink, gelatinous mass swiped at Thomas. He ducked under the blow, the scents of sea life passing overhead in a blur of goo and tentacles before it struck another two fighters and dragged them to their deaths. Thomas looked over his shoulder to see that Eleanor had flattened herself against the deck moments before the attack and was safe.

"Brace yourselves!" Thomas ordered, and rammed the tug onto the beach.

The brass hull screeched in tandem with the squid as it dragged against the jagged shale and granite and everyone on the boat was knocked to the deck. Madam Brune stood calmly, undisturbed by the ordeal.

"Would someone help an old lady off this blasted boat?"

Alexander rose first and took her hand, helping her to offload as the rest of the crew righted themselves.

"Get off now, it'll try and drag us back!" Thomas had just managed to say before dozens of tentacles burst from the water in a frenzy, grabbing props, railings ... and reaching for Eleanor. She screamed as the horrid, suckered monstrosities split into a dozen branching tendrils and grabbed for her.

So it is not just a squid, Thomas thought, *but a SWiGS.*

Thomas launched himself onto Eleanor and blinked away. They landed roughly on the beach a ways from the boat in a heap. Thomas was on top, looking down into her bewildered eyes.

"You okay?" he asked.

"Yes," she said softly.

They held each other's gaze.

The moment was fleeting, and he blinked away, materialising next to his boat with the taser he had acquired from the Establishment in hand.

"Off the boat, don't touch any metal!" he ordered the crew as he cranked the mechanism.

It whirred and sparked while the SWiGS dragged more of its insidious mass out of the water and onto the boat, reaching for the retreating group with suckered, sinewy tentacles that split and grew and split again until it was a churning, writhing mass that made the air taste of brine.

"That was a new boat!" Thomas screamed and jabbed the end of the taser into the hull.

The whole thing hummed and sparked and seared the squid; it squealed and convulsed in agony, retreating back into the waters, which returned to a deceptively calm surface within seconds.

"Away from the water, now!" The group upped themselves and scrambled over the uneven surface of the beach to where Eleanor was now sitting with her mother.

"You said the chances of getting attacked by a giant squid were nil!" she said.

"I said they were low … We're safe now," Thomas said.

"And minus a boat!" Madam Brune said. "How are we to get to the slave drop-off now?"

"There is a second smuggler's boat in the compound, Mother, not to worry," Eleanor answered.

"I'm not getting back into that water. That thing took Jack, Grace, and Earnest," one of the Islanders said.

"I can tinker something to make the charge go through the hull and not us," Thomas said. "It'll take the night, but it'll keep us safe."

"How inventive," Alexander responded. "I can see why Eleanor says you're useful."

"I do my best. Come now, there is food and tea in our hideout."

"There's someone else here." Alexander gestured ahead of them, where a group of men were rushing towards them. "Enemies?"

Thomas squinted through the dimness. "No, that's Matchins's men, constables from Quartrant, friendly."

"You lot all right there?" Matchins's deep voice called out before he and his handful of constables reached the party of Baul Islanders.

"We are, Matchins, just some trouble with the local wildlife. Were you waiting long for us?" Eleanor asked.

"Just a few hours. We got more from that magistrate about that slave ring. Thought we should share."

"That sounds intriguing, Constable," Madam Brune said coldly, "but we already know what we need."

Matchins straightened, realising who the group of Baul Islanders were—you don't get to the point of being a freedom fighter matriarch without developing a reputation. "Ah, very good, ma'am. Let's get inside?"

"Didn't think we would ever work alongside constables." Alexander laughed, clapping Matchins on the shoulder as they marched on.

The weary group picked their way tentatively through the boulder-strewn beach towards the bunker. When they were halfway across, Madam Brune stopped in her tracks and looked to the ridge, and the broken village beyond it.

"What is it, Mother?" Alexander asked, the group stopping in staggered fashion along their path.

"We are not alone," she answered, not taking her eyes from the ridge.

The party crouched and scurried behind the boulders strewn along the beach, all except for Madam Brune.

"You are quite the perceptive adversary." A chilling voice crept over the ridge and flooded over the beach. "It will be a shame to kill someone so attuned to our ways."

From the derelict buildings and the brush and stone upon the ridge, assassins melded into view, as if from shadow. Then, from farther back, an assorted brigade of mercenaries and bounty hunters also emerged. Finally, *she* emerged herself, the Night Mother, a beacon of death in her black robes. Even at her apparent age, she drifted past the deathly vigil like a wraith.

"It would be a shame to sully my blade against the likes of you!" Madam Brune spat on the ground. "I've heard that the Night Mother is a fickle bitch. It will dull the edge."

The Night Mother chuckled, a haunting echo that reached the ears of the warriors hiding on the beach.

"What business do you have with the Brunes?" Alexander asked.

"I have business with one Brune, boy!" the Night Mother answered. "My business is with the Symbicate; you were just unfortunate enough to be here."

The patchwork force of assassins and mercenaries readied their weapons along the ridge, drawing blades, cocking hammers on blunderbusses, and crouching to spring into action.

Thomas drew his own blade, glancing at Eleanor as she flexed her sword-shield into a defensive stance alongside her brother.

"And what business does a murderer have with the Symbicate?" Thomas asked.

"Ah, is that Hooks, the great Hero for Hire who blundered into vengeance? What makes you think that you are any better than I?" the Night Mother said.

"Answer the question, you bleating banshee," Thomas said. "I know what horrors you bestowed upon my friend, upon my sister—are you here to seek their forgiveness?"

"And where are my children?" the Night Mother said. "I can see they aren't here. What useless endeavours have you diverted them to?"

"Answer the question!" Eleanor's voice roared.

There was a silence as the two forces squared off against one another.

"The Night Assassins have a new client," the Night Mother said, "a new ally, I should say. And he has galvanised us against the budding threat your organisation poses. We will slaughter you like sheep, and he will feast on your corpses."

"Who?" Thomas asked.

"The time for talk is done, young Hooks; now is time to die. ATTACK!" The ridge erupted in explosions as a volley of blunderbusses rang out in the night.

Assassins dropped smoke bombs to cover their charge, and the Baul Islanders and constables returned fire as they retreated towards the cliff bunker.

"She's the head of the snake!" Alexander shouted while shots pinged off his sword-shield. "Cut it off and the body will flounder."

"Worth a shot!" Thomas blinked out of existence and appeared upon the ridge, in line with a group of marksmen mercenaries.

He moved through them, charging their flank, and they fell under his swift onslaught. One, two, three, four before they noticed his presence amongst the din. The fifth in the line turned to face him, but Thomas blinked behind him, stabbing him in the back.

He ducked under the swing of an assassin, scrunched his nose as the killer dropped a smoke bomb, and he thrusted haphazardly into the cloud to where Billie taught him an assassin would strike from. The cry of his opponent was confirmation that his anti-assassin training had paid off.

He blinked from the cloud. His disappearing presence sucked the smoke into the vacuum his body left and churned the cloud into a vortex which obscured the other marksmen on the ridge. He appeared up in the air—a necessity in spite of his fear of heights—taking in the battle in an instant.

Constables and Baul Islanders were fighting a desperate skirmish among the boulders as the Night Assassins swarmed through every nook and cranny. Eleanor and Alexander led the retreat, keeping most of their people in a tight fall-back pattern as they seamlessly fought as one, switching their sword-shields in tandem to attack and defend at the same time. The Night Mother was watching from atop a jutting ridge. Before gravity took hold of his instant in the air, Thomas swiped and blinked at the same time, appearing behind her mid-strike.

His sword sliced through shadow and air as her form morphed into black, sinewy tendrils. Without turning physically she was suddenly facing him, with a wrinkled, sinister smile shadowed beneath her hood.

"How cute," she said.

Thomas's eyes widened, and he blinked behind her again, but up in the air. Without moving, the shadowy, sinewy tendrils of the symbioid she was woven with had her facing him seamlessly. He slashed down at her breast and hit nothing but shifting shadow smoke yet again. She shifted to gut him.

Thomas swore and blinked back across the boulder, squaring up against his opponent.

"What symbioid is that?" he asked, blinking his eyes through sweat. "I can't read your movements."

She chuckled. "It allows me to shadow-form. Much in the same manner yours allows you to blink, it allows me to morph my form into whatever position I choose, and all that is left in my previous form is shadow and sinew." She chuckled some more. "You'll never kill this old bird, mercenary!"

She lunged with a snarl, knives in each hand, and Thomas lunged forward to meet her. As the shadow-form emerged to boggle his mind, he rolled forward. She struck down, and he blinked behind her, coming up mid-roll. She had twisted in shadow-form to face him, and he had already blinked away, emerging from his roll *above* her, driving his blade down.

It impacted the stone ridge as she danced away and slashed his cheek. His blade fell from his hand, and he gasped at the sudden cut to his face; he blinked away, sprawling over the ridge, winded and in terror as she was upon him within an instant.

She held a blade to his eye.

"You have her eyes, you know?" she said in her taunting tone. "I nearly cut them from her when she was a child for failing me once. But she pulled through, and hid behind those goggles ... perhaps I'll take your eyes instead, and force her to feed on them?"

Thomas cried, in rage and in terror, and blinked, dragging her with him like drifting smoke. He blinked into the sky, high above the losing battle below. And they fell. Thomas drew his long knife and slashed at her. She writhed in shadow-form, parrying and riposting as he blinked again and again. They fell, embroiled in battle, a sporadic, twisted mess.

The Night Mother gained the upper hand and jabbed shallowly between his brass plating. The cut stung and he blinked away—breaking contact and sprawling over the ridge, defeated a second time. She landed in wisps of shadow by him.

"That was a thrilling battle, I must admit, but now it's over," she said.

Thomas spun onto his back, breathless, disoriented and in pain, as the Night Mother picked up his discarded sword and held it high to strike. He closed his eyes and waited for the inevitable.

The Night Mother screamed in rage as she struck. The air displaced from the blade ruffled Thomas's hair, and he winced at a clang as it stopped inches above his head. He opened his eyes to see Madam Brune standing over him, her gnarled blade halting the Night Mother's killing blow.

"Where did you come from?" he gasped.

Madam Brune kicked the Night Mother back with ferocious speed and attacked. Her movements were as fast as a blur, striking as fast as Thomas could blink, and the Night Mother struggled even in her shadow-form to keep up with it all.

Madam Brune then slashed at the Night Mother's wrist, and she dropped Thomas's sword with a cry. Brune kicked it over to Thomas, who clambered to his feet.

The cry from the Night Mother caused other assassins—intent to watch until now—to move up onto the ridge, circling around the two challengers.

"Whenever you're ready, Mister Marrow." Madam Brune blurred towards him and grabbed his arm.

Thomas nodded and steeled himself to blink with the last of his energy.

The two appeared at the base of the cliff bunker, with the other defenders who were making a last-ditch defence under an overhang against the cliff wall. The path to the entrance was cut off by mercenaries who had closed in with blunderbusses.

The place was littered with the assorted bodies of their enemies, several Baul Islanders, and two of Matchins's constables.

"We'll never last!" Matchins shouted as Eleanor knelt over Thomas's panting form.

"Are you all right?" She took his face in her hands and wiped the blood seeping down his cheek.

"Your mother is woven?" Thomas asked breathlessly.

Eleanor smiled in reply.

"MOVE IN AND PULL THEIR SPLEENS FROM THEIR BODIES! MAKE THEM WATCH AS YOU CRACK THEIR SHINS, AS YOU TEAR THEIR TONGUES FROM THEIR MOUTHS!" The Night Mother's voice screeched terribly from the ridge, and the assassins and bounty hunters closed in.

"We're done for!" one of the Islanders cried.

"Not yet," Madam Brune said. "Many more of them will perish before we draw our last ragged breaths. Our people have suffered worse than this lot, and this lot will suffer worse than that to get to us."

Thomas gripped his sword and took a loaded blunderbuss from the fallen Islander beside him. He aimed at a brazen assassin who leaped above the stony barricade that the Islanders had formed and pulled the trigger.

With a loud blast and a wet grunt, the assassin went rocketing back, copping the blast in the gut.

"They will suffer indeed," Thomas said, discarding the weapon. "Let's give them the Three Perversities!"

CHAPTER 9

Tara Night ... a convenient distance away

ara and Frogman slogged wearily through the highlands—sodden into a marsh by the seeping waters from the Barcos. Their destination was the nearest coastal town which was as far from their attackers as possible. Mud clung to their legs and coats, and exhaustion clung to their souls. The light of dawn crept over the horizon, through the smoke and fog, highlighting the dark misery around them with ghastly grey light.

There were other refugees too; all of them shell shocked and distant, from whimpering children who had long since stopped screaming, to old husks coming to grips with what happened.

The more alert ones nervously glanced over shoulders, back towards the river and Crankod, which still burned a beacon of ruin even when the light rain started falling. The ship—the Light Wizards—hovered in the distance, their course taking them down the river. The tone of their light cannons resonated dully at this distance. It was random and sporadic as they targeted other symbioids. Some of the refugees could not quite get used to it and jumped and ducked into the knee-high, squelching bog whenever the ominous tone sounded.

But Tara and Frogman slogged on.

"How far away is it?" Tara asked.

"We should be nearing it soon," he said, with his odd accent; it wasn't quite Inlander. His family must have immigrated through The Great Pass relatively recently. He was a strange man, sporting a lean build with pale skin and black, braided hair. His getup was all sealed leathers, and his bulbous helm dangled on his shoulders like a baggy hood. "It's a small byway town," he continued. "Really just a train station with the disguise of a town around it." He chuckled. "It's a rust hole, but the river from the Copper Cobble range swings by it on the far side, so it gives us options."

"Mmm." Tara tried to focus on what he was saying, but all she heard was gibberish.

Flashes of Regen tore through her mind at random.

She wanted to collapse and let the bog take her.

But her friends—her family—needed to be warned.

The whistle of steam ahead caught their attention, and a train approached. Tara squinted into the brightening sky and found the trail of steam indicating the train thundering slowly to a halt. A sense of childish glee swept through her as it sounded its high-pitched "choo-choo" horn, and she immediately chastised herself for it.

"Sounded like a large train." Frogman seemed quizzical. "This far up north, and coming from that direction? If you follow the line down the path it's taking, it bisects the Copper Cobble range on its way past Bronstone, but the terminus is at some abandoned fishing village. And the line is *really* badly maintained ... It doesn't make any sense for a train of that size to pass through here."

Tara's incessant tingling returned, and she perked up. "And why would a large train be heading that way?" she asked.

Frogman turned to her and shrugged.

Tara took off across the squelching bog as quickly as her weary form would allow.

"Hey, wait!" Frogman called out, chasing after her.

A half hour of slogging later, the ground rose from the muck, forming a plateau against the bog, giving Tara's burning muscles much-needed relief. The waystation town was built upon it, a collection of storehouses, sheds, and basic amenities for travellers and the few people who lived there. There were several roads which converged on it, one which was chock-full of steam wagons.

Tara halted mid-stride. Dozens, no, scores of warriors in maroon cloaks were disembarking from the steam wagon train and loading onto the actual train, which hissed and steamed like a wounded beast. The train itself was odd, thick with bronze and copper plating, sleek, and the carriages had whole walls lowered down, forming ramparts so that the hustling warriors could load into it. Within the carriages there were harnesses strapped to the ceiling, and on the roofs what looked like squat watchtower turrets that could be manned by gunmen.

One of the warriors noticed her—noticed her instinctively gripping her blades—and he strode over cautiously. He wore the same maroon cloak as the others—the same as Thomas wore—and had pale skin and short red hair and carried a strange-looking blunderbuss.

"Can I help you?" he asked with a thick Soth accent.

Frogman caught up a moment later, cresting the plateau breathlessly. The warrior's eyes widened as he shouldered his gun.

"Frogman?" he said.

"Snipes?" Frogman flicked his blades from his wrists, catching them in a practiced motion.

"You two know each other?" Tara asked.

"We're from rival organisations," Frogman said, lowering his knives, "and he has the drop on me."

"This your new protégé?" Snipes gestured to Tara.

"No, we found our company to be mutually beneficial along our journey."

"And what journey is that? Not that I care, but you look like you've just gone through Moon-fall itself."

"I don't have time for this!" Tara snapped. "Put that weapon down. We aren't a threat—the threat is on its way." She marched up to Snipes as he trained his weapon on her; she pressed her head right up against the barrel.

"Er," Snipes floundered, "stand back?"

"No!" The commotion was drawing attention from the other warriors who were gathering around, watching with morbid curiosity.

"Put that weapon down, David." A squat man emerged from the crowd, dark skinned, from Masonville, but his accent had blended into Weznin. He had been here a long time. "Hello, Frogman. I'm afraid we can't be enemies today."

Snipes cautiously lowered his weapon from Tara's fierce gaze as Frogman spoke. "That's fine by me, Boss. We've had a hard go anyway, and so have a lot of people behind us who need help."

"What happened?" Boss asked.

"Crankod was sacked," Tara said.

The crowding warriors gasped and murmured among themselves.

"How?" Boss muttered, disbelieving.

"It doesn't matter. I need to get to Tinrod to warn my friends."

Boss's eyes widened, his monocle falling off his face with the motion. "Your friends? Who are you?"

Tara took a breath, already weary and aware that she would need to play twenty questions before she could proceed.

"She is Tara Nightingale." Billie stepped between the warriors. "And she is a member of the New Symbicate, a member of my family."

Tara's heart flew as she stumbled forward. "Billie!" She collapsed into her arms. "Billie." She began to sob.

She didn't care that Billie might not approve, or that the people around her were watching on intently. All she cared about was that she was with her family.

Billie stiffened in her embrace, but quickly forced herself to relax. "Shh," she cooed and caressed Tara's head. "What happened?"

"Enemies!" Tara snapped up. "Enemies that target symbioids. They're tracking down the Barcos, and if they turn south, they'll happen upon Tinrod. Thomas, Eleanor, you, symbioids! We have to warn them."

Billie's lenses whirred. With a flick of her head, the goggles flipped up so she could look at Tara with her naked eye. Her eye was calm, but beneath the calm her anxieties were a churning rage. She squeezed Tara and helped her to stand. "Boss, we need to accelerate our schedule."

"We were already pushing it, Miss Marrow," Boss replied. "We were lucky to even get the train out here in time."

"Then we leave the week's supplies, load up what you can carry. We must be on."

"But all of this food?" Boss gestured to the crates that were waiting to be loaded onto the train.

"They will need it more." Billie gestured over her shoulder to the mass of refugees ambling across the plains. "Come, we have a mission to complete."

"What is happening?" Tara still sobbed.

"I will explain all on the train, little Night, come."

Billie hefted her along as Boss shouted orders, and the Hired Heroes doubled their pace, abandoning their food stores and loading onto the train.

Snipes tentatively eyed Frogman. "If this mission goes sour, it will affect your people too. Come along."

Frogman cautiously followed him with Billie and Tara.

Twenty minutes later, the armoured assault train was roaring to life, the coals were smoking, and the steam was spewing. It let off its whistle to the giddy cheers of the Heroes on board, and it lurched out of the tiny town, onto rickety tracks not maintained in years. As the Heroes left, the refugees swarmed the town, ravenously clutching at the discarded food.

121

The New Symbicate

The ringing vibrations as shots pinged off Eleanor's sword-shield blended in with the ringing in Thomas's ears. They had managed to hold here for most of the night, pressing into a depression in the cliff face and fighting off waves of ill-tempered bounty hunters and undisciplined thugs.

All the while the Night Assassins slinked in, taking pot shots from strategic locations or attempting to scale down from the overhang above.

The assassins were the ones who were gradually wearing down the superior skill of the Baul Island warriors and the cool-headedness of the constables. The bounty hunters and mercenaries were just distractions, fodder for the Night Assassins' main goal—the extermination of the Symbicate.

One of them leaped over the barricade, a fragmentation bomb in hand, and Thomas blinked by her. He tackled the assassin to the side and slit her throat, grabbing the bomb. He lobbed it at a boulder where an assassin was taking position to fire. The fragmentation bomb "disappeared" the assassin in a hail of shrapnel, and viscera rained down on a charging group of mercenaries who winced and faltered under the gruesome shower.

A volley from the Islanders finished off the failed charge as it retreated.

The enemy forces pulled back.

"They aren't making it through here," Alexander breathed in the respite. "Yet they keep dying by the dozens. What's driving them?"

"At first it was greed," Madam Brune answered, relaxing on a squat rock as if she were spending a leisurely day at the beach, a successful image if not for her crimson-drenched hands and gown. "Now it is fear. The Night, they are more reckless than they ought to be. A pitched battle isn't their way."

"Well, they aren't getting in here," Alexander repeated. "They can keep trying all they like."

"Not unless the Night Mother enters the fray," Thomas said, peeking over his rocky cover and spotting several enemies doing the same across the makeshift no-man's land.

"I can keep her at bay long enough," Madam Brune said. "I am concerned that the one that drives them may become fed up with their lack of progress and push matters further."

"Who leads them if not for the Night Mother?" Eleanor asked.

"Who indeed?" a sinister voice answered from the enemy lines, a drawn-out drawl of sick malice.

The defenders peeked over cover to see a lone man standing in the clearing before them, clusters of uneasy mercs gathered in the gaps of the rock formations behind him as the assassins kept overwatch above.

He wore black coattails, with a tall top hat and monocle. He bore a bushy white moustache which exceeded the rim of his hat and held an umbrella under one arm.

Thomas and Eleanor exchanged a worried glance.

"Rella?" Eleanor whispered. "Wasn't he Mason? This man has pale skin, not dark. Didn't Tara tag him with the Symbicate device? Didn't he retreat out of Masonville with his hordes under fire from their soldiers?"

Thomas didn't take his eyes off the man before them for a second, recognising the disjointed, animated movements of a creature playing at being a man. "Rella was the symbioid that wove with a Mason man ... he has found a new host."

"A new host who has a gripe with you, Thomas. I am wearing the butler of Eric Futruble ... you remember Eric, don't you? You made him drive his own knife into his heart; must have been a painful way for your friend to go. His butler sought me out and removed the Symbicate orb to exact revenge on you."

Thomas's heart fluttered as if it were about to fail, and his breath caught in his throat. "Eric?" he gasped, unable to form more words.

Eleanor sensed his anxiety and spoke for him. "Eric Futruble died defending the man who slaughtered Thomas's father, a criminal! The butler you now inhabit would have been as vile as Eric's uncle; you will meet the same fate."

"And aren't you yourself a criminal, a killer? Aren't the other members of the New Symbicate assassins?" Rella cackled. "It seems Thomas has a double standard. He would betray a friend, but not his sister, not a lovely Baul Islander lady such as yourself. I wonder how hard he had to reason with himself to work so closely with a pretty woman such as you?"

Thomas slumped down against the stony barricade. Images of Eric's lifeless body flashed through his mind, accompanied by the sound of fear as the Blink symbioid left him for its true host, the horrid, dull, wet sound of the knife entering his body, the look of shock in his eyes ...

"The butler freed me from that bitch Tara's trappings, and allowed me to enter him on the condition he is aware enough to slaughter Thomas. Then afterwards, I am going for the girl Tara, and oh how I will make her suffer for what she did to me!"

Madam Brune knelt before the slumped Thomas as Rella rattled off more threats of pain and torment. She gripped his chin, forcing him to focus on her. "Eleanor told me your story on the boat. Your friend Eric chose his path, you yours, and Eleanor hers. He did not die because you murdered him. He died because he crossed paths with justice, and justice had claimed you as her agent. Eric defended that which tore your family to bits, sold your sister into servitude, thrust you into a life of violence when all you wanted was to tinker, to create. I understand what it is to suffer these things, and I understand how those that oppose me will twist the story to make me hesitate. This creature called Rella will sow doubt into your mind. Do not let it.

"You are a Hero."

"H-how …" Thomas stammered. "How would you know?"

"I sized you up the very moment we met Weznin, as did my daughter; otherwise, she would not have followed you. Now, I may have had some misgivings about you, but they were superficial. It is folly to try and claim we are wrong about you; you must instead try to see yourself as my daughter does."

Thomas's lip quivered and he took a deep breath. He nodded and stood, turning to face Rella in his new form.

"You claim to know me, Rella, but I also know you." His voice wavered, but— thinking on Madam Brune's words, holding to the man he knew himself to be, deep, deep down, the man who Eleanor had somehow seen—his resolve gathered. "Most of what you told me from the moment we met was cogrust, and this is no different. You claimed to be a conscious symbioid hard done by, but were instead a parasite. You are only living off the manipulation of symbioids, off the corpse of a servant of evil; you will not subsist on my suffering! I am not afraid of you, or anything you have to say!"

Rella tutted, cocking his head. "Ah, Thomas. There is more in this universe than you have the capacity to be terrified of." His grin broadened into a sinister leer. "But I will allow you the terror of being rushed by my husks." He flexed his fingers.

There was a commotion behind the mercs in the gaps in the boulders. A terrible cry and jostle as a frenzied group surged through the hapless warriors.

"Cogrust," Thomas said, realising what was happening.

He had seen these things before, in the Zombie Quarter in Masonville. They were symbioid woven husks—poor bodies of men and women who Rella had taken over a decade ago.

Their flesh was gaunt and clung to the bone, and their teeth gnashed and mouths foamed as they pushed forward. Their will bent wholly towards following Rella's every whim.

And Rella's whim was to kill.

The horde surged past Rella's extended arms and into the clearing.

The defenders opened fire.

As furious battle was joined, a train whistle cut through the din. Everyone—even the husks—snapped their attention up to the ridge on the beach. Thomas's brow furrowed as he contemplated the thundering of what sounded like an onrushing locomotive. The station here at Tinrod was as derelict, abandoned, and disused as the town. The track could barely hold a stationary train let alone a moving one, and this one was showing no signs of slowing down.

The opposing forces watched in awe as the chugging steam rose above the ridge in the night. They flinched as the wheels screeched and the earth shook when a great train slammed through the terminus barricade. The train derailed, smashing through the town and soaring over the ridge, over the beach between the two armies.

"What the fu…"

The train crashed onto the battlefield beach with a colossal tremor, and Thomas dove for cover back up against the cliff wall. Rending metal shrieked against the shale boulders and matched the ghoulish cries of a swathe of husks who were crushed. Rock disintegrated and showered the gasping onlookers.

Thomas peeked out from his covering arms and over the barricade once more. The train had launched itself over the ridge and now cut them off from the enemy, forming an armoured wall. It was on its side, wheels facing them as it steamed and hissed and smouldered.

"Who is moon rock moron enough to ram a train off the tracks?" Alexander asked.

* * *

From within the first carriage, Billie allowed her eyes to unclench, holding the harness which kept her suspended in place safely.

"You're a mad woman." Boss coughed. "Nearly wiped out my whole company."

"Well," Tara groaned, "you saw the battle raging from the periscope. We had no choice."

"Head count!" Snipes barked.

Down along the carriages there was a chorus of groans, grunts, and swears.

He turned to Boss as he disengaged his harness. "Good enough for you is good enough for me, Boss."

Boss sighed. "Disengage!"

The carriages were filled with the sound of quick releases being triggered on harnesses, and the Heroes readied for battle.

"Are we at least facing the right way?" Frogman asked. "This assault train may be versatile, but if the door opens on the wrong side ..."

"We are ... open the top door," Billie said, reorienting herself in the tumbled compartment to look up through the window and sighting the cliff bunker looming over the underside of the train.

A lever was pulled, and a hiss sounded as hydraulics turned gears and the roof of the train grinded open. The phalanx of Heroes found themselves facing down a mismatched group of bewildered husks, mercenaries, and assassins.

"Nicholas." Billie sighted her former partner among their ranks.

"Billie!" he roared back.

"Boss, Billie? How good to see you all." The Night Mother drifted into view as a cloud of black tendrils and smoke.

"Night Mother," Boss said curtly. "You ruined my liquor."

"Cogrust!" Tara screamed, spotting who she assumed could only be Rella.

"TARA!" Rella bellowed.

"Well, so long as we all know each other," Boss said. "Attack!"

The Heroes surged forth with a battle cry, firing and stabbing and using their various woven abilities on the hapless force before them. Many of the enemy force crumbled, still bewildered by the Heroes' sudden appearance.

To add to their feverous attack, Thomas, Eleanor, the constables, and the Baul Islanders clambered over the overturned train and charged alongside the Heroes. The battle was a close and furious brawl of blades, smoke, limbs, and blunderbuss fire. Somewhere in the fray, Madam Brune and the Night Mother reengaged their furious duel from earlier, moving in blurs and shadows around the tumultuous and diverse melee along the beach.

"You crashed a train over the beach!" Thomas cried, astounded as he blinked down to Billie and Tara.

As soon as he did, the assassin Nicholas and the creature Rella were upon them.

Nicholas quickly separated Billie from the others and duelled with her along the train's wreckage while Thomas and Tara fought fiercely against Rella.

"You have no device to stop me this time, girl!" Rella sneered.

He extended his umbrella, knocking them both onto their backs, and made to stab at them with its tip, but Eleanor was there in a flash with Alexander at her side. Their shifting sword-shield formation held him off long enough for Tara and Thomas to stand and circle around behind him.

A husk loomed up on Thomas's rear and its head exploded. Thomas sighted the source of his salvation and found Snipes expertly picking off enemies who were about to overwhelm warriors among their ragtag gang. While he was distracted an assassin rushed Thomas, but Frogman charged in and tackled them aside. Thomas gaped, two former rivals having just saved his life, then ducked from Rella's next strike. The arrival of the Hired Heroes, Snipes, and Frogman was a question for another time.

Tara, Eleanor, and Alexander grappled with Rella's limbs as Thomas moved in for the kill, stabbing Rella in the heart.

There was a wet sound as his blade entered Rella, who cocked his head. "Is that all you have?" he roared and extended his symbioid-woven umbrella. The four were knocked back by the force.

Thomas blinked around and grabbed Rella from behind.

"This isn't working!" Tara screamed, and before Rella could react to dislodge Thomas from his rear, she slammed a smoke bomb in his face.

Rella cried out and coughed as Eleanor slid in and swiped at his leg with her sword-shield expanded to its full width; it chopped through skin, muscle, and shin, but no blood came forth. Alexander leaped over her and kicked Rella in the side, toppling him over amid the smoke as Thomas repeatedly stabbed him in the neck.

"He won't die!" Thomas cried.

Rella's dismembered foot reattached with thousands of searching tendrils, he rose and flung Thomas from him, and the battle continued.

"Alex, beware of his tendrils—they can take control of your sword-shield," Eleanor warned as Alexander tried to swipe at the sinews of the relatching leg. He danced back when they lashed for his blade.

The brawl raged on, with Rella holding his own against the four of them.

* * *

Closer to the water, Billie was trading a flurry of knife blurs with Nicholas, the man she had not seen face-to-face since before she left for Masonville—what felt like a lifetime ago. He was taller than she was, bigger and stronger, but she was faster. She grappled up a boulder and then backflipped off it, using the grapple as a flail to swipe at his head. It hit hard and knocked him forward against the boulder she had sprung from.

She pressed up to him, knife at his throat. "Nicholas, stop this. There is another way!"

"You betrayed everything, your family, your way of life!" he spat at her.

"No, that is my family." She gestured to Thomas, who was fighting the losing battle with Rella, and gasped.

Nicholas took her moment of distraction to shove her from him and slink away between the boulders. Billie let him go and rushed to aid her brother.

She took stock as she sprinted through the rest of the battle. As it was going, things were fairly even. But Rella was making headway against the New Symbicate, and once he was through with them, he would tear through the rest like wet paper.

* * *

Tara was knocked down with a hard slap from Rella. Eleanor and Alexander charged in as she fell, with Billie rushing in to join the fray from the far side.

Rella flipped around, knocking Billie, Eleanor, and Alexander in the face simultaneously. He sucker punched Thomas in the head when he reappeared from a blink—taking him out with a grunt, and as Tara pulled herself to her feet, she found herself standing alone against the twisted creature. He swiped forcefully, breaking past her guard. He pressed the tip of his umbrella to her chest, a fierce, vengeful glee leaking through his insidious visage. Tara backed away, the panic rising with a feverish panting, and Rella pressed forward until she was backed up against a boulder.

"Do you know how much pain I was in?" he spat. "For weeks I writhed with that cursed device latched onto my cheek! I have thought of nothing else but dismantling you, piece by piece, as you watched. That's why I haven't possessed the symbioids of your friends here. I wanted to defeat you as I am, at my leisure, for you to feel the desperation build as you slowly lost ground, knowing you could never beat me!"

Tara was trying to force her breathing to slow, but it was impossible with the tip of the umbrella driving with more and more pressure into her chest as she tried to back away. She knew that Rella had a blade that extended from the tip, and she waited for him to trigger it, hoping for such a quick death from a monster like him.

Then, the tingling sensation tore down her spine, and it was a strange comfort, enough to make her look him in his lifeless eyes and utter weakly, "The Three Perversities are too good for you, fiend."

He grunted a laugh and pulled back to ram her through.

There was a flash of light in the sky, freezing the combatants mid-fight as their attention was drawn heavenwards.

The Light Wizards had appeared.

Their chrome ship hung ominously, and the crimson sails pulsed in the dark sky; wisps of fractal light streaked from the hull as they phased out from whatever magic allowed them to travel so quickly.

"Oh, cogrust!" Tara said, more strongly now.

The ship's gun ports opened up with a thunderous clanking, and the prism-imbued cannons extended out from them, drawing crimson beams of light upon their target. All the lights homed in on Rella.

"Those bastards!" Rella cried. "How? They ..."

Every single cannon rang out with a humming charge that lit up at once, painting the battle-strewn beach in brilliant white light as Rella was blown back under the terrible force.

The heat of the light made Tara wince, and images of when Regen was incinerated flashed through her mind. She slumped back against the boulder. The cannons all targeted different points now. The husks, some of the Heroes and assassins, *everyone with a symbioid*, Tara assumed.

The combatants scrambled for cover as the ship lit up the field, killing dozens at a time. The New Symbicate collected themselves in a mad dash and made for under the crashed train while the smell of concentrated, burning death reached them.

"What is that thing?" Thomas yelled.

"The Light Wizards!" Tara yelled back.

Some on the beach returned fire, but like the defences at Crankod, the shots rang off the chrome hull or pinged off the amber, pulsing sails. They would all die here on this beach.

The Symbicate huddled down; thunder and light assailed the beach, strafed it with impunity as the warriors died or scattered for cover. And then suddenly there was darkness. The thunderous sound halted and was replaced by an extended humming charge of the prism cannons. Tara looked out from their little piece of cover. The red beams of searching light all traced the beach to the lapping waters, grouping upon a single point.

The ship's charging cannons sounded out like a rising cry and then fired, lighting up the water, sizzling the surface in a jet of steam, and the water screamed back ... a monstrous scream from the depths.

Tentacles upon tentacles shot up and lashed at the ship hovering over the water, breaking and bending the cannons. The tentacles entered the gun holes and gripped tightly, dragging the ship down into the depths. Within minutes it was submerged, pulled into the icy waters with steaming flashes of white and red.

The combatants tentatively moved from cover, friend and foe alike eyeing each other cautiously as they looked to the water.

There was another explosion of light and steam, and the Light Wizards' ship jettisoned from the water, half crumpled and inflamed. It arced up and out over the sea, falling past the horizon with a trail of thick smoke.

A pained cry came from Rella. "RETREAT!"

He staggered out of a smoking crater, scorched and malformed, but alive. He bounded away from the battlefield, up the ridge, and through the derelict fishing village, followed by his ambling husks, the few surviving mercs and remaining assassins.

"This isn't over!" the Night Mother cried before dissolving over the ridge.

"Should we pursue?" a constable asked Matchins.

"We're in bad shape, lad," he replied.

"We have medical supplies in the compound." Tara shook herself from her shock, seeing a way to help those around her. "We should set up a triage and get everyone here fed too."

"And while we are doing that," Boss cut in, "someone can explain just what in the Three Perversities is going on!"

CHAPTER 11

The New Symbicate

All members of the New Symbicate had been in their fair share of fights. They had been in scraps so severe, done things so brutal, that it sometimes kept them up at night. But the aftermath of a real, pitched battle was a strange new horror to them.

All of the warriors, from Hired Hero mercenary, to freedom fighter, to constable were tough, brave, and ferocious, and now they were brought low, weak, and infirm. Triage was a mess, set up in rooms and cots along the hallways as the diverse crowd tried to save the dying and soothe the wounded.

Tara walked through the mess of bloodied rags and haphazard arrangement of cots with an absent look on her face. She was numb to the horrors, ever since Crankod, ever since she witnessed the destruction of an entire city.

Eleanor was the only one of the Symbicate who seemed to have been in this situation before, treating the wounded with deft skill, her visage that of a competent battlefield physician in the wake of disaster. Thomas wondered just how young she was when she fought her first battle.

He wanted to help, to take charge, be of use, but the Brune family and their warriors were on top of things; they took the lead and Thomas followed.

Boss and Matchins were happy to follow along too, deferring to other leaders in the treatment of their people. They had to as they were somewhat scrapped up themselves.

Out of a hundred fighters in total, twenty-three were dead, thirty were wounded beyond the point of incapacitation, and only one had suffered not even a minor scuff—that was, of course, Madam Brune.

The sun was high into late morning once the wounded were stabilised and the dying were mercifully on their way. The assault train was a broken, steaming wreck upon the smouldering beach, and the enemy dead were now being collected by the able grunts from Matchins's constable force. The beach stunk of decay, burned flesh, and expelled wastes. The salt on the air did nothing to mitigate this. Gulls and birds of prey hovered around the town, their horrid cries accompanied by the gentle lapping of the sea as they swooped in to pick at what they could among the body gatherers who shooed them off. They had a harder time shooing off the crabs that emerged from the smouldering gouges in the stone.

As the morbid work was done, the last few crumbles of the moon were drifting below the horizon, barely visible in the brightening day—the celestial tendrils that trailed after the crumbled sections were a fading backdrop to the line of smoke on the edge of the world.

Ending where the Light Wizard's ship crash landed.

The New Symbicate, along with Boss, Snipes, Madam Brune, Alexander, Matchins, and Frogman, were all sitting around the round table in a large room in the cliff bunker. It was what Thomas assumed was the cliff jumpers' main meeting place, before they ousted the smugglers.

Thomas gave a rundown on the attack on the beach, then Billie recounted her tale recruiting the Hired Heroes to her cause, and they all sat in stunned silence as Tara retold the devastation of Crankod, of the terror of the Light Wizards.

"Rella seemed to know who they were," Thomas murmured.

"Right before they blasted him into oblivion," Billie added.

"He survived." Tara slammed her fist against the table. "All of that terrible firepower, and *he* survived!"

"How is that possible when it even killed Regen?" Eleanor asked.

"He knew what they were," Thomas repeated. "He is not from this world. I don't even think he is a true symbioid. If anything could have survived their onslaught, it's him … it."

"Then how do we kill him?" Matchins said. "He is clearly an enormous threat to the safety of Weznin's people."

"Of all people," Alexander added.

"As are these wizards," Boss said. "We have two big-bads to deal with."

"The wizards might be dead," Matchins suggested. "What could survive a giant squid attack like that *and* a crash into the sea?"

"They didn't crash into the sea," Eleanor said. "Their trajectory was steered, controlled, even as they fell from the sky. If they were smart they would have aimed for land away from their current combatants. All that is out there are the Baul Islands. They are alive."

"We need to concentrate our actions, focus fire, one enemy at a time," Snipes said. "We aren't really in any shape to fight them if we are divided, not as we are."

"Then who is the bigger threat? Who do we go after first?" Alexander asked.

Out of the assembled, many answered at once, and the serious decorum erupted into a raucous chorus of conflicting responses.

"The Light Wizards," Tara, Boss, and Frogman said.

"Rella," Billie and Matchins said.

Thomas remained silent, contemplating the brewing dissonance, dissonance he felt himself.

"Neither." Madam Brune turned from the window facing out the sea, and the room turned to face her. "My goal was to intercept a slave transport carrying my people into forced servitude. That is my only concern."

"Mother," Eleanor said, "the Light Wizards landed out near the Baul Islands. Our people are in danger."

"Which is why I am not asking you to come with me, my dear, nor Alexander," Madam Brune said. "I will travel alone—I'm faster that way—and head off the slavers."

"We need you," Thomas said, quietly. "You are the reason we weren't slaughtered before the Heroes arrived."

"You *needed* me," she corrected. "Now there are others who do. As for my wounded ..."

"They will be safe here," Eleanor said.

"If we aren't attacked again," Billie added.

"We won't be attacked again because we are going after Rella!" Matchins shouted. "His people slaughtered my constables!"

"And what about our people!" Boss rose in anger.

Thomas eyed Madam Brune leaving the room as the discourse devolved into argument.

"Enough!" Thomas stood and all combative eyes turned to him. "Both of these threats have been weakened. I want nothing more than to track Rella down and rip out whatever he calls a heart. But according to Tara, one of these threats is capable and willing enough to destroy cities. Yes, Rella wants to kill all humanity and enslave all symbioids to do it for whatever twisted reason, but he is too weak to achieve his task without the help of assassins, without removing us. The wizards are the bigger threat, and we can't risk them repairing their ship."

"So you want me to take my men and leave Weznin waters?" Matchins asked. "We have no authority there, it'll be seen as an invasion by the Islanders, and they have good reason to retaliate as it is."

"No," Thomas answered. "I am going to take a force out to the Baul Islands, and we will finish what is left of these ... aliens. While we're doing that, Matchins, I want you to head to Copper Cobble. It's where the assassins' den is. I want you to press the constable force there for aid. I want you to observe, run interference, and plan an assault for capturing them, but don't act until we return."

"The Copper Cobble bastards won't help us!" Matchins protested. "The municipalities still work like the cities are separate city-states, with no cooperation between them. And they would not dare challenge the Night Assassins for fear of reprisal."

"That's why you'll explain to them how the Night Assassins launched a brazen assault on the constables from Quartrant," Thomas said. "Surely they'll share some fear then, thinking that they are next, that their turning of blind eyes to the assassins will no longer keep them safe. Surely there is some solidarity between constables you can rely on?"

Matchins was silent, considering this. "Fine." He crossed his arms.

"That place will be a death trap," Tara said.

"An assassin should go with him," Billie added. "Let me."

Thomas and Billie eyed each other. "You stay safe," he finally said.

Billie nodded. "You too." She clapped Matchins on the shoulder. "Come, Sergeant." They rose and left the room.

"Don't attack until we're there to back you up!" Thomas called out to them. "Observe and plan! That's all!"

"You really want us to boat out there with a squid in the waters?" Boss asked as the door swung closed. "It's suicide."

"Give me a day to rig the hull of our spare boat with the taser; the squid didn't like it," Thomas said.

"So ..." Snipes said, "we will leave in the morning?"

"We leave in the morning," Thomas confirmed.

"Are you two going to be all right working together?" Boss asked.

Thomas and Snipes regarded each other for a long moment. "I think it is maybe time I stopped blaming you for what happened in Foundton," Thomas said.

"Don't worry," Snipes answered. "I have blamed myself enough for the both of us."

Thomas sighed, and nodded.

Boss laughed. "Now we may just be unstoppable!"

* * *

It was a hard day for Thomas—exhausted as he was—to tinker with the boat hull, installing a cage of sorts to the exterior, insulated with rubber padding and attached to the taser crank by the helm. Billie helped as Matchins readied his few remaining constables to travel.

The next morning, after a night of fever dreams for most of the warriors, they set out from the New Symbicate hideout. The force on the boat included Thomas, Tara, Eleanor, Boss, Snipes, Frogman, Alexander, and an assortment of Heroes, freedom fighters, and a handful of constables left over by Matchins. This boat was larger than the one Thomas and Eleanor took from Drifton, but it was still cramped with all of those fighters.

The smoke in the distance still wafted up from the horizon. It would take the better part of two days to get there. They passed the time mostly in sullen silence.

CHAPTER 12

Rella

The convoy of steam wagons roared out the end of the tunnel and into Copper Cobble, screeching around the tight cobblestoned streets, which were slick with ice, before stopping at an inconspicuous high-rise wedged amongst a dense city block.

The Den.

It was a place with many outlets to nearby buildings and blocks from high, as well as from sewer and tunnel paths below, the perfect fortress for the Night Assassins in this mountain metropolis. There was some strike going on, on the far side of the city; the copper mines were deemed unsafe by the union, and the municipality was struggling to regain control of the city's artery of wealth.

This left few witnesses on the streets around the Den to see the deformed body of Rella emerge, roasted and charred like some hideous monster, nor his surviving husks along with the other assassins and finally the Night Mother, who may well have been out for a stroll, judging by her composure.

"So who were they?" she finally asked, once they entered her suite up above.

"The Prismath!" Rella smashed a glass table to bits.

"That was expensive," she said calmly. "A gift from a bureaucrat whose family I spared ... he suffered an accident shortly afterwards, and I don't know where he sourced it from." She tutted. "Expensive, like that failed attack. I'm used to losing assassin recruits, Rella, but I've only lost three full-fledged assassins these past few years, and two of those were Tara and Billie ..."

Rella screamed at the mention of Tara.

"But I lost twenty full-fledged assassins in that battle." She shook her head.

Rella raged again, tearing at the walls, smashing paintings and vases. Nicholas made to intervene, but a subtle head tilt from the Night Mother stopped him.

"And who are the Prismath?" she asked calmly, taking a seat on the only couch Rella had not yet overturned. "Some tea please," she asked Nicholas.

"I was so close to slaughtering her!" Rella growled through clenched teeth and halted before smashing a glass cabinet, regaining control. "Your sun-well has two habitable planets," he whispered as he squeezed his fists, but turned to face the Night Mother as if he was not horribly burned and enraged. "Prisma is slightly farther from the sun than this cesspool."

"A sun-well is?"

"Let's call it the gravitational jurisdiction of your star." Rella turned from her and stalked to the ceiling-high window, gazing up into the sky. "My progenitor attacked the Guardian of Prisma first, used its sinews to turn against its people to be consumed ..."

The Night Mother had just accepted her tea from Nicholas and paused half sip. "So you aren't a symbioid after all."

"No," Rella growled. "I am a scion of my true form, a scion of the scion that sacked their planet. I was sent ahead of time to infect your Guardian."

"Well," the Night Mother put down her saucer and rose, "you succeeded, I guess."

"No, I failed, and I failed again trusting your kind. I will have to expend more energy and do this myself." He turned to face the Night Mother, who had drawn her blade.

She sighed. "I was hoping our alliance would serve us both in the long run. But it seems to only serve me in the short term, at the detriment to my future plans ... it's a shame."

"It is ... it is difficult controlling many symbioids at once, but to fight the Prismath as well as the New Symbicate, I will need all the fodder I can muster." He was staring at the Night Mother with stilled features and intense focus, like a predator; his geriatric, twitching motions were gone. She hardly flinched under his gaze. "Your services are no longer required." He lunged forward, and the Night Mother blurred in shadow-form to greet his attack.

He plunged his fist into her shadowy form, and sickly tendrils sprouted from his limbs, stabbing and intertwining with the Night Mother as she became solid and went into spasms.

"W-what ..."

"I am infecting your symbioid, Night Mother. Your body will now be a vessel for my will, and soon, so will this whole festering city!"

CHAPTER 13

The New Symbicate

It was cramped, and many lamented Thomas's decision to pack the aero-breaks in the bow of the boat. Going up against a flying ship, you had no idea what you might need, but it did make things more crowded.

Despite the discomfort, the crossing in pursuit of the plume of black smoke was mostly uneventful ... mostly. The SWiGS attacked in the early evening of the first night. Thomas cranked the taser from the helm, and it whirred and shot through the insulated cage he had fitted to the hull.

There was a high-pitched scream and the smell of burning seafood; then the monster slinked back into the unfathomable depths out here in the deep.

On the morning of the third day, land was sighted.

The closest island was Bauttuon, one of the larger ones with sandy yellow beaches and palm trees along the low coast, which quickly rose up into a plateau of red rock. There was a fishing village to the south, and craggy boulders punctuated the sandy paths up onto the heights of the inlands.

"It's Baul, friends!" one of the freedom fighters cheered and jostled the others. "Baul!"

The cheers from them were stifled, however, when the source of the plume of smoke slowly became clear as they drew closer.

On the north side of the coast, wedged in the bottom of the cliff face several hundred metres from the shore, the Light Wizards' wrecked ship loomed in a shimmer of steam and smoke.

It was precariously placed—half embedded, half sunken—into the bottom of a now disrupted waterfall which cascaded onto the sizzling hull and steamed and sprayed everywhere before trickling back into the squat, winding stream that led out into the ocean.

The cliff itself was perhaps a few metres out of reach from the highest point of the now dull, crimson sails. Upon crashing, the ship had caused a minor landslide. Ramparts of strewn red rock and rubble had slid around the ship from the surrounding cliff face, mottling the waterfall further and damming parts of the misplaced water as it tried to make its way back into the stream.

Baul Islanders from the nearby village were busy trying to dig the ship out, some standing upon the hull a third of the way up the cliff, looking for survivors.

Thomas wiped sweat from his brow, the heat of the mid sea a punishing sensation as the sun rose. He regretted his long maroon cloak and the brass plating beneath it. Or at least he would regret it until the fighting started.

From the fire posts set up around the excavation site, the Baul Islanders sighted the approaching vessel and began to signal them.

"If there are any survivors in that wreck, the fools will set them loose," Snipes cursed.

"They mean well." Eleanor glared at him.

"They can't mean well if they're incinerated," Tara said coldly. "We need to accelerate."

The increased hum of the boat and the spewing of more steam from the engine was Thomas's answer to Tara's request.

"Start flagging them down!" Boss cried to the crammed warriors on the boat. "Get them away from that thing!"

As the vessel surged closer, the men and women of their war party at the prow began waving and shouting back to the Baul Islanders on the shore, shouting warnings of danger.

Thomas bit his lip. He knew it wouldn't make a difference until they got close enough to battle the wizards anyway.

As he had this thought, up in the thick of the rescue effort, a Baul Islander working to free the wreckage hammered at a stubborn lump of boulder wedged into what he thought was an opening into the ship. It cracked and rattled, tumbling out of place, and in its absence a gun extended forth from the opening, swivelling with a groan on weary cogs as it attempted to aim towards the approaching vessel.

"Cogrust," Snipes whispered, looking through his scope. "Hooks," he yelled, "that thing is going to sink us!"

"You think I don't know that?" Thomas steered the boat at an angle to deny the wizards a straight shot, but what else could he do? It would still be minutes before they could make landfall. "Everyone be ready to bail out!"

The red tracking light shone out from the cannon's red prism tip as the ship rumbled and mini rockslides caused the Baul Islander rescue group to flee. The tracking light swept the ocean, homing in on the vessel.

"It's targeting the symbioids on board," Tara breathed.

Thomas resisted the urge to blink. Eleanor and Tara would still be trapped on the vessel even if he got away. The light beam swept past them, homing in on the water by their vessel, and fired a white beam of bright light.

A high-pitched squeal erupted from the water, and a large dark shape thrashed to the surface and sped away.

"That squid was tailing us!" Boss cried. "Good thing we froze and didn't bail out … hah …"

More cannons emerged from the hull of the ship, broken and gnarled out of shape, but able enough to deal some serious damage. Thomas pushed the vessel as hard as it would tolerate from the wheelhouse, and they grinded onto shore.

"Find cover in the landslide!" someone barked.

Thomas grabbed Tara and Eleanor and blinked to the rockslide as the beams tore through the vessel.

The Hired Heroes and freedom fighters scattered off the ruptured boat, taking cover from the fortress of beam dispensing death that was the Light Wizards' ship. It kept rumbling and it lurched, keeling in towards the island at an angle, but remained lodged in place.

"It's not going anywhere, lads," Alexander said.

Tara risked a peek over cover and saw what she needed to do. "There's some kind of loading ramp partially open at the back, and there's that small stream jutting from the cliff face along the hull. I can get inside from there or from the hatches on top of it and deal some damage. Frogman can go along the stream and place charges beneath their gun emplacements. We will need cover."

Thomas drew his blade. "You say they target symbioids?" he asked. Tara nodded, her jaw set, grim determination in her brow. "Then I'll give you your cover." Eleanor reached to Thomas before he moved to blink. "Yes?" he asked.

"Be careful." She leaned in and kissed him on the lips.

He froze, and stunned ecstasy crept across his face. "Well," he finally managed to say as she pulled back from him, lost in her scent and taste, "I'll certainly have to." He blinked out of existence, and the next beam of light tore out from the ship, pursuing his flittering form.

"Concentrate your fire!" Boss ordered as he advanced to a boulder closer to the ship, risking a stray glancing blow from a wizard who had emerged on top of the vessel and was taking pot shots to cover others emerging alongside him. His weapon was a handheld version of the huge cannons their ship sported. "Keep the fight down here!"

Eleanor glanced at her brother and nodded. They fanned out their sword-shields and readied to advance as the Baul Islanders clustered behind them.

"Tara," she called before their manoeuvre. When no reply came she looked back over her shoulder. Tara was nowhere to be seen, and Frogman was disappearing into the surf.

"Ninjas." Alexander shrugged. "Let's go."

They stepped out of cover with their shields up and were immediately pushed back by a prism cannon which scattered their formation.

* * *

Thomas blinked erratically from cover to exposed ground to the peaks of the boulders, drawing the fire of the Light Wizards to the right flank as the villagers fled. He was breathing fast, sweating, exhausted, but that kiss ... it exhilarated him in a way he was afraid to explain.

He could keep going.

* * *

Snipes took aim at a wizard who was pinning down a group of Heroes moving up to the stream passing before the wrecked ship. He exhaled and fired with a crack from his modified blunderbuss, and the wizard fell back.

They wore stiff grey or brown military winter coats of some kind of sheepskin. Their heads bore steel-looking helmets that encased their whole face, with wide, shining, rectangular goggles. Snipes marvelled at how similarly they moved to people here on this world, but his musings were interrupted as two other of their shooters trained sights on him. With a yelp he recoiled when the boulder he was perched on sizzled and crumbled under their fire.

"Not used to other people taking aim at you, Snipes?" Boss laughed.

Snipes laughed back. "I guess not!"

* * *

Bobbing along the stream below, the sounds of the battle were muffled for Frogman, his way lit by a small, encased oil lantern on his shoulder and by the stray beams of light up from the surface which silhouetted the symbioid-powered breathing buoy that filtered air down to him through a tube.

He halted as a cannon embedded into the lower hull beneath the water lit him up in red, ghastly light, then relaxed as the white light caused the water to steam and fizzle, creating enough cover for him to skitter along the bottom like a crustacean who had just been exposed, and place a saboteur bomb to the ship's underside. He continued to bob along the dank stream bottom, placing charges, when a hatch opened and one of the wizards in a rounded, fully encased metal suit popped its head out, spotted him, and drew a long knife.

"Oi," Frogman said in surprise to himself within his helmet. He gazed up his own breathing tube to his buoy and back down to the emerging wizard. The wizard had his own air supply from tanks strapped to his back. "Never fought another scuba warrior before," he said.

He launched at the wizard before he could jump up and swipe at Frogman's lifeline, and they wrestled in the disturbed water.

* * *

Up on the red cliff face by the top of the waterfall, Tara panted, having scrambled around and up the battlefield. She looked down at the battle which had spread across the beach; the New

Symbicate warband was spreading out to avoid the beams and concentrating their fire on the effectively immobilised wizards upon the hull. Thomas blinked sporadically across the area, drawing most of the wizards' fire. But despite his efforts, there was a steady build-up of friendly casualties. There seemed to be hardly any casualties from the wizards so far.

Not for long.

Tara's mind swam with the horrors of Crankod. The screams, the smell, the crushing depths of the Barcos as the weir was destroyed ... and of Regen burning into ashes, atomised, only to be swept out to sea. The rage bubbled within her as she stood over the vessel that caused such devastation. The wizards were now brought low, their ship wrecked upon a cliff face and its crew exposed upon its hull. She was going to kill them; she was going to kill them all.

With a snarl, Tara leaped off the ridge, aiming for the now crumpled rust-hued sail which had ushered these terrible people to her world's gravital shores. She scaled down, over half a dozen wizard shooters.

The vibrating zipping of her sliding down the mechanical rigging at speed caused one of the masked aliens to look up. His cry was silenced as her smoke bomb engulfed the group. Tara landed and rolled up into the bloody work, slashing out at the respirator of the hapless wizard who spotted her initially.

In a gasp, a large swathe of her smoke was inhaled into the battle mask, and he started choking. A light in the smoke came towards her, and she deflected a thrust from the beam rifle of the next wizard in the haze. Her opponent cried out as Tara's knife imbedded into her gut, and she drew back her blade, which was slick with ink-blue blood.

One of the snipers dropped a device which whirred and sucked the smoke into it, so Tara stomped it, and it cracked with a shower of sparks. She kicked it away, her veil partially broken as she leaped up and fly-kicked the gadget-wielder in the face, sending him screaming over the banister and into the shallow stream below.

A beam of light strobed over her shoulder, and with a swear Tara ducked and scrambled into a roll; she flung a knife that knocked her attacker's next shot off mark and rushed to engage him. He brought his rifle around to block her stabs, and they engaged in a deadly grapple upon the deck as the battle raged below.

* * *

Thomas blinked onto a boulder and slipped when one of the cannons shot where he had landed. He stumbled forward and landed heavily onto the beach, his fall softened by sand and the charred corpse of what he assumed was one of his former Hero comrades. His position lit up red as a cannon took aim, and he scrambled behind cover, watching in horror as the charred body that had saved him was burned further into oblivion.

He took a breath, trying to steady his shaking limbs. The blink symbioid accepted him, unlike its previous user—Eric— so using it did not drain him as quickly as it did his former friend. But he had never used it this much before, not after continuous days of intense toil. It was taking its toll, and the cannons were cluing in to his movements, following him to where he would blink almost before he got there.

He couldn't keep this up for long.

Another strafe of light and he heard Eleanor's cry as she crouched behind her shield somewhere in the fray.

He had to keep going.

He took another breath and blinked again.

* * *

Beneath the churning waters in the stream where Frogman was battling with his better equipped opponent, he was knocked back and bobbed onto the riverbed, sediment rising around him. He fumbled for his blade and held it up, expecting the wizard to launch down on top of him to strangle his oxygen cord.

But the sediment cleared with the stream just enough for him to see the dark figure holding an alien-looking pistol with a crystal set into its barrel. It shone as the wizard charged the light energy within it to fire. Frogman's eyes widened, knowing that if he survived the blast, it would compromise his suit and he would drown down here.

That's when a figure splashed the water, another wizard who Tara had knocked down from above. He landed on top of Frogman's assailant and pushed him forward, down onto Frogman's blade.

There was a cry, muffled by the water and the dulled explosions from above, and Frogman realised that he would be surviving down here after all. He pushed the two bodies from him, who were dragged listlessly along the riverbed by the current, and went about his work.

* * *

Snipes ducked under a stray sniper's beam and aimed down his scope to return fire, only to find no available targets. Tara had dropped her smoke bomb.

"Cogrust," he swore.

"What is it?" Boss said as he desperately held a field dressing over a Hero's scorched eye.

"That assassin girl dropped a smoke bomb. I can't cover her and now none of us have any targets that aren't an armoured hull. We're useless until she does her job."

"Keep a steady eye on her battle," Eleanor grunted from another boulder. "Tara is capable but sometimes bites off more than she can chew!"

"Roger," Snipes said, and peered through his scope into the smoke cloud, which began to clear rapidly.

* * *

Tara pivoted and threw her opponent over her shoulder, keeping hold of the alien rifle—it was sleek dark-grey metal, with indicator lights along the barrel that led to the crystal set into the end—this was the tool they used to slaughter a city. She flipped it over and aimed at the downed wizard, the crystal in the barrel flashing as she squeezed the trigger. Something rose in her throat, her breath hard and rapid as she clenched her jaw tight, baring her teeth even though her scarf and hood covered her face.

The wizard panicked, tried to rise, tried to roll away, tried to beg, but he was not fast enough for Tara's wrath.

The beam burst from the rifle and burned into the wizard's writhing form.

"How does it feel?" Tara spat, keeping pressure on the trigger as the beam of light tore perpetually into the body. The white light burned through his coat, his armour, and his flesh, sizzling and sputtering until the body stopped writhing and burst into flames. "How does it feel?" she screamed.

A wizard emerged from a hatch behind her, but she could not hear him in her bloodlust, could not hear him over the sound of the battle and her focus on the burning body beneath her, which she continued to fry in fury.

She could not feel the change in the air pressure when he moved on her rear, drawing an angular blade to run her through.

All she felt was a tingling and then the blood splatter as it hit her.

She gasped and turned. The wizard had been sniped from the beach, dead before he hit the ground, blade clattering away.

From the beach, Snipes reloaded his rifle.

Tara looked down at the body of the enemy she had failed to detect, looked at the body she had charred into a smoking, stinking mess, and instead of bubbling rage, a bile rose in her throat. She dropped the rifle and retched, pulling Eric's yellow scarf from her mouth and copping a lung full of the charred, smoked smell of the wizard's body.

Not for the first time the thought of monster-hood passed through her mind, *a killer, born and trained.* She trembled and collapsed onto the deck of the ship, weeping in anguish.

Beside the hatch where the wizard had emerged, a contraption rose, haltingly, with a screeching of ruined metal mechanisms. It was a turret, two prongs of prism set rifles secured to a central casing. The turret swivelled slowly towards her. It was badly damaged; they had only just managed to fix it, she figured. In her distress she hesitated, and capitalising on her slowness, it took aim at her. Another shot from Snipes pinged off the turret uselessly, and Tara lit up with red light as it readied to fire.

She nodded to herself. "This is what I deserve." The turret's guns whined as they charged to fire, and she closed her eyes.

The tingling down her spine intensified.

From below, there was an explosion—Frogman's charges.

The ship rocked and Tara fell from the turret's line of fire, tumbling into a tear in the side of the hull that had opened under the stress of the explosions from below, and she slipped inside in a blundering state.

* * *

Watching the ship rock and sway as its underside exploded was a sight to see, and it gave Thomas some breathing room. He blinked onto a boulder while the ship screeched and a second rockslide cascaded over it from the cliff, battering the already gnarled hull and sending more cascading water flowing over it from the increasingly damaged waterfall.

"Don't tell me I have to thank Frogman for something?" Thomas panted, hunched over and gripping his knees as he tried to catch his breath.

The Heroes and freedom fighters taking cover among the boulders started cheering, but were soon cut short when the rockslide abated. In the silence and clearing dust, the ship appeared to be in much the same condition as it was before.

It shuddered, the cannons protruding from its hull reorienting, sweeping red aiming lights through the haze.

"All right, lads," Boss yelled. "Nobody said this would be easy!"

The first cannon beam streaked towards Thomas, so he blinked away. The second beam streaked towards him, and then the third, and fourth.

Thomas blinked towards a boulder, and before he touched down, it exploded into rubble as the Light Wizards concentrated all of their fire upon him.

"Cogrust!" He blinked away. The sand where he alighted next lit up with red light, and he dove aside; an instant later the sand was sizzled into shimmering glass.

More red lights traced his position.

He blinked up—there was nowhere else to go—and the cannons followed.

Eleanor looked on in bewildered horror as Thomas blinked sporadically higher into the air, and the increasing concentration of beams followed, the white lights fracturing through the steam and smoke into technicoloured lashings. It would have been beautiful in the night, if she did not know that Thomas was in danger, being targeted, and forced into an area that was not his strength.

Heights ...

Thomas blinked haphazardly upwards as the cannons kept track, his gut dropping each time he looked through the strobing sky to the ground, which pulled farther away from him in his evading path. One beam singed his side, and he floundered, falling towards the hull, which rushed up to greet him.

The panic took him; his breathing quickened as the air rushed past him. He tried to blink to safety, but another cannon struck the plating on his back beneath his cloak, and he was knocked into a smoking, spiralling plummet. He was too weary and too dizzy to do anything but fall. The chrome hull filled his vision as he fell towards it, and he shut his eyes, waiting for the end.

He could have sworn he heard Eleanor screaming.

* * *

Tara pushed herself up from the hard floor, shaking her head in bewilderment as the ship rumbled.

"What?" she mumbled, looking around through the haze. "Was I unconscious?"

She was in a narrow corridor lined with chrome plating and a grated metal floor. The battle still raged outside the tear in the hull. Frogman's charges had saved her pathetic life but failed to kill the enemy.

She coughed, trying to dismiss the thought from her mind, the thought of what she had just done to another living being. She remembered what was at stake. Her friends were risking their lives outside, the threat to the world was here, and elsewhere other threats in the form of Rella and the Night Assassins were regrouping. She shook off her apathy and rose, peering through the murky corridor which had strobing red lights along the curving ceiling, casting a flickering sense of dread through the smoke.

The air was circulating through vents, being recycled and purified to the point it tasted stale once the dust cleared. But it was much easier to breathe after a few minutes, and she tried to think. *This place is being controlled from somewhere. I must find the bridge and shut it down, and then the New Symbicate can move in and kill* ... she shuddered, remembering the burning body on the deck above, *no*, capture *the wizards*.

She clutched her blade closely and shuffled down the corridor, pressed against the wall to keep her standing despite her sheer exhaustion.

She quickly came to a partition and a narrow opening heading deeper into the bowels of the ship. *A vent?* She looked around, thinking this was some sort of maintenance corridor, which explained the lack of enemies. The tingling down her spine intensified, and she decided to trust it as she would her gut. Vents she knew, vents she could deal with. She took a deep breath and shuffled into the narrow space, crawling deeper into the belly of the beast.

The air was cooler in here, channelled down the shaft as the floor turned from steel grating to opaque chrome panels. Her sweat from her exertions began to chill her beneath her jacket as it clung to her skin. She pushed the discomfort aside and crawled through the little tunnel, until she stumbled upon what she was after.

There was more grated flooring ahead and beneath it a strange room, a control centre—a bridge. A man in wizard attire stood up from a leather swivel chair and approached a wall of consoles and impossible windows that flashed with images from outside, manned by staff with strange headsets and miniature microphones.

The man's uniform was different from the others: bluish grey with silver bars on his broad shoulders. The coat hugged his chest, which highlighted his strong frame, but he was also lean at the same time. He had black skin, not Mason black, not the beautiful umber tone of the people from the north, but a pitch black—a night black—accented by short-cropped silver hair.

They were not all the same. One of the technicians by the strange consoles had peach-coloured skin with hints of rose and off-green long hair tied into a tight bun. Another had skin that was bronzed, like a Soth man had applied fake tanning lotion in ludicrous quantities, and his hair was copper coloured.

So they are as diverse as we are, Tara thought curiously—uselessly. *They still need to be defeated.*

She took a quick look at the room; the technicians weren't dressed like the fighters she had seen, wearing thick jumpsuits of bronze or red, and seemed like easy enough foes, but they had pistols set with crystals on their hips. She could not see the edges of the room, and had no awareness of any guards who may be present. The proud-looking man with silver hair—a captain, she assumed—looked like a fight and a half.

"I want an update," he said.

Tara almost gasped—she could understand him. The accent was odd, and the vowels were hollowed out, as if he was struggling not to burst into a deep song—his voice was incredibly deep. But she could understand him.

"Captain Mallel," the rosy-peach-skinned technician said, "our snipers have been routed. I would not advise sending more out there until that ninja Stemcog is repelled."

"Where is she, Votly?" Mallel responded.

"She's disappeared, Captain," Votly answered. Her voice was airy, delicate, frantic. "I don't think we can count on that explosion taking her out."

"Lower hull is inaccessible from the stream from the blast," the bronze-skinned one said, "so no hope of that flanking squad from the ocean."

Mallel grunted. "Then continue to use our available cannons, Bromean. We must hold them off until our maintenance crew can repair the engines."

"We *are* using them, sir," a technician Tara could not see said. "The majority of our attackers have found cover though; only the one that is infected is presenting himself as a target."

"Infected?" Tara breathed.

"The teleporter?" Mallel asked.

"Yes sir. We have analysed his pattern of movement, and he seems to be sticking close to the ground, as if he's adverse to the heights. I have plotted a solution that would drive him upwards, maybe catch him off guard and out in the open?"

"Cogrust, Thomas." Tara's mind raced. *He hates heights, can't think straight at them; he'll get hit eventually.*

Mallel nodded. "Do it. He may be drawing our fire from something, but he seems to be the most capable of catching us off guard should we turn our attention elsewhere. Finish him quickly."

"Implementing solution. We now have forty-five percent of our starboard cannons operational. This will be over quickly."

"Cogrust!" Tara raged quietly. "Gear-jamming crap!" She had to act, *now*.

She lifted her body, bracing herself against the vent's sides to slam down through the grating and break into the bridge.

A tone sounded by Votly's console.

"Captain!" her airy voice squeaked. "Scion detected within the ship!"

"Where?" Mallel spun, flourishing an angular cutlass which bristled with sparkling energy.

Tara slammed down through the vent and landed within the bridge, brandishing her long dagger.

"I am here to accept your surrender!" she roared.

The captain paused, sizing her up. He was head and shoulders taller than she was, broader, and he held himself with the confidence born of innumerable battles, but he gazed at her seriously, ready for anything. "Continue with the battle," he ordered, before lunging in to strike.

His sword smashed Tara's blade right out of her hand; as contact was made, it vibrated the metal and shook it uncontrollably until she lost her grip. He kicked her back and she rolled over her shoulder to come up in a crouch, pulling two throwing knives and holding them underarm.

"You won't win," he said. "I simply can't let you win."

"You can't survive," she countered, heat and fury overriding her previous revulsion at what she did to the wizard upon the hull. *This one is in charge; this one would have ordered the attack on Crankod.* "I simply can't let you survive." She leaped forward.

She dived over his swing, rolling again, and swiped at the back of his leg. It glanced off the fabric—some kind of hardened fibre—and he backhanded her across the face. She flinched back and spun, hook-kicking him in the jaw. He stumbled into his chair with a roar.

The one called Bromean rose and fired his pistol. Tara dodged and weaved forward, easily avoiding the panicked beam, and leaped to kick the technician in the face. His body embedded into the strange window, which cracked and went dark.

Votly screamed—fumbling for her pistol with clammy hands—and the other technician she could not see before ran from the room.

Mallel was up again, his fists clenched so hard that his black knuckles turned a faint hue of blue.

With a roar he launched forward, and Tara sidestepped him. Mallel stopped just before ramming into the unconscious Bromean and turned to follow Tara as she leaped and rolled out of his way.

Tire him out, she kept thinking. Mallel wasn't the biggest man she had ever fought, but she knew she could not match him in a close quarter battle. She had to tire him out.

The doors that the other technician fled through slid open, and an older man strode in. He had rose-tinted skin with a long white beard down to his belly and wore loose brown robes. He carried a bulky, technological-looking staff with a prism set into its top, around which spun whirring gears and cogs and lit-up contraptions.

"Mallel, cover your eyes!" the newcomer bellowed.

The staff in his hands shone with amazing light, and Tara went blind. Then she was smacked to the ground. Powerful limbs embraced her, lifted her, and slammed her back down into the floor.

Coughing through winded agony, her vision returned enough for her to find Mallel standing over her, with Bromean's pistol in hand.

"Forgive me, please," he said.

Her spine's tingling spiked.

The roof seemed to collapse, a figure in maroon appearing on the ceiling before tumbling down.

It was Thomas.

He slammed into the elderly wizard, knocking the staff from his hands. Mallel was taken aback and stepped away in shock. Tara pushed off the ground, leaping to her feet, and bit Mallel's hand. Blue blood seeped into her mouth, and he cried in pain, dropping the pistol. She put her throwing knife to his throat, pressing him up against the wall.

She spat inky blood from her mouth and addressed Votly, the technician who was frozen in shock. "Disarm the ship now or your captain dies!" she snarled, blue-blooded teeth stunning the woman into compliance.

Without hesitation, Votly hit a switch, and the sounds of battle from outside subdued; the ship hummed, powering down weapons and the like.

Wizard soldiers—mostly in brown coats like the one Tara had burned—burst into the room, and Tara ducked behind Mallel as Thomas rose and held the elderly wizard by the neck.

"Surrender now or your leaders die," she snarled. "Do it now, you bastards!"

The soldiers glanced at one another, and one stepped forward, lowering his weapon as he held up his free hand in surrender. "Scrond?" he said to the wizard in Thomas's grip.

"They aren't what we expected," the wizard replied.

"And what did you expect?" Thomas asked, tightening his hold.

"Captain," Scrond struggled to face Mallel, "I think we can trust them for the moment."

"Do it then, lay down your weapons," Mallel ordered, "and let's hear them out."

"Why should we talk after you slaughtered a whole city!" Tara spat. "Innocent people!"

"They were infected," Mallel replied calmly, ignoring the increased pressure of Tara's blade on his neck, ignoring the sharp pain and the thin blue line of his blood. "The Rel had them, or it soon would."

"The Rel?" Thomas asked, loosening his grip on the elderly wizard. "You mean Rella?"

"Who?" one of the soldiers asked.

"Shut up!" Tara screamed and they all flinched back.

"Tara," Thomas cautioned, "we are outnumbered here. Calm yourself until they've fully surrendered."

Tara seethed at him and then growled, snapping her attention to Votly. "Open all of the hatches, and once we have you all submitted, we will have that talk."

"Okay, okay!" Votly said, pushing a button. The creaking of hatches opening sounded throughout the ship.

"Good," Tara said, keeping her blade to Mallel's throat. Then she said to Thomas, "I didn't know you could blink through walls?"

Thomas smiled. "Until then, neither did I." He laughed nervously.

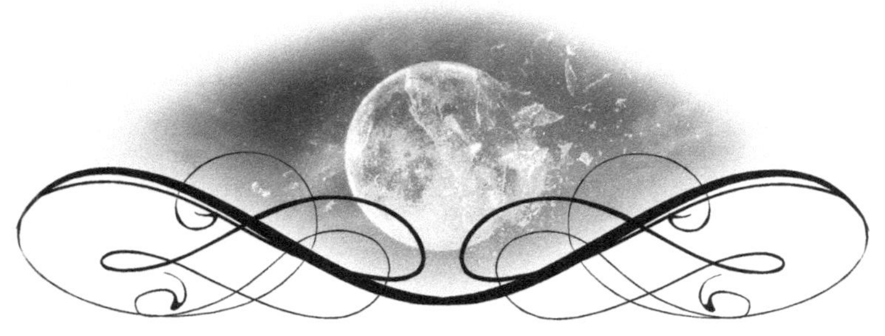

CHAPTER 14

The Light Wizards

Despite the cruel malice that Tara had described the Light Wizards with while struggling in the depths of her churning rage, their surrender and disarmament was a relatively civilised affair. Apart from the technicians and noncombative crew, there were two castes of warrior among them: prism marines in the grey coats who were less in number and seemed more proficient in combat, and the more numerous but less disciplined riflemen in the brown coats. They were stripped of their weapons—which they called prism rifles—and sat down in a line at the mess hall of the ship, guarded by the less zealous Heroes and Islanders.

Seeing them without their breathing masks and their alien, rectangular eyepieces was disarming. They looked just like people, despite the odd colours of their skin and hair. There seemed to be four ethnicities among them. There were ones with pitch-black skin and varying shades of silver hair, some had the rosy-peach skin with green or reddish hair, and there were the bronzed ones with copper-coloured hair as well as the rose-tinted ones who had an assortment of pale brown, grey, or white hair. They were quite calm, looking at their captors with curious suspicion, and their civility made Tara all the more furious.

There were two apparent leaders, Captain Mallel and the elder one, whose title was High Prismatist Scrond—the riflemen seemed to respect Scrond more than their captain, but the marines were deferent to both.

After Boss struggled to say "High Prismatist," Scrond smiled warmly and said that "just Scrond is fine."

Thomas, Tara, Eleanor, and Boss stood before the kneeling Mallel and Scrond on the bridge, with two Baul Islanders guarding the door.

"So," Thomas said, as they considered each other for a while, "how can we understand you?"

"There is actually an interesting theory for that," Scrond started. His voice was frail but carried the wisdom of a long life. His eyes scrunched with glee at Thomas's question, an opportunity to teach and nurture. "It is said, that in the time before ..."

"To Moon-Fall with this!" Tara surged forward and struck Mallel hard across the face; he grunted and Scrond flinched back as Tara screamed at their faces. "Hundreds, *thousands* of innocents died when you razed Crankod! My friend! All of those children!" She reared to strike Mallel again, but Thomas was there in a blink, restraining her.

"Easy, Tara, easy."

"Let go of me!" She struggled half in earnest against Thomas but ultimately let him lead her away.

"You make sure she's okay," Eleanor said. "Boss and I can handle this."

Thomas nodded as he carried Tara from the room and sat her down in the chrome hall once the doors slid shut.

"Tara, hitting a bound man ... it isn't you."

She glared up at him. "How about burning a man alive as he screamed and struggled to flee? Huh? Is that not me?" Thomas opened his mouth to speak, but she spoke over him. "Whatever you're about to say is cogrust. I'm a monster, Thomas. Raised to kill, trained to be good at it, even to like it. There is no point in denying what I am." She pushed herself up and made to walk away when Thomas grabbed her by the arm.

"Do you think me a monster for killing Eric?" he said softly, in barely a whisper.

She rounded on him, her eyes flashing with shock and fury and concern all in the space of a breath. "Of course not," she said. "That situation was forced on you. He was responsible for that battle as much as you; he could have helped bring his uncle to justice without further bloodshed. Your hand was forced in a horrible, ugly moment."

"Then could I ask you a favour?" he asked. She looked away, so he continued. "That compassion and understanding you use for me, use it for yourself."

Her tears flowed freely, dropping from her cheeks and onto the cold, sterile floors.

"You were put into a terrible situation too, Tara, at such a young age, like me. You overcame that and then had to face this." He gestured around the ship. "Allow yourself to not be perfect, okay?"

"What I did was horrible!" she cried, leaning into his embrace. "I can still smell the burned flesh." She reached for his arm and hesitated before caressing the burned skin showing at the cuff of his sleeves. *Large swathes of his body must be marred*, she thought, *from the trauma he went through as a child*. And she hated herself for using those words in front of him.

"It'll take time," Thomas held her closer, sensing her thoughts, "but you *can* heal. Have faith in yourself. You are not the monster you think yourself to be. Are you able to come with me to find answers? Or would you like to be left alone?"

Tara sniffed. "No, I can do it."

Thomas smiled, pulling back from her. "That's my ninja!"

With a deep breath, Tara followed him back onto the bridge.

Mallel eyed Tara warily, but did not shirk away. He held himself with deep stoicism.

"Your friends here tell us that you were in the city we attacked," Scrond said.

"Crankod," Tara said quietly, as she shuffled to the darker corners of the room.

"It was a feat you survived," Mallel said. "It is no wonder you could overcome our defences."

"I did not survive alone, nor take you down alone," Tara replied. "Now tell me why."

"Perhaps it is best we start at the beginning?" Scrond said. "May I stand? This floor is hurting my knees."

Boss hefted him up and guided him to the captain's chair. "Speak, and keep it brief; we have other enemies to battle."

"Yes, I bet, the Rel," Scrond said with a wrinkled smile, his long white beard swaying as he shook his head.

"You mean Rella?" Thomas asked.

"So that is what this scion calls itself—very well, Rella. My cousins, we come from a sister planet to yours here in this sun well. Your astronomers have sighted it many times, I'm sure. I am not sure what you call it, but we call our planet Prisma. We call yours Stemcog. What do you call it?"

There was an awkward silence as the members of the New Symbicate and Boss glanced at each other.

"The ones before you aren't the most academic bunch," Boss said, "but as far as I am concerned, we have always just referred to it as the world."

"Ah." Scrond looked aside, contemplating this. "Not a very forward-looking society then; at least, not yet."

"You would do well not to insult us given the situation," Eleanor said, sensing Tara's tension. "And perhaps we have not looked to the stars so much since our moon shattered and littered our world with ruin. Great perversities were endured and many terrible wars were fought in the aftermath and as people migrated from the affected lands and resources were fought over."

"Ah ..." Scrond trailed off, and his shoulders dropped. He glanced at Mallel, who nodded solemnly, and Scrond continued. "Well, both of our worlds once had similarly sized moons. They were inhabited with cosmic creatures that we called Guardians; ours and yours were probably some form of sibling, I am sure. Our Guardian defended us from threats, cosmic beasts, and dangers. We believe they took up sentry on their own volition out of benevolence or were entreated—designed—for the task by some higher power we do not yet understand. However, whatever power the Guardians held to was challenged. The cosmic entity we call the Rel tried to attack many times; we have many legends of our Guardian fending this evil off over the ages. I'm sure if you looked at your own myths, you would find similar stories of beasts from the void.

"Anyway, I digress. The Rel crafted a new evil, an infection, which turned our Guardian against us, split it apart in a civil self-war that ravaged our moon. And the miniature entities that split off from it descended onto our world. The Rel beings would weave into us, infect us, and turn us against each other. It was a war that lasted generations. And we were losing. The Rel was infecting more and more of our Guardian by the year, and once that battle was lost, we feared that the whole moon would be driven down onto our planet.

"So we developed a weapon, a great staff of power which would absorb the very energy of light and then transmute that energy into solid form with infinite momentum and power. We call the technology that makes it possible wave-form.

"As the moon passed over our capital city, we revealed our last bastion of defence, drawing out what we believed to be the nerve centre of the Rel. We destroyed it at great cost to our city and our people in a titanic battle ..." Scrond took a deep breath.

"It is okay, High Prismatist, the battle is over," Mallel said.

"Once the battle was done," Scrond continued, "eventually the Rel creatures died, everyone who was tainted died, and sadly, so did our Guardian. It is now a dead husk that orbits our world as a bitter reminder. We knew that Stemcog's moon, your moon, also had a Guardian, so we turned our attention to it. We were horrified to find that the Rel was in the process of infecting it too ... so we launched our ultimate weapon against it."

Thomas's eyes widened. "The cubes ... you fired an infinite cube at our moon, and it shattered?"

"You know of the cubes?" Mallel raised an eyebrow.

Boss and Thomas produced their cubes, a smattering of colours from amber to green. "We use them as currency."

"Ah ... strange," Scrond said.

"So you caused the destruction," Eleanor said. "The flooding of the inlands, the meteor showers that lasted generations, the wars as people vied to control symbioid and cube alike only to realise how widespread they were? You did all of it? You shattered our moon!"

Scrond sighed. "Yes, to our everlasting shame, yes we did."

"And you are alive because of it," Mallel said. "But we knew your world wasn't safe yet, showered with potential infections. We developed a ship to come and finish off any surviving traces of the Rel. When we came closer, to our horror we realised that many of you were infected, and we homed in on the largest population of the Guardian tendrils to begin our purge.

"If your planet was overrun, if the meat of your people and your Guardian was turned against us, we might not survive." He looked at Tara. "When we attacked your city, we thought it lost to monsters. If you had witnessed the atrocities they committed ... if you had seen what terror that the Rel had wrought ... I am so sorry." Mallel looked down at the deck and shuddered, a motion that broke his stoic demeanour for only an instant.

Tara said nothing.

"Mallel was just a boy during that fateful battle on Prisma." Scrond eyed Tara intently. "And on the day I struck the Rel down, he fought more terrors than many can comprehend in their entire lifetime."

"So Rella," Thomas said, "I was hoping he was just trying to frighten us with his tales of infecting the symbioids. But it turns out it's true; he wants us and the symbioids all dead."

"Symbioids?" Scrond asked.

"What we call the pieces of your guardian moon," Boss explained. "They can weave with us and devices to provide useful properties and powers. And you say Rella can infect them, which explains how he has turned people into husks ..." He looked at Thomas. "And we sent your sister after them with Matchins."

Thomas gasped. "And if Rella has revealed himself, if he knows the Wizards are here to finish him off ... he will react rashly, maybe husk the whole city. Billie is in danger."

"Wizards?" Mallel asked.

"That's what we've been calling you." Boss shrugged.

"Silence!" Tara strode forward, and the room turned their attention to her. "Rella, why hasn't he taken over already?"

"He was incredibly weak. He wasn't even conscious until the original Symbicate tried to gather the symbioids," Thomas said. "And even then they essentially held him hostage in Masonville as he feared their orb device. But now he is regaining his strength. The device must have been destroyed by Eric's butler. We have to get to Copper Cobble and destroy every tendril of his being."

"How?" Boss asked. "It would take too long."

"If we had a chance to repair our ship?" Mallel ventured. Tara seethed at him, and he met her glare without flinching. "We see now that not all of your ... symbioids are infected, that we now have a chance to carve this cancer out in one fell swoop ... our interests are aligned."

Thomas and Eleanor looked to Tara as she crouched down in front of Mallel, drawing her knife slowly.

With a quick slash his bonds were cut.

"We are allies then, but once this is over, I will make you pay for what you did to Crankod."

Mallel massaged his wrists as he rose. "I will pay any cost to atone for my sins, Stemcog ... as I am sure you would too."

Tara glanced away, to Thomas, and then back to Mallel. "We'll see."

CHAPTER 15

Billie Marrow

It was a long journey to Copper Cobble—*only two days by steam wagon*, some would think—but the entire time Billie fretted over the fate of her family. Every jolt of the already rumbling carriage on the poorly maintained, winding mountain road sent her mind spiralling into despair.

She was constantly fidgeting with her nails, and when they started to bleed, she pulled out a multi-tool to tinker with her grappling hooks. Tinkering was a strong word for what she was doing, constantly screwing and unscrewing a bolt with her ratchet.

Matchins talked quietly with the two other officers in the trundling carriage, leaving Billie to her devices. They occasionally glanced at her with an air of suspicion, knowing what she was. She ignored that—she already had enough to fret on.

The air grew chilly as they zigzagged up the mountain paths, and they had to hold their cloaks tightly to their necks when they stopped to rest at the dirty, dingy waystations. Their road wound around and between the mountain ranges of Copper Cobble. She could have done it quicker through other roads and lifts and carefully disguised zip-lines if she didn't have to come with the constables.

The higher they climbed the more the icy gusts would buffet the carriage, whipping at the flames in the engine, which caused it to sputter and stall. The snow caps were gradually unloading upon them in the gales, littering the grey mountainsides. As they progressed, scattered all around the mountain range was evidence of the mining industry. Shafts and tunnels bored into the mountainsides with tracks and gondolas crisscrossing the peaks, marring the pristine vista along the main road that made its way into Copper Cobble.

Billie's ratchet broke at the socket. She had been straining it against the case of her grapple housing as her mind imagined Thomas, Tara, and Eleanor being vaporised by a beam of light from the Wizards.

The constables jolted at the sudden, sharp snap and Matchins laughed. "A lot on our mind?" The first direct communication she thought they had ever shared.

"You could tell?" she said with a weak smirk.

"I recognise emotion when I am feeling it myself." Matchins shrugged. "We are going into unknown territory."

"It's well known to me, Sergeant," she replied. "I was worried about my friends."

"Ah, maybe we should take your mind off that then? Worrying about them will do nothing, especially given how capable they all are. I'm more worried about our task ahead."

"How would you take my mind off them?" Billie asked.

Matchins stroked his moustache thoughtfully, and his eyes lit up. "Those hooks, they have a dead symbioid, yes?"

"Mechanical symbioids," Billie corrected.

"Yes, yes of course. And the symbioid is woven into the mechanism and throughout your muscle and skeletal structure, which is why your arms don't tear off when you use them?"

"Yes?" Billie raised an eyebrow.

"So you never take them off?" Matchins asked.

"No."

"Ever?" he smirked.

"Is that a problem for you?" she smirked back.

"Not at all. You're not my type anyway. Wouldn't they rust when you wash?"

"You aren't my type either," Billie said. "The casings are a special brass alloy; they'll tarnish slowly over time if I don't care for them. As for the mechanisms, the symbioid keeps them in good repair, and I like to tinker with it anyway."

"What of your goggles?" the constable next to Billie asked. His name was Bettly. "Do they not come off?"

"When I wear them the symbioid weaves into my cranium so I can control them with my thoughts. But this is not a structural weave and can be removed and rewoven relatively quickly," Billie answered. "Do you boys require more classroom teachings?"

"I would like to know how we are going to survive on the streets of Copper Cobble," the other constable—Rutters— said. "The assassins we're going after know Quartrant constables were at the battle at Tinrod. They will pick us off on the street."

"Do not worry about that," Billie said. "I know their ways."

"What's the plan?" Matchins asked. "We will be arriving very shortly." He gestured out the window; they passed a sign that read, *Welcome to Copper Cobble, the mineral capital of Weznin,* as they passed between two short peaks and into a raucous hubbub. "The steam wagon will only take us as far as the station on the edge of the caldera, and we heard no reply from their municipality before we left, so an escort is not likely."

"You three will follow the most direct route to the constable's station. Just follow the main street, bear right at the fork, and take a left at the next main intersection," Billie said.

"We'll be sitting ducks," Bettly said.

"You'll draw out their sentries, and I will deal with them," Billie replied.

"They know what you look like too," Rutters countered.

"I have my ways, constable."

"A fake moustache?" Matchins smiled, and his gruff demeanour broke again momentarily. "Might look out of place next to mine."

Billie stifled a giggle. "I'll make do."

The steam wagon hissed to a halt, and the constables disembarked onto the arrivals bay. Copper Cobble was built onto a flat plain carved out of the mountain's peaks. The treads on the steam wagon were built for the shoddy mountain roads, but the steam wagon wasn't allowed up onto the city platform to muddy and destroy the delicately cobbled paths. The three constables found themselves standing below the lip of that vast, citywide platform; it rose to head height, and they found a staircase to ascend into the city proper.

"Where will we meet?" Matchins turned to Billie to find she had disappeared. "Well, lads, let's hop to it."

They milled against the crowds as they ascended the stairs, past destitute miners and cargo workers who held out cups filled with pale blue cubes, begging for more. The steam wagon terminals were busy with thousands of people trying to leave in an exodus.

"What's going on here, Sergeant?" Bettly asked.

"I have no idea." Matchins was scanning the area for Copper Cobble constables; he saw some green uniforms—the Copper Cobble Municipality colours—amongst the crowds, but the constables were too busy to offer any assistance. "Let's just stick to the girl's plan, shall we?" They set off.

The buildings were built in tight, tall blocks of red brick and metal-laced masonry with wide-paned, iron-barred windows that were shuttered closed, and heavily slanted roofs to combat the build-up of snow.

The three men fought a crowd of traffic down the main street. Poorly salted frost clung to the edges of the road, and everything had a sheen about it, as if freshly frozen.

Out of the corner of Matchins's eye, a figure leaped from one rooftop to the next, training a crossbow on their position. His breath caught in his throat, about to cry out, but the marksman was pulled from an alley-side ledge.

"Did you see that?" Matchins asked.

"Huh?" Bettly replied.

"We've been spotted," Rutters said, gesturing to a black-robed figure shadowing them from the side of the street.

"Keep an eye on them," Matchins ordered with a puff of misted breath, struggling to ford through the crowds. "And we'll keep our heads about us, fork's coming up."

"I lost our tail."

"Cogrust," Bettly said.

"Keep. Your. Heads," Matchins said sternly, fighting to keep his own.

There was the ringing sound of a knife being drawn and a wet grunt behind them. The three spun, seeing nothing but the backs of the crowds bustling past them.

"Did she just tag another one?" Bettly asked.

"But she was on the roof!" Rutters said.

Matchins let out a gasp as someone bustled into him from behind. "Keep moving," they said in a hush. It was Billie.

"Well, lads." Matchins nudged the shoulders of his men and turned back down the road.

"How can she move like that?" Rutters asked.

"She's a trained assassin," Bettly answered.

"So are they," Rutters retorted.

"Quiet!" Matchins grunted as another robed figure approached them from the side of the throng they were battling through.

Their new assailant stumbled and grabbed her neck in pain. She looked down at her hand, as if expecting blood, but found nothing, and she stumbled away in a daze.

"What jus ..." Bettly started but Matchins cut him off.

"Look, son, we are going to see a lot we can't explain. Just trust our girl Billie."

"Sir," Bettly said, humbled.

They bore right at the fork. The streets were still crowded with people trying to leave the city, and they neared a street bench with a lone figure reading a paper. He stood as they passed, but another figure emerged from the crowd to meet them. There was a blurred exchange, and the newcomer sat the figure down, taking the paper and blending into the stream of people.

The constables reached the next intersection without any visible incident, but Matchins was sure a terrifying battle was being raged in secret around them. A street urchin selling papers was on the corner.

"Read all about it!" he yelled. "Mining union turns to violent riots, city entering lockdown! Could this be The Fourth Perversity?" The child approached Matchins, "On the house, sir," and handed him a folded paper.

Matchins took the parcel with a suspicious eye, but the child was already peddling to other uninterested passers-by.

"She said left here, yes?" Rutters suggested.

"Not anymore." Matchins unfurled the paper, which had a note folded up inside of it.

"*Nearest* alley—*B*."

"It could be a trap," Bettly said. "But then I guess we'd be dead already."

"Agreed. Batons at the ready, lads." Matchins and his men trod into the nearest alley, and the hubbub of the street died out in an instant as they entered the sheer, enclosing cliffs of the adjacent buildings. "You hear that?"

There was a strangled cry from around the next corner.

"She's in trouble!" Rutters shouted, and made around the corner.

"Rutters!" Matchins called after him but was also spurred into action.

The constables rounded the corner to find an assassin suspended by the neck from a garrotte wire tied to a windowsill while letting out her death throes. Billie stood by her squirming feet, casually reading the paper she had acquired from the assassin on the bench.

"That was incredible," Matchins said.

"You didn't see most of it," Billie scoffed without looking up. "Most of the spotters are taken care of; one or two retreated to report back to the Den. Have you read this?"

Matchins looked down at his own free copy. "Crazed miners tear through Copper Cobble?"

"The miners tried to organise union action as a peaceful protest against their working conditions until we took out their leader," Billie said. "They're tough bastards, but not up to causing a ruckus. This sounds a lot like Rella's husks by the read of it. It's lucky we came."

"Right, shall we?" Matchins said.

"Station's this way." She gestured down another alley; there was a blunderbuss shot and the scream of petrified crowds. "But I think we'll be the ones helping them."

She took off after the sound, and with a glance at each other, the constables followed.

CHAPTER 16

The New Symbicate and the Light Wizards.

It took the better part of the day, and the following night, but with the help of Thomas's expert tinkering, the Light Wizards retrofitted a steam engine to their ship, the *Motebeam*. It used power harnessed from the sun through their amber, pulsing sails, but their circuits were all damaged in the crash. The flight mechanisms were still operational; all they needed was a reliable power source. Thomas had the idea to rig the steam engine from his boat to crank his taser—enhanced by Light Wizardry—to power the ship.

It had been a hard slog, but with tentatively cooperative efforts, they got the *Motebeam* airborne. They stripped the tugboat of parts and equipment, and with the help of tamed baulsaws, the Islanders hauled the gear from one boat to another, including the fleet of aero-breaks Thomas had packed.

They were now chugging along over the ocean towards Weznin at a height just out of tentacle range.

During the whole repair and refit, Tara kept a close eye on the former-enemies-now-tentative-friends with her hand firmly on the hilt of her blade.

Out of all of the battle-ready warriors at the time of castoff, they had a force consisting of twenty-three Prismath soldiers—who everyone still referred to as Wizards—twelve Heroes, seventeen Baul Islander freedom fighters, and four constables. Not including Mallel, Scrond—who they referred to as the "High Wizard" to his amusement—Boss, Snipes, Frogman, Alexander, and the three core members of the New Symbicate.

"Sixty-five warriors … not a comforting force if we are going to battle against an infestation of those husk things," Boss tutted.

They were in the briefing room by the bridge, a long chamber in the chrome interior with a long, red-hued table in the centre. It was lit by prism crystal lights in sconces on the walls.

"We'll need to focus on our target then," Thomas said, before whimpering and grabbing the table as the whole ship rattled with a bout of turbulence.

The belching steam engine made for a bumpy ride, but it was still safe, Scrond had said. It didn't make Thomas feel any more secure.

Snipes smirked to himself, and Eleanor gripped Thomas's arm.

"Focus how?" Frogman asked.

"We need to fight them like we did in Crisza, our capital," Scrond said, holding his staff on high. "Once we drew the Rel out into the open, drew out the brain at the top of the stem, so to speak, we obliterated it with this weapon. The same weapon we used to destroy your moon once our astronomers observed the Rel's influence over it."

"You mean that thing created all the currency we now have in this world?" Boss said, nervously looking around, along with several other people at the briefing table. "Well, as well as creating an ... object of mass destruction?"

Scrond smiled. "The fact that you use scattered cubes as currency is amusing. It is more a by-product of our technology, but yes, this prism," he pointed to the crystal mechanism in the tip of his staff, "absorbs light-wave energy and converts it into physical form; the longer it draws energy, the denser the form ... the wave-form. The denser the cube it creates, the more deadly its impact is as it is launched."

"Why don't all of your warriors use them?" Eleanor asked.

"Because what I am holding is powerful enough to destroy celestial bodies, young miss," Scrond said.

"Why didn't you just launch it at us? Why come to our planet at all?" Thomas followed up.

"We did not know for sure if there was an infection," Mallel answered for Scrond.

"You wanted to see the people you killed, more like it," Tara said under her breath. Mallel ignored her.

"So, we target Rella, and then the infected symbioids die?" Alexander asked.

"If only it were so simple," Scrond said with a warm smile. "It will remove the controlling intelligence that ... Rella ...

exerts over them. They won't be able to spread the infection and will become like mindless animals, much easier for a dedicated force to clean up. Once we killed the central Rel node on our planet, the fighting lasted years more against the husks and deformed guardian bodies. Although, it was more a hunt than a fight; we lost very few of our precious people in the wake, thankfully." His smile faded into a weary look. "Luckily we know where the brains of your infection will be, do we not?"

Tara stepped from the wall she was sulking on. "If they really did pull back to Copper Cobble, the Night Mother would have gone to the Den."

There was a murmuring and a frazzled tapping by Votly as she typed on a console by the wall. The room darkened from her typed commands, and the table lit up with a three-dimensional map of Copper Cobble, made entirely out of golden light.

"What magic is this, wizard?" Snipes asked.

"Not magic, silly." Votly giggled. "Technology, like your tinkering but just years more advanced. Which building is the Den, miss?"

Tara pointed to the Den, the tall building on the corner of a nondescript but wealthy area of Copper Cobble; it highlighted red.

"Hmm, not very defensible," Boss said, stroking his chin. "I can see many lines of sight and entry points from surrounding buildings it's so closely packed."

"Not defensible, accessible," Tara said. "The assassins use the surrounding buildings and rooftops as discreet exits, and no one has ever attacked it, at least not without encountering a den of assassins." She gave Boss a pointed look. "Besides, you are the first outside the Night Assassins to know of its true existence ... unless you count Rella."

"I don't see any open landing points," Mallel said.

"We'd be swarmed as the more pressing threat if we even tried to land in that plaza over the next few streets," Scrond agreed.

"That's even if Rella is taking over the city like you said," Tara snapped. "So far he has remained clandestine, underground; the only apocalyptic threat so far has been you!"

"Tara," Eleanor said, "let's just plan for the worst."

"The worst can't happen," Thomas said. "Billie is there."

"Is this Billie powerful enough to stop Rella on her own?" Mallel asked.

"No ..." Thomas said. "She's my sister."

"Ah," Mallel replied. "Prepare yourself for potential heartbreak, warrior. Rella will react to our presence now; he will be making preparations to defend against our wrath."

"What preparations should the city make for your wrath?" Tara spat.

"Tara," Eleanor said again.

"Look," Thomas cut in, exasperated, "even if it is being overrun, Billie went there with Matchins to organise their constables against an aggressive assassin ring. She would be organising a defence if battle had broken out already."

"Then she'd be here." Tara pointed to the constable station. Votly highlighted it green.

"Two blocks from the Den?" Snipes raised an eyebrow. "These assassins are ballsy."

"No one would have dared stand against them before now," Tara said.

"It's not far from where Rella would be either," Thomas said, concerned. "But if she is hauled up there, we can reinforce her and then coordinate an assault."

"But we can't land!" Mallel said. "And you won't allow us to torch the city with what few cannons we have."

"If you even tried," Tara said through her teeth, "I'd tear your throat out!"

"Exactly!" Mallel raised his hands in vindication.

"We aren't landing and we aren't torching the city!" Thomas stumbled between the two who were positioning themselves to fight. "I have about forty aero-breaks from my tug; their previous owners liked to run cliff raids. We can drop in without landing, and the *Motebeam* can carry on."

"So by necessity, enough of our warriors won't have these aero-breaks and will have to remain on board the *Motebeam* to defend it," Mallel said. "This could work to our advantage; the Rel would focus the bulk of his swarms on the *Motebeam*, thinking it the greater threat. It could pull the enemy away for us to take it out before it infects too many people."

"Yes," Thomas said.

"Very well." Scrond rose, and Mallel stood to help steady him. "I will let you young ones draw up the plans. I grow weary; another battle with the Rel on the horizon is a prospect that taxes my mind." He was helped out by Mallel. "Good lad," Scrond said.

When Mallel returned they drew up their battle plans and dispersed. Thomas went to the cabin he was offered by Mallel as repayment for getting the *Motebeam* off the ground. Tara followed Mallel onto the bridge to observe him closely.

"I should go check on Thomas," Eleanor said.

"You two play nice." Tara was surprised by the mirth in her voice. Eleanor blushed and ushered herself from the room. Tara's venom returned quickly as she noticed Mallel eyeing her. "What?" she said.

"You hate us so much?" Mallel said.

"I was on the ground in Crankod," Tara said.

"And yet you survived, such luck."

"I am not a lucky person," Tara said. "I heard the screams, smelled the burning flesh, and saw my friend vaporise before my very eyes."

"Is that why you hate me? I was trying to save the majority of your world from what I thought was an infection," Mallel said easily. "You would have done the same if you had seen what I had seen. Scrond's weariness is not from age. He was in the thick of it the whole time, the only of his caste to survive, which is why he was the one to battle through the hordes that invaded our city. He was the one who smote the Rel. Seeing another city fall almost broke him."

"I'm sure that's a comfort to the children who burned," Tara said.

Mallel nodded solemnly. "I do not enjoy what I do, assassin. Sometimes I even hate myself, but I don't think you really hate me."

"Oh?" Tara said, rising with the gall in her throat. "You think I wouldn't kill you in an instant?"

Mallel laughed. "Oh I'm sure, but you'll still be hateful after that, because I think you really hate yourself, and see in me an outlet for that." He shifted almost imperceptibly as Tara drew her dagger and strode towards him. "I sense you have committed great sins," he added. She paused. "I know this because I, too, have committed them. I feel it, what you feel. It's why my crew fear me, but you don't. You have killed the innocent as well."

Tara remembered her first kill under the Night Assassins, Mart "The Log" Logran, a man whose only crime was standing up to injustices in his own little way. She had poisoned him and left his corpse in his office.

"You may have been compelled to, as I have, but it still haunts you all the same. You must forgive yourself, Tara."

"How?" Tara whispered.

Mallel laughed. "If you ever figure it out, let me know."

He turned his back on her—her knife still drawn—and moved to the display consoles, where the technicians were diligently pretending to ignore their interaction.

After a moment's thought, Tara sheathed her knife.

* * *

Eleanor found Thomas huddled in his bunk, gripping the edge with every slight bit of turbulence the *Motebeam* rattled with. Eleanor laid down her sword-shield and slipped into the bed with him. She embraced him from his back, threading her limbs through the clutches of his; she leaned over his shoulder and kissed him on the temple.

"I bet I look like some mighty warrior." Thomas laughed.

Eleanor laughed with him. "But you are. I find this quite endearing." She squeezed tighter.

There was another jolt of turbulence, and Thomas let go of the bed post to grip her arms.

"You better let go. Alexander might waltz in here any moment. He wouldn't take kindly to finding me with his sister like this," Thomas said.

"Nah, he likes you. So do I." She kissed his cheek this time, and it sent tingles rippling down his skin.

"When we fight Rella, he'll try and drum up my guilt for killing Eric," Thomas said.

"Your duel with Eric was terrible," Eleanor said. "Two friends, both fighting for their families and found at cross blades. But ultimately, he was defending a murderer, even if it was his uncle. You were just trying to find justice for your father, for your sister. Eric forced your hand, Thomas. You may have killed him, but the blame is not all yours."

"I know, I know," Thomas said. "I just feel like this fight might take a lot from us."

"Then we should enjoy our time here together, while we can," Eleanor whispered in his ear.

She leaned in to kiss him again, and he turned to meet her.

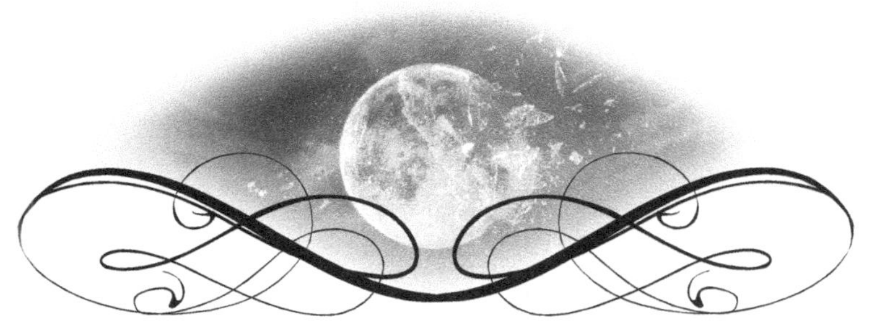

Billie Marrow

Snowflakes blew in flurries throughout the dark, unlit streets as cold gas lamps stood inert in frozen vigil, unlit. The green luminescence of the shattered moon seeped weakly through the snowstorm over the city, highlighting the frosted cobblestone, brick, and steel in ghastly light. There was a wailing on the air, but it was not the wind. A young couple and their six-year-old daughter sped down a narrow street, pursued by a horde of ravenous husks.

Billie crouched in wait on the ledge of a high window, mouthing to herself as she counted down from ten. "... two, one, NOW!"

Dark buildings lining the street erupted with blunderbuss fire, and the horde of husks crumbled with indifferent gasps and wet cracks as the shots tore through sinew and flesh.

Constables rushed from the ground floors with batons in hand to bludgeon the stragglers into submission.

The little girl with her parents screamed as one of the felled husks reached out suddenly and gripped her ankle, pulling her foot towards its gaping, wheezing maw. Billie launched her grapple across the street and leaped from her vantage point, swooping down, gathering the girl in one arm, and alighting safely a dozen metres away as the constables swarmed the disagreeable husk.

Grateful parents rushed to Billie, praising her with their thanks as they took the shivering girl from her arms.

"Please, don't mention it," Billie said to them as she tousled the girl's hair. "Were there many more stragglers your way?"

"We got separated from our group when the horde attacked. We think they fled in the other direction," the mother said breathlessly.

"Then we can offer them no help," a man dressed in the dark green of the Copper Cobble constables said. He was decorated with many medals and adornments—the commissioner.

"I agree. We should regroup at the station and prepare it as best we can for a prolonged siege," Matchins said, wiping the coagulated blood from his baton with a dirty cloth.

"The girl was bitten," another Copper Cobble constable gasped; he was removing the ramrod from his blunderbuss and training the weapon on the family.

The parents paled and held their daughter close.

"She was not!" the father protested.

"I got to her first, Constable," Billie said sternly. "Lay down your weapon."

"How can you be sure?"

"We can just check?" Matchins offered.

"The bites don't spread the husk infection anyway," Billie said. "We've seen as much. Most are simply slaughtered."

"Then how are the husks multiplying?" the constable said, the muzzle of his blunderbuss shaking as he aimed at the family.

Billie slowly stepped between them. "Constable, if you don't lower your weapon, I am going to rip it from your hands and use it to bludgeon your knees to bits. You can be bait for our next ambush and find out how they spread the husk infection yourself."

"She's going to turn into one of those things!" the constable cried. "We need to finish her quickly."

"So far only those woven with symbioids are infected by bites," another constable said silently behind the commotion.

"Constable," the commissioner said, "I will have you flogged for your cowardice."

"We're wasting time here," Matchins said.

There was a shout from one of the sentries, and all eyes snapped back down the street where a swarm surged around the corner.

"Open fire!" the commissioner ordered, and the onrushing horde was torn by the sporadic volley of blunderbuss fire from the half-prepared police force.

Many shots missed their mark, impacting uselessly into the road, the lamp posts, or surrounding buildings. Those that did hit toppled several husks, but the dozens and hundreds that were now surging past their fallen comrades were indomitable.

"Time to go," Billie said to Matchins.

The family had already bolted, as had the constable who threatened to kill the little girl.

After a smaller, second salvo from the constables who hesitated to fire on command, the commissioner ordered a full retreat. The staggered formation broke away from the rushing horde. Billie and Matchins—at the back of the group to begin with—pulled out ahead of the rest quickly, overtaking the twitchy constable and the family, making it to the next intersection.

"Which way is the station?" Matchins yelled.

"Left!" Billie turned to him to point when a harrowing scream pierced through the night.

They homed in on the source of the sound, where a grotesque mass launched itself from the rooftops and sailed down through the now lightly falling snowflakes. It impacted the centre of the intersection with a sickening squelch, and the hideous, tumour-esque growths that protruded from it wobbled and sloshed with inertia. The creature reared itself to its full height upon spindly, all too human-looking legs that supported the gross mass against all logic. It screamed again, spreading its limbs out, and forks of sinewy tendrils lashed out from its extremities like lightning bolts.

One of the sinewy bolts arced towards Billie, who ducked under it and swiped up with her blade, severing the strange tongue-like appendage. The base of it withered and retreated, and Billie rose with a smile. Her smile turned as sour as the bile that rose in her throat when she took stock of the fight. Dozens of lashed-out tongues had spread almost all around the square, embedding into the girl's parents, into the cowardly constable, and into a few of his comrades who were still retreating.

Their eyes rolled back into their heads, the whites turning grey and lifeless with black, bloodshot veins. They writhed as the sinewy tongues invaded their bodies and caused them to spasm and twitch with the rasping of husks.

"Cogrust," Billie swore.

Behind them the constables who fired the second volley were being overrun, with the commissioner making a valiant account of himself with his baton on the front line. She had precious seconds to act.

The parents turned on their daughter, clawing at her sluggishly, and Matchins was there with his baton, bludgeoning away the husks before they could fully act on their new appetite. The husk of the cowardly constable assailed him next, and Matchins backhanded him with a quick strike. He took the girl in his arms and made down the road towards the station, which left Billie to tackle the sinewy node mass on her own.

It retracted its sinewy tongues, and even without a discernible face, it seemed to focus its attention on her. She bit back her bile and leaped into action, sprinting forward, and shot her grapples to the upper levels of the buildings behind it. It screamed and launched a concentrated mass of tongues at her, and she leaped over them—allowing the grapples to pull her high above their reach—arching into the air while flipping, before releasing her grapples and landing with a solid kick to the head area of the node mass.

It stumbled and Billie landed spryly on her feet; she spun and slashed at one of the thing's protruding growths. The innards spilled open with a combined smell of bad breath and sulphur, but the wound lashed itself together almost instantly.

Almost.

Billie produced a flash bomb from one of her many pockets and lobbed it into the open wound before it fully sealed. She kicked the creature away and turned, dashing away as fast as she could.

Within the horrid insides of the node mass, the flash bomb exploded. Phosphorous powders ignited and spread along the dead, half-dried sinew that made up its body. The creature exploded in flames with another high-pitched scream, and the surrounding husks faltered as if they were physically struck.

It gave some of the retreating constables who were about to be overwhelmed the seconds they needed to gain ground on the fiends. Billie looked back to check on them, and her heart fell upon seeing the pile where the commissioner had fallen—she was too late to save him. With a curse she sprinted along the street with the other retreating constables. The husks quickly recovered and tore after them.

Billie and her surviving group reached the end of the street and came to a new intersection. The station was the three-storey corner building on the far side, and the clearing was littered with bodies, either from husks or those fortunate enough to be torn apart instead of being infected by a node mass.

The station's dark windows were alive with movement and the protruding ends of flashing blunderbusses which were firing down the approaching streets as the hordes flowed throughout them. The defence produced a continuous chorus of thunderous gunshots to challenge the growing wailing of the swarming husks.

The door to the station swung open, and two Copper Cobble constables, as well as Rutters, came out urging the retreating constables to hurry inside. The majority sprinted towards the doors, but Matchins was slowing down. Billie slowed as she passed him and turned quizzically.

"Safety is just over there, Sergeant; we cannot slow now," she said.

A husk rushed them from a side alley, and its head exploded with a well-placed shot from the upper windows of the station— followed by a cursed exclamation urging them to get moving.

"Sergeant?" He had doubled down and was placing the girl on the ground, telling her to run inside. She ran past Billie with tears in her eyes. "Are you well?"

Two more husks rushed at her—the hordes behind them were surging closer and closer despite the continuous fire from the station. With one motion, two knives flew from her robes and embedded into their heads. They collapsed, sliding across the icy street.

"The tongue you dodged from that ugly blighter," Matchins pulled his hand from his shoulder, revealing a protruding barb, "you dodged too fast, I think. The sinews are taking a while to weave with me since you severed them, I reckon. It gave me a few moments of clarity."

"No, Matchins ... I'm so sorry." Billie stepped forward. Three husks now ran at them, and two were felled by shots from the station. Billie slashed the last one with her sword before turning back to Matchins.

"It's quite all right," he said as if slightly inconvenienced. "I ... I got to save the girl." He laughed, pulling a blunderbuss from a corpse nearby and handing it to her. "I just don't want to cause any more of a fuss, if you get my meaning?"

Billie took the blunderbuss and levelled it at his head; the sprinting monsters behind him blurred out of her awareness as she focused on him. He was sickly, the colour draining from his skin. His eyes had lost their lustre, and the blue veins of the barb were making their mark beneath his paling flesh.

"I'm sorry," she said.

There was another exacerbated shout from the station.

"My first name is Walter," he said with a smile, a weak, charming smile that curled his moustache.

"Walter," she flicked up her goggles, blinking away a tear, "it was a pleasure." She fired.

Her arm jolted and Sergeant Walter Matchins toppled to the ground. She did not hear the blast. In a state of shock she turned and sprinted through the station's doors as the swarm entered the intersection, flooding towards the impromptu bastion. The constables slammed the doors shut behind her and heaved a heavy writing desk against it just as it shuddered under the charging horde outside. Some fired through the side windows as they piled more furniture and the like to barricade the door.

"What took you so long?" Rutters said. "What happened to Matchins?"

"Where is the commissioner?" a Copper Cobble constable asked.

"They didn't make it," Billie said coldly. "We must look to our defences, constables. Our lives depend on it."

Rutters went pale, gripping his blunderbuss grimly. The little girl Matchins saved rushed in to embrace Billie, crying uncontrollably.

"Can we survive?" she sobbed.

Billie stroked her hair. "We can, but we need more Heroes."

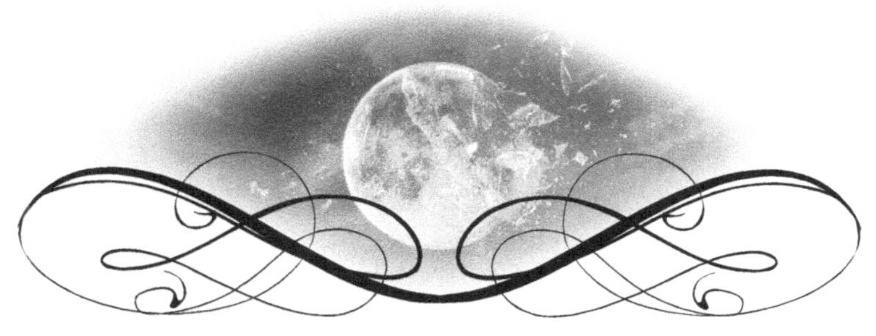

CHAPTER 18

The Battle for Copper Cobble

As the sun rose over the mountain peaks—casting pink hues across the dispersing clouds and lighting the snow with golden rays—the *Motebeam* floated over the ranges and into sight of Copper Cobble.

"Is that what Crankod looked like on your ... scanners?" Tara said, aghast.

The monitors—Votly had explained to her the windows were called monitors—on the bridge showed a wire frame layout of the city. Swarms of red, globular shapes swarmed through it like a writhing tumour with many tendrils.

"It was," Mallel said, his face stoic. "Our technology tracks the Guardian signature, not the Rel's. The city we attacked was a red, writhing mass like you see here, only not as embroiled."

"But surely not all of them are husks," Eleanor said. "Some of them are untainted symbioids?"

"This is true," Scrond replied. "But you can see from the way they move en masse that these ones are clearly infected."

"Enough," Thomas said. "Billie is down there, and so is Rella."

"Hooks is right," Snipes said. "We need to save her and all of those people down there. It's time we end this."

"Hah!" Boss laughed and clapped them on the back. "I always wanted you two to agree on something. Shame it took the end of the world."

The assembled warriors shuffled out of the bridge, their aero-breaks already donned. Aero-breaks were worn like a heavy-set equipment vest, and were made of plates of tin with vents and thrusters that had a mechanical symbioid woven throughout them. The symbioid would suck in the rushing air through the vents as the wearer fell and jettison it through the thrusters to slow their fall.

Tara let the warriors filter out before her, watching Mallel through the throng as his eyes watered and twitched; then they glanced towards her. He nodded, she nodded back, and they followed the warriors down into the cargo hold.

It was a dim, cavernous room—the lights cutting out as they readied to deploy—filled with the ready warriors standing in formation, shoulder to shoulder. The tremors in the hold from the air buffeting the *Motebeam* were more intense than other parts of the ship. They rattled the floors as well as Thomas's resolve, and he squeezed his eyes shut, planting his feet as best he could. It was cold here; the steam from the breath of the sixty-odd warriors filled the space in the tense, brooding quiet before the storm.

A tone sounded, then Votly's voice spoke over a speaker above. "Entering the target zone, lowering into bait altitude. Scans show many swarms breaking from their current targets and converging on the *Dustmote's* position ..."

Dustmote? Thomas wondered.

"... Good luck," Votly finished.

A red light flashed by the cargo doors. It was ominous, strobing across the stoic wizards in their stiff military attire. It washed over the grim determination of the Baul Islanders, who shivered in their fur coats, highlighted the bravado of the Hired Heroes, reflected off the beads sweating off the constables, and strobed over the grim concern of the New Symbicate.

"You all know your targets," Boss said. "Ship team, keep this bucket of jammed gears and rusted bolts alive long enough to get to safety."

"Aye!" a section at the back replied in chorus.

"Snipes, overwatch by the Den with the prism rifle sharpshooters."

"Aye, Boss," Snipes said.

"Hooks, grab ground support and rendezvous at the target."

"Aye," Thomas replied.

"Ninja, take your team through the roof."

"Aye," Tara said.

"Islanders, take your team through the middle-level entrances."

"Aye," Eleanor and Alexander said as one.

"Frog ..."

"Frogman," Frogman corrected.

"Down the sewers and through the basements."

" ... Aye."

"Grand Wizard Scrond."

"High Prismatist ... oh well, yes, I know the plan ..." Scrond said.

"You and Captain Mallel hit the adjacent roof entrance on the other side, then follow in with your team."

"Aye, Boss," Mallel replied.

"And I," Boss smiled with crazed determination, "I will breach the lobby. Ha hah!"

The red light flashed green; Thomas approached the loading bay door, where a wizard hit a switch.

"Remember the stakes," Thomas bellowed. "We've all walked different paths. Sometimes running at odds with each other, but they all brought us here, to quell evil and the horrors of the void, to defend the innocent from those who would oppress them, abuse them, consume them. Remember why you are fighting, and we will succeed!"

The assembled warriors cried out in unison, a mesh of different threads now woven into a single tapestry. They were ready.

A warning tone sounded as the cargo bay door creaked open, and torrents of high winds assaulted the interior as white light pierced the dim, cavernous space, illuminating the ranks of warriors.

As the door creaked down, it revealed the destruction that ravaged Copper Cobble. Buildings were aflame, bodies littered the streets, and there was a constant battle, a brawl more like. Whatever it was, it presented as a vicious melee along failing lines from pockets of resistance. The pockets were finding a reprieve as the *Motebeam* lowered into the city, and the husks, responding to Rella's call, swarmed away from their prey and towards the new threat.

Thomas knew they wouldn't have long. "DIVE, DIVE, DIVE!" he ordered.

The ranks of fighters—some hesitant, some brazen—charged down the loading bay ramp and leaped into the skies, spreading out into a free fall over the city. With a dry throat, Thomas leaped out after them.

They slowed instantly thanks to the aero-breaks, like softly falling snow. The wizards fired into the streets with their prism rifles as they descended, scorching the swarming husks in tandem with the few working prism cannons on the ship.

Thomas plummeted past them all—wearing no aero-break himself—and he banked towards the building Tara had pointed out, the constable's station, which was besieged by husks. He didn't need to slow down; he needed his emotions high to do what he did next.

"We're clear, *Motebeam!*" Mallel's voice sounded in Thomas's ear from one of the strange earphones the wizards had distributed among the strike force. Mallel was yelling over the torrents of air rushing past his face. "Get out of here!"

Swarms of infected symbioids and foul, powered creatures were already firing up at the *Motebeam* or launching off the taller buildings to grasp at it, some making their way into the cargo bay before the doors shut. The fighting was instantaneous inside, and the sharpshooters on the gun decks above were busy fending off the boarders as the *Motebeam* rose back into the air and drifted away while firing back at the piling husks on the rooftops. Many of the single-minded beasts thankfully followed its path, away from the Den, away from the real attack.

The descending warriors drifted into distinguishable groups and made for their objectives. Thomas found the roof of the constable station rushing up to him.

He flinched at the last moment and blinked, appearing inside the top level of the station in a flurry as he bumbled into a group of civilians who screamed at his arrival. Thomas struggled up in a daze to realise several blunderbusses were pointed at him.

He raised his hands. "Ah, I'm looking for my sister."

"Stand down, you fools, he isn't infected!" Billie pushed through them. "Thomas?"

"Billie!" He rushed to embrace her.

"I didn't know you could blink through walls!"

"I discovered that I have to be frightened ... Look, that's not important. Things are worse than they seem."

"What?" One of the constables blanched.

"But the wizards are on our side now," Thomas explained.

"What?" Billie asked. "How does Tara feel about that?"

Thomas scoffed. "It's iffy, but we have a plan of attack, and I need you by my side. Any warriors who can fight, I need a party to make for the muscle-for-hire building on the corner of Brass Avenue and Picklin Street."

"With those things out there?" a constable said.

"I came with reinforcements. We have sharpshooters covering the route between here and there. We need as many guns and blades as we can muster while Billie and I get inside and cut the brain from these husks. We will need you to help hold off any of the enemy from coming in behind us," Thomas said.

"We can spare a dozen men," one constable said. "We can't leave the civilians here undefended."

"It'll do. Meet us there and watch for friendlies … Some of them … well, they look different."

"So we're going for the Den?" Billie asked.

"We have a weapon that can kill Rella. If we get the High Wizard to him, we can turn the husks into just that—husks. Then it will be easy-ish to eliminate them, and they won't be infectious anymore," Thomas said.

"Good plan, let's go," Billie said.

Thomas grabbed her by the arm and blinked them onto the roof. He steadied her as she was hit by a bout of wooziness. "You all right?"

Billie grabbed his shoulder. "Whistling steam." She relaxed her grip as she took in the scene.

The *Motebeam* was rising up above the city, swarming with creatures that had found a purchase before it had risen too high, and a vicious battle was being fought on the gun decks. The husks in the streets were swarming towards it, piling over one another in a useless attempt to head the wizards off should they try to land again, and the descending New Symbicate warriors fell gently to their positions. The wizard sharpshooters within the precipitating Heroes beamed out rays of red or white light at the husks that swarmed their respective landing zones.

Snipes's group landed atop a taller building opposite from the Den and set up a sniping roost, covering Boss and his team as they landed in front and stormed the lobby. Tara landed on top, dispatching some hidden assassins with her team, and moved inside. Mallel, Scrond, and Eleanor with their teams landed on adjacent buildings and immediately moved inside.

Below Thomas and Billie, a team of constables broke out onto the clearing intersection and made through the streets to support Boss's team.

"We're needed," Billie said. "Can you blink me again?"

"Probably? But blinking others takes a bit of a toll on me as well as the blink-ee."

"Then don't risk it. We'll need to be as fit as we can be in there. Make sure you enter the Den in a point where our allies most need you." She raised an arm to grapple. "And Thomas?"

"Yes?"

"I love you. Be careful."

"I love you too, Billie. See you there."

She grappled across the street, and Thomas steadied himself to blink. The fighting around the Den intensified as more husks peeled off from pursuing the *Motebeam*, realising it was a diversion. Billie swung down the middle of the street over the constables, who struck up a brutal melee with a group of husks about to attack Boss's rear. She detached her grapple mid-air, flying through the sky, and shot both hooks at either side of a window on the second floor of the Den. Then she spooled herself in with a dynamic, window-shattering entry.

"Whistling steam," Thomas said, before blinking from rooftop to rooftop.

He blinked behind Snipes's position. A wizard sharpshooter spun wildly and fired, and Thomas ducked under the beam with his hands up. "Cease fire, you moon rock moron!"

"Moron?" Snipes said between shots. "Who blinks on the flank of friendlies with no warning?"

"That's fair." Thomas took cover by the lip of the roof and peeked into the Den. Several floors were embroiled in savage fighting, with windows breaking, flashes lighting silhouettes in the recesses, and there was the general sound of chaos. "Where am I most needed?"

"Fighting is most intense on the upper levels. Tara is there," Snipes said.

"Thanks—stay safe all the way up here far from harm." Thomas tapped him on the shoulder and blinked away.

Snipes shook his head. "I *will* shoot you," he said to himself.

Thomas leaped forward before he blinked, appearing before the top floor window of the Den and letting his momentum carry him through in an explosion of shards. He broke out into a roll and came up with his swords out to find Tara and her team in a brawl with a squad of assassins.

He stomped the knee of an assassin who turned at his entrance and then slammed his elbow into his face. The assassin fell with a cry. Tara cartwheeled over a swipe to her leg and pranced around to be back-to-back with Thomas.

"Hey," she said, giving a hand signal command to her team of Heroes and Islanders to spread out. There was a lull in the fighting as the assassins and New Symbicate forces squared up against one another.

"Hey," Thomas replied.

"Find Billie?"

"She was leading a successful resistance until I interrupted her." Thomas smirked grimly.

"That's our Billie."

"Are we interrupting something?" One of the assassins stepped forward.

"Oh, sorry," Tara said. "Attack!"

The brawl erupted again, with Tara and Thomas leading the carnage against their lithe enemy.

* * *

Billie exploded through the window, fly-kicking the katana-wielding novice who charged her. He fell back head over heels down the main stairway to the lobby, and a number of enemies whirled on her.

"Howdy." She flourished her blade with a smile. "Miss me?"

"Billie!" one sneered. "You've made a grave error."

"Not as grave as allying with the literal plague. About that, why aren't you guys husked by the way?"

One of the assassins stiffened. "We ... we are more useful as we are."

"For now," Billie replied. "How long after Rella has his victory do you think he'll wait before munching on you?"

"Pay no heed to her words, my family." A new assassin trod up from the stairway, dragging the bewildered novice who Billie had fly-kicked by the cuff.

"Nicholas," Billie said.

"A group of Hired Heroes are trying to knock down our front door. Go secure it." His eyes were grey, bloodshot, and lifeless; the skin above his face-covering scarf was throbbing with blue tendrils.

"What about her?" one assassin inquired.

"She's mine." Nicholas dropped the novice assassin, who scrambled to his feet. The assassins arrayed on the floor quickly lowered their weapons and filed downstairs.

"So this is what it has come to," Billie said, as she circled Nicholas. "I expected a bitter duel with my former Night brother. Instead I must put a diseased fool out of his misery."

"You found a new brother. I remained loyal to Mother," Nicholas spat. "Your brother failed to protect you when it mattered most, but the Night Mother has now assured the Night's strength!"

"No, she has betrayed you to that filth!" Billie said. "My brother was a child when I was taken and sold to you bastards. The failure was always with the crime syndicates. I am here to end them, to end Rella, and to save you from this life." She clicked her grapple hook out from her gauntlet, forming a spiked mace. "However I have to do it."

Nicholas hissed and leaped to attack her.

Billie gasped and leaped to meet him.

* * *

Frogman hit the streets with two masked wizards flanking him. The rubble beside them chipped as pot shots erupted from the windows of the Den. Boss's group landed and returned fire, blunderbuss shots, crossbow bolts, and prism beams mixing together in the return volley. The fighting in the street intensified as Boss organised his group to start battering down the main entrance.

The two wizards with Frogman returned fire too.

"No," he said, removing the grate from a manhole and ushering them in. "If Tara is to be believed, we have to trigger the door to open from the inside. Our comrades will fight, we will infiltrate."

He triggered the symbioid in his buoy—strapped to his back—to suck in an air supply. It would last him a good ten minutes before he would need to refill it. He hopped down into the coursing filth of the city sewers, splashing into excrement and blood, and waded into the dark junctions beneath the city.

The two wizards followed him, the lights from their prism rifles sweeping the coursing sludge for enemies as they made their way to a churning sewer junction with an outlet pipe from the building. It spewed a constant flow of sickly fluids.

Frogman pointed to the outlet. "There."

The three leaped into the raging lake of sewage—their masks sealing them against the smell—and waded with murky brown, veiled lights to the base of the pipe outlet. The three in single file shimmied up it, their suits and weapons scraping against the edge of the pipe which closed in around them.

"Here," a wizard said over the strange device in Frogman's ear.

The wizard pulled a contraption from his belt and set it on the side of the pipe; it thrummed and sizzled and all of a sudden the wall of the pipe crumbled. The three infiltrators fell in a heap onto a basement floor, the flow of the sewage pipe spilling out around them.

"I can smell it through my regulator," one wizard said, the grimace on his face evident through his voice.

"Just the standard smell of espionage," Frogman replied as he stood and made a show of dusting himself down. "Come, our people are trapped out in the open."

The three picked themselves up—weapons at the ready—and made for the stairs. Frogman was muttering the directions that Tara had painstakingly laid out for him as they crept by a door in a darkened hallway.

"No assassins?" one wizard asked.

"They are all too distracted by our friends. Through here." Frogman pulled a flash bomb that Tara had made for him from a protective pouch. "We will have seconds to get the door open."

The wizards nodded.

Frogman counted down with his fingers so the wizards could see: *three, two, one.* He ignited the flash bomb, and a wizard kicked down the door. Frogman lobbed the bomb into the fortified lobby of bewildered assassins, and the three infiltrators shut their eyes.

The bomb went off with the accompanying sound of shouts and expletives, and Frogman—with the wizards—sprinted through the writhing assassins to the door. The two wizards kicked the bracing assassins out of the way while Frogman lifted the locking beam, and Boss burst through with his team.

"Time for a true scrap, boys!" Boss yelled.

One of the female Heroes shoved past him, cocking the hammer of her blunderbuss with a glare.

"… and girls!" Boss corrected, laughing so hard his monocle popped off his face.

* * *

Eleanor and Alexander landed with their team on what Tara called "the short roof." It was a building one-third the height of the Den, which was pressed in no more than a child's leap from the fourth-storey window.

The windows surrounding their entry point immediately erupted with projectile fire, and Eleanor and Alexander expanded their sword-shields to create a moving wall.

"Just like old times, eh, sis?" Alexander said.

The shield formation reverberated with pings and ricochets as their team huddled behind them; some from the Hired Heroes held smaller brass shields of their own and formed a testudo on the top and the sides, while wizards and Baul Islander shooters at the back returned fire.

"I prefer fighting slavers," Eleanor said with a wry smile. "They always back down when you show some fight." She turned to the makeshift testudo and gestured through the crack in the sword-shields towards a window. "Don't trip!"

The loose formation picked itself up from a crouch and started an awkward shuffle towards the edge of the building with all of the grace of a ballet-trained battering ram. Once they were a single bound from the edge, Alexander gave the order.

"LEAP!"

The formation crumbled forward as Eleanor and Alexander broke into a sprint and leaped the distance through the nearest window. Several of their team were cut down as the testudo dispersed, and one tripped on the ledge of the building, falling to their death, but the majority of the patchwork group leaped through the windows and found themselves immediately engaged in fierce combat.

* * *

On the "tall roof"—a building opposite the short roof which was in line with the seventh storey of the Den—Mallel and Scrond touched down.

"These aero-breaks are ingenious," Scrond commented as one of the Prism Marines helped him to remove it. "Thank you, lad."

Mallel was scanning the face of the building; their entrance was a patio on this side. Despite the sounds of the embattled city, all was quiet on their front.

"Thoughts, Captain?" Scrond asked.

"I expect our enemy is inviting us in. Perhaps they want the battle done and over with," Mallel replied. He held up his binocs. The device whirred and an x-ray image of the Den appeared on the screen projecting into his eyes. "Hmm."

"What are we heading into, sir?" one of the marines asked.

"The Rel Scion itself awaits us. And two assassins. They've been husked, but their infection isn't as severe as the other husks we've faced," Mallel said.

"Minions," Scrond explained solemnly. "People who willingly accepted the Rel's plight in exchange for some petty goal. They retain more autonomy, slight improvements to speed, and a dulling of pain, so they make ferocious enemies. Ultimately they are consumed like the rest."

The doors to the patio from the Den were opened, and the prism marines and riflemen aimed their weapons. Two assassins walked out, pushing a makeshift drawbridge on wheels, constructed of wood and mechanised by pulleys and copper gears. It lowered across the narrow gap.

"Rella would like to invite you in for tea," one of the assassins said, beckoning them with a friendly gesture.

"Marines," Mallel said, "remove the guards."

Two of his warriors brought up their weapons and executed the waiting assassins without question. They fired quick, direct shots to the head which vaporised their brains instantly.

"Is it a trap?" one of the riflemen asked.

"Yes," Scrond said. "The Rel Scion in Crisza did something similar. But it did give me a chance to use this." He patted the staff. "Let's exploit that same hubris."

They sheepishly crossed the bridge, tense and alert for threats. They passed through the open doors, sweeping the area in a leapfrog-like pattern as Scrond and Mallel waltzed through the centre of their formation. Mallel's vibrating energy cutlass was brimming at the ready.

They found themselves in a lavish sitting room, with a high ceiling, chandelier casting delicate light over marble floors. A lone figure sat on a luxurious red couch in the centre. On the low table before him was a tea tray with a steaming pot and an assortment of cups and saucers.

"How rude of you to kill my entourage," the sole occupant on the couch said. "They were going to pour you all drinks."

"Rella, I assume?" Mallel said, aiming his pistol at the top-hat and monocle-wearing, moustached man.

"Indeed, you may call me Rel if you wish. That is what my counterpart called themselves, no? Or Relqua, if you will, or ..." He puffed air out of his cheeks. "I don't know how many variations of the name I have now." He went to sip from his cup, but paused. His monocle fell from his eye as his gaze hardened on Scrond. "Oh, you're the one who did it, aren't you, the Prismath who halted the purge at Crisza?" He placed the cup down. "What was it like; to win at such great a cost, to become so fearful you would destroy your neighbour's moon?" He chuckled. "Do you have any idea how much suffering that devastation inflicted on these *fine* people?"

"Rel ... Rella," Scrond said, "for your crimes against this world, I must sentence you to die." He hefted his staff. "Do you have any final words?"

"Did you give my counterpart such an offer? I don't think you did." Rella leaned back on the lounge.

"It was hard to give such an offer while my city was eviscerated around me," Scrond all but spat.

"It doesn't really matter. When I arrive again ... when I *really* arrive, you will be consumed nonetheless. It doesn't matter whether it's through me and my fellow scions, whether I repurpose those filthy Symdian Guardians to cannibalise their charges, or if it's through the *real* me. The Symdians will pay for their transgressions, and so will their precious pets. It is just a matter of how much it's going to hurt." He sipped from his tea, placed the cup down, and flipped the table at the Prismath party.

They dove for cover, and a few stray bursts from their prism rifles burned through the table, but some at the rear who could not react in time were clobbered down.

The chandelier went dark, thick shutters fell to obscure the windows, and the room was blanketed in darkness other than from the lights on the wizards' weapons.

"Up!" Mallel ordered, pulling Scrond up with him, prism pistol and energy cutlass at the ready as they scanned the room.

"Where is it?" one of the riflemen asked, searching the room frantically. "Where is it?" He screamed when a long, sinewy limb reached down from the dark ceiling and grabbed him by the face, pulling him up into the cavernous abyss.

"OPEN FIRE!" a marine bellowed.

The roof was strafed by light beams, and plaster crumbled down around them as Rella skittered across it and into the dark recesses to strike again.

He dropped down by Scrond, expanded his umbrella, and knocked Mallel back from intervening. He made to strangle the high wizard. Scrond brought the shaft of his light staff down, it clobbered Rella in the face with an explosion of technicoloured sparks, and Rella shrieked and leaped away.

"Start charging the wave-form," Mallel ordered, stumbling after Rella.

"I need more light!" Scrond answered.

* * *

On the top level, Thomas, Tara, and her team had the upper hand. The New Symbicate forces cut down the lesser trained assassins and routed the ones with enough experience to know the fight was going badly. They quickly retreated through shafts and vents to the lower levels.

"They weren't so tough," a Hero said.

"Mustn't have known we would be dropping down through the roof and placed their novices up here on guard," a Baul Islander replied. "Give me a real challenge!" he jeered and the other Islanders jeered with him.

"Hey!" Tara snapped at him. "Members of our party are dead or wounded. Tend to them." The admonished Islander nodded and ran to the closest wounded comrade he could find to provide assistance.

"He has got the right idea though. Not likely that the Night Assassins knew we would attack here," Thomas said.

"Then why post guards here at all?" Tara asked.

"Why indeed?" a weathered woman's voice replied from a darkened corridor. The Night Mother emerged.

Tara went stiff, her jaw trembling as her breath quickened.

"Ah cogrust, ah wet coal!" Thomas brought up his blade and readied to blink. "What's wrong with her?"

The Night Mother's robes were torn, her face sullen with blue and black sinewy barbs sprouting from her skin.

"Ah, Tara." She smiled. It was uncanny enough to make the hardened warriors arrayed against her wince.

Tara found her strength and stared her tormentor down with steely-eyed resolve. "Mother," she said through clenched teeth, "you've had some work done."

"It was a mistake to trust that fiend," the Night Mother said. "He … he has done something to me, taken my will … maybe that's how you felt, I wonder? I always pushed you so hard, tried to wring that gentle streak from you. I thought I succeeded with your sister," she said to Thomas, who started forward, but Tara caught him by the shoulder. "Tara, I guess I didn't need to push you so hard. I mean after all," her smile turned cruel, "you have become such a grand killer all in your own right." She gestured to the carnage around her and cackled.

"Mother," Tara said, the tremble returning to her voice, "where is Rella?"

"Our new overlord is dealing with the Prismath as we speak … we will be consumed in short order." She seemed to droop. She quivered and her voice turned, doubled over itself, waned from human to ... something else. "BUT HE'LL ALLOW ME THE SATISFACTION OF FEEDING YOU TO HIM FIRST!"

She screeched and blurred into shadow-form, filling the room and reconstituting in front of the boasting Baul Islander long enough to slit his throat, and then she dissipated and moved to the Hero behind him.

The room erupted into chaos as the warriors fretted and cried in terror. They shot at the walls, the floor, the ceiling, and even at each other if they were in the way, lashing out, crawling over one another to escape the terrible wrath of the Night Mother.

Tara dashed through gun smoke and shadow. She reached the nearest Hero as the Night Mother appeared behind him, and Tara shoulder-charged her when she became corporeal. The Night Mother collapsed with a grunt and exploded into smoke as Tara tackled her into the ground. Her shadow-form blurred past Tara and made to strike her exposed back. When she reconstituted, Thomas blinked by her side, scoring a cut to her arm.

She shrieked in rage and slapped Thomas down, then dispersed to take out another of Tara's team.

What followed was a panicked scramble, every shadow providing a target, every twitch a possible apparition of the monster assassin. In a valiant, adrenaline-fuelled battle, Tara and Thomas found themselves back-to-back, fighting off multiple apparitions of the Mother, who screamed and wailed in and out of existence.

Before they knew it, their whole team was dead, and they stood alone in the blood-soaked room, panting.

"Where is she?" Thomas panted. "Tara, where is ..."

"Quiet!" Tara snapped. "Now that it's just us, you can hear the air move when she appears."

There was a gentle hushing of air; the shadow-form congealed, and Tara lobbed a flash bomb. It ignited as the Mother appeared, and she screamed, grabbing her eyes in pain when Thomas blinked behind her and drove his blade into her kidney. Tara leaped onto her from the front, stabbing repeatedly with her knives in the neck, chest, and face.

"Is that brutal enough for you, you bitch!" Tara screamed.

The Night Mother croaked a pained laugh and spun into shadow-form, causing Tara to nearly stab Thomas as he staggered back.

"How is she still alive?" Thomas asked.

"She was never fully human," Tara said. "It's just now she has an excuse for that."

"Such harsh words, my sweet daughter. Was it all so bad? I gave you food, power—who has dared cross you lately and lived? I took the killer in you, and made you who you are today!"

The Night Mother appeared between them and swept Tara's leg, then shot up and side-kicked Thomas in the head. She flipped in the air and came down on Tara's gut with the hook of her boot and then disappeared into shadow-form again, reconstituting behind Thomas as he tried to blink away.

He blinked by Tara and grabbed her to carry her to safety, but the Night Mother was upon them, a blade around Thomas's neck, her foot pinning Tara's arm to the ground.

"Now it is time to kill this one, this man who made you think you could have a life outside of us."

"It wasn't him." Tara struggled to move, but beneath the weight of two people, she was helpless. Thomas was frozen, with the blade to his neck, another prodding his kidney; he knew he was not fast enough to blink away before her superhuman reflexes plunged each blade into his flesh. "It was five minutes outside of your charge, it was realising that you were all insane, and it was Billie as well. You failed, as a trainer, as an assassin, and as a mother!"

"Well, that hurts, Tara," the Night Mother said. "Not as bad as it's gonna hurt watching me kill your friend before your eyes. I wonder, does he treat you as a sister too? Are you about to lose a brother, a brother that you chose? That might be just enough to break your spirit, before Rella breaks your pathetic little body! You are no one, nothing but food. You have no name, and now you have no family!"

The Night Mother made to ram her blade into Thomas's back as she began to slide her other blade across his throat.

* * *

Boss vaulted over the barricade, clobbered a husk with his pistol, and shot down an assassin as they leaped to kill the wizard to his side.

"Fresh wave coming downstairs, Boss!" Frogman yelled at the base of the stairs.

"Smudge!" the wizard exclaimed as he strafed the stairs with his prism rifle, causing spot fires to erupt on the carpet.

"Will you stop burning our potential defensive positions?" Boss dodged a swipe from an assassin's blade and pulled a fresh pistol from his harness to blast him away.

"We won't be able to use them as defensive positions while they're still teeming with ninjas!" the wizard retorted before clicking a switch that jettisoned a crackling bayonet from his beam rifle, which he used to eviscerate an assassin who had sprung up from a trapdoor.

A Baul Islander was thrown into their barricade with a blow dart's barb sticking from his shoulder. "We're being overwhelmed!" he warned.

"I can see that!" Boss kicked back another husk that charged in through the opening they themselves had made and took cover from the fresh assassins tearing down the main stairs. "It's been an honour fighting alongside you!" He gave the wizard a pointed look and raised an eyebrow over his monocle in mirth. "Well, most of you."

He couldn't see the wizard's face behind his helmet and battle mask, but Boss liked to think that he was smiling back.

* * *

Billie grappled from ceiling, to stairway, to shaft, using the network of passageways and secret halls that riddled the Den in her battle with Nicholas. They dropped bombs, swiped through the smoke, flash bombed, launched darts from hidden devices in their wrists, threw knives, and ran across the walls trying to gain an advantage over each other.

"Your infection has made you a bit more fit." Billie alighted on a stairwell landing, a flight down from Nicholas. She was panting. "It's a shame it did nothing to increase your skill."

"I have skill enough to kill you, Billie. We were supposed to be partners before you grew soft for that whelp Tara. You betrayed us," Nicholas said.

"Nicholas!" Billie cried. "You have literally been taken over by a parasite—that's what loyalty to the Night gets you. You have been led down a dark path, and I have to destroy it."

"You will have to destroy that path with me on it, sister."

"Then so be it!" She grappled up to meet him at his level, and came down hard, kicking him in the head.

There was a sickening crack and his head lolled back, but his body remained upright, swaying. His breathing became raspy, and with meandering arms, he—to Billie's horror—grabbed his dislocated head and cricked it back into place.

"Don't you see, sister, I am more powerful than you can ever dream." He lunged forward and grabbed her. "And now you will join us again!" His jaw widened to clamp down on her face.

She shot up with a flash bomb and planted it in his gaping maw, then uppercut it shut. It burst and his head exploded in flames. She cried out as the bright light lashed out at her, and her goggles were instinctively flipped down to protect her sight.

Nicholas brayed and squealed like a stuck pig as the flames consumed him and he tumbled down the stairs. Billie fell back against the wall, grabbing her face and sobbing. She tried to stand, but her vision was still disoriented, and she fumbled and fell. Then the doors around her burst open, and several husks ambled out. She kicked and struck out at them blindly, but it was no use as they closed in, chomping at the bit to consume her.

Her vision recovered in time to witness the first bite, and when the husk bit down on her, her vision went white again.

* * *

Eleanor and Alexander's team were scattered throughout the hallway they had entered through the window, fighting a mismatched force of assassins, husks, and the half-husked assassins, which were relatively unskilled yet almost un-killable foes.

One assassin clambered up the wall like a spider and dropped down between the two siblings. Alexander twirled on instinct and expanded his sword to a shield.

"Mortar and pestle!" he screamed.

Eleanor spun and drove her blade into the assassin as Alexander pressed his shield up against him. They each twisted and pushed in different directions, and the assassin died with a pained cry, torn to bits.

"We're getting cut to pieces!" a wizard shouted.

"Rounded testudo!" Eleanor ordered.

The Heroes with shields banded around Eleanor and Alexander, and the wizards and Baul Islanders slipped into their defensive wall, lashing out at assassins and husks that came too close as their shooters strafed the walls and ceilings.

The husks filled the hallway and clambered over the defensive formation. The shield wall shook and buckled under their weight, chipped away at from projectiles lobbed from the assassins above. Eleanor peeked over her shield to see an assassin light up a flaming cocktail, and her eyes widened in horror.

The assassin wound up the throw, and all Eleanor could do was look to her brother.

They were finished. This whole operation was doomed from the start.

In her last moment, she thought of Thomas.

Everything went white.

* * *

Rella dropped from the high, dark ceiling and knocked Mallel's pistol from his grasp. Mallel responded by letting him taste the might of his energy cutlass. As Rella recoiled with a howl, a marine rushed from behind and rammed his bayonet into his back.

Rella spun, ripping the embedded gun from the marine's hand, and grabbed his neck. He squeezed, breaking the marine's neck with a sickening pop.

Rella dropped the corpse and spun, kicking out Mallel's legs and smacking him in the head while he was down. Mallel grunted, sprawled against the hard floor in a state of pained half consciousness.

"Is that it? Is that all of the might the Prismath can conjure?" Rella spun to face Scrond, who was worriedly looking to the walls, to the shuttered windows, to the dimmed lights. "Didn't you think I would be smart enough to remove your strength, *Light* Wizard? Is that what the people of this world call you? Light Wizard? So primitive, hah!"

"Yes, well, I can still cause you a great deal of pain before I expire. I can promise you that, Rel." Scrond readied his staff; the prism in the top crackled with power, and the geared mechanisms spun and whirred around it.

Behind Rella, Mallel gasped back into a state of awareness. He searched around the room. Among his fellow crew who had been slaughtered or rendered unconscious by Rella's ferocity, he found his pistol.

Rella cackled as he approached Scrond. "You will wish to expire long before you have stopped experiencing pain, old man. I owe my fellow scion that much at least."

"You are all talk, beast!" Scrond struck the floor with his staff.

It impacted the ground and caused it to crumble with sparks that tore towards Rella. Rella dodged the blow by leaping into the air, flipping over Scrond. Scrond stabbed backwards with the butt of the staff and clobbered Rella in the gut as he landed.

"So much fight for a frail one!" Rella grabbed the staff still pressing into his gut but recoiled when it sparked.

Scrond brought the head piece of the staff around and smashed Rella in the face. Rella spun and snarled, surging forward to knock Scrond onto his back.

"You weak little thing! You will see the true horror of what you're facing!" Rella expanded, horrible, sinewy tentacles shooting from his form as he bloated and swelled in the darkened space, filling the room. The tendrils wrapped around Scrond's feet, pulling him towards the churning, chomping mass that was Rella.

"Once I am done with this world, I am going to go back to yours, and I am going to relish the screams of your young as I tear them from their loved ones and ingest them, slowly, at my leisure, leaving the parents to watch in horror knowing they're next!"

Rella stabbed down with a barbed tendril into Scrond's chest, who cried a rasped, painful breath and bit down with resolve.

Scrond gripped the staff and spat his final words along with the inky blood that flooded his mouth. "You will never touch my people again, you filth!"

Mallel grabbed his pistol and fired at the shutter mechanism that Rella had tripped on the windows. They fell open, letting the pale morning light pour into the large room, and Rella flinched with the sudden brightening.

Scrond activated the staff. The prism shone and pulsated as the newly lit room dimmed and the wave energy flowed into the brightening gem, converting into form.

"No!" Rella recoiled from the staff. "You can't!"

The staff ignited.

* * *

The floor below Tara collapsed in bright light, and she, Thomas, and the Night Mother tumbled through.

The assassin lobbing the flaming cocktail at the Brunes was annihilated in a beam of light from above, and the whole hallway crumbled. The Brune siblings fled to the side of the building as the husks fell away and assassins retreated like cockroaches in sudden light.

The stairway lit up brilliantly, the building's structure was shaken, and the husks tearing at Billie tumbled and fell. She reached up and grappled out of the collapsing staircase.

It was as if the whole building collapsed on the lobby stairs, crushing the reinforcing assassins, and the front facade of the building crumpled as well, crushing the fresh horde of husks that had just rushed in to flank Boss and his team.

Boss peeked out from between his fingers. The entrance to the lobby had completely collapsed, with a ramp of rubble spilling out into the ruined street.

"Well, how in the Three Perversities are we going to defend this?" he said.

There were cubes of all colours littered everywhere. Boss had to smack a Hero across the head who was pocketing an amber-coloured one.

"Friendlies!" A small group of Copper Cobble constables entered the rubble ramp. "We were sent by Billie. There are hordes of those creatures massing in the streets; they seemed disoriented but are about to attack."

"Well, get in here and help us construct a barricade!" Boss bellowed.

The Hunt for Rella

The Brune twins clung to the windowsills as the floor stopped shaking.

"Are those cubes?" one Hero asked.

"It was from the staff! Scrond was able to get a shot off," one of the wizards said.

"Damn." Alexander picked up an opaque, ink-black cube from the scattered detritus of rubble and colourful cubes. "This is more money than was in this entire city."

"It was," Eleanor said, standing and dusting herself off.

"We have more enemies coming in from the roof entrance," an Islander pointed out.

Sure enough, a swarm of husks was flowing from the adjacent buildings' roofs and into the Den.

"Symbicate?" Eleanor tapped the wizard device in her ear.

There was a pang of static in response.

"The blast had to absorb wave radiation to work," a wizard explained. "Comms will be down until it can reboot."

"What?" Alexander asked.

"No remote communication for at least an hour," the wizard explained.

"Well, if the husks are swarming, then Rella isn't dead. I have to warn the Symbicate," Eleanor said.

"You go, sister. I will hold this point."

Eleanor hugged him. "I will kill Rella, and that'll give you the edge to survive the horde."

* * *

After the blinding light the world spun for Thomas, and something flittered past him as he tumbled. *Was that Scrond's staff?* he wondered, plummeting through chaos.

After surviving the earth-shattering storm, as things stopped swaying and rumbling, Thomas coughed and heaved the dust from his lungs, trying to take in the situation. In the chaos he had blinked—or fallen—several stories through the Den. The building was still trembling, but it held for now. Each floor had a ruined, central hole from where some mighty blast had shot upwards ... and downwards.

Thomas scanned the smoky, ruined room for threats, and for signs of Tara or the Night Mother—he found none. There were cubes everywhere of different colours, lighting the hazy darkness in a dim and disjointed rainbow. He found himself on the edge of the huge, crumbling hole in the floor on his level and peered into it.

The room one level down through the hole was the ornate sitting room where Mallel and his beleaguered wizards were regrouping after battling Rella. Thomas blinked down to them.

Mallel rounded with his gun up at his arrival, his teeth bared in aggression.

"What happened?" Thomas asked.

Mallel held his pistol up, pointing the prism in its barrel away from Thomas, and he knelt by Scrond's body, burned and with a barb embedded in his chest. He placed Scrond's hands over his chest with reverence. "Scrond got the shot off, but he missed. His staff must have flown away, being so close to the cataclysm."

"Captain, husks are massing on the far rooftop," a wizard reported, his eyes never leaving Scrond's body.

"Destroy that bridge, and hold this point; we need time to find the Rel," Mallel ordered.

"Captain." The wizard saluted and turned with the others to obey Mallel's orders.

Mallel turned to Thomas. "You and I must continue the hunt alone."

"But Tara, I lost Tara," Thomas said.

"We can't help her unless we can weaken the Rel's grasp on the city. Come, Hero, we have work to do."

* * *

Billie stumbled through the debris-littered floor, fumbling over bodies, jumping at shadows, and avoiding the crumbling hole in the middle of the building. Clumps of ruin still fell from higher parts of the structure in lumps and clouds, through the gaping central hole that penetrated all the way to the bottom floors.

Billie jumped when one of the bodies shifted, grey matter falling from it like sand.

"Tara?"

"Where is she!" Tara shot up wide awake, knives in hand.

"Who?"

"The Night Mother, she had Thomas!"

"And I will have him again." The Night Mother appeared before them both. She was silhouetted in the beams of light from the broken windows, each ray suspended in the dust, choking the air. "Ah, here I find both of my treacherous daughters. I will make you both pay, together."

Tara and Billie braced against each other; they were both wounded, but so was Mother. Half of her face was burnt, and the edges of her corporeal form were constantly flowing like black fire, dissipating into shadow-form and then oblivion. She was losing control of her symbioid.

"She isn't in good sorts," Billie said. "We can take her."

Tara laughed. "We aren't in good sorts either."

"A good match then." Billie steadied Tara and let go, flexing and un-flexing her grapple hook latches as if clenching and unclenching her fists.

"Ah, that's sweet, Billie," the Night Mother said as she strode forward, gliding through the debris as if it wasn't there. "I thought I had wrung the sweetness from you." She readied her knives and Tara did the same. "Now I'll wring your guts from your writhing body!"

She shifted, differently this time, her form not dissipating like it had so many other times before. Instead it kept hold of its central mass as she charged forward, and Billie and Tara dove out of the way.

The Night Mother reconstituted and caught herself, panting. She snarled in a rage and leaped forward again. As Tara and Billie leaped out of the way, falling back under her onslaught, they flung knives and bombs to slow her down.

With each attack the Night Mother would shadow-form a portion of her body to avoid harm, but the edges of the shifting shadow were caught, diced, and burned ever more with each slightly less effective evasion.

Billie grappled her hooks into an overturned desk and swung it at the Night Mother, who shifted through it as Tara charged forward and skidded into a feet-first dive at the Night Mother's legs.

Tara struck corporeal feet, and the Night Mother cried out and tumbled forward. Instead of rolling over her shoulder—like another assassin would have—she shifted across the ground in shadow-form and came out in a crouch. Billie grappled the collapsing ceiling above and yanked hard, pulling crumbling stone down upon the Night Mother as she struggled to right herself. Tara rose cautiously, watching the pile of rubble intently, and Billie circled around to stand beside her.

"Did we just get her?" Billie panted.

"I didn't think it would be as easy as that," Tara answered, scanning the shadowy recesses of the broken floor.

"It wasn't!" The Night Mother dropped from the ceiling in a cloud of black smoke and attacked.

Tara swiped through her bosom with her blade and hit nothing but shadow, while Billie stabbed with a throwing knife. She grabbed Billie's wrist and Tara's neck, expanding her limbs in shadow-form to grapple and lock the two young assassins in place. She was strong, and despite how much Billie resisted, the Night Mother inched her captured blade hand closer to Tara's heart.

"I will have you dispatch this traitor, and then I'll dispatch you!" the Night Mother said through gritted teeth. Sweat poured down her brow as she struggled to maintain her hold over her two resisting daughters.

"You never really had allies," Tara coughed. The tip of Billie's blade began to pierce her jacket and scratch at her flesh. "But we assembled ours, and now you find yourself alone."

"And who will help you out of this predicament, naive child?" The Night Mother laughed through strain.

Billie smirked, clicked down her goggles, and looked out the window, nodding as much as she dared. "His name is Snipes."

There was a crack from outside, and the Night Mother's head exploded. Her shadow-form condensed into a corporeal, lifeless body which slumped to the ground alongside Billie and Tara in a heap. Billie dragged herself up and gave a thumbs-up through the window.

From his position on the opposite rooftop, Snipes gave a thumbs-up back, then punched out a husk who had clambered up over the edge of his building. They were massing on the street and climbing over each other to get to him.

"Whatever you're going to do, Goggles," Snipes said, "do it fast."

* * *

Thomas and Mallel picked their way carefully through a crumbling hallway, lit dimly by the multicoloured cubes scattered about the place. The door in the side opened and they brought up their blades in readiness as Eleanor rushed through, ready for war.

"Eleanor!" Thomas sagged and they embraced one another. "I'm guessing you haven't seen Rella either?"

"You must have—you look awful," she replied.

"No, I ran into the Night Mother again. Lost sight of Tara when the staff went off. You haven't seen Tara, have you?" Thomas said.

"No, I left Alexander to defend from the horde bashing down our entry point."

"I left my men to defend the other one. We can only hope that the *Boss* is doing his part in the lobby," Mallel said.

"He'll get the job done. We need to focus on ours," Thomas retorted.

"Where is the High Wizard?" Eleanor asked. "We'll need him to finish Rella, won't we?"

"He gave his last breath to vanquish the beast," Mallel said stoically. "Sadly it only seemed to delay our defeat."

"Then we need his staff," Eleanor said, "... I mean, I'm sorry for your loss."

"We can mourn after we have vanquished the cosmic consuming horror," Mallel said.

"The staff," Thomas said, "I could have sworn I saw it as I fell from the top floor."

A grappling hook shot up from the hole in the floor ahead of them. Billie spooled herself up with Tara under her arm.

"Billie, Tara!" Thomas said. "I lost track of the Night Mother."

"She's dead, thanks to Snipes," Billie said, giving Thomas a pointed look at his mixed expression.

"Well ... I shall have to thank him ..." Thomas said.

"You won't get your chance." Rella's voice came from everywhere and nowhere. "So you lot don't have your *High Wizard* anymore!" He laughed. "You don't have his staff, your allies are on the brink of being overwhelmed, and the surviving mortals that I hate most are assembled together in this one place. What have I done for the universe to reward me so?"

"The universe has just laid us out as bait, you rat. The spring is wound and ready to snap the trap closed, snapping your neck," Tara responded.

The five warriors stood in a circle facing outwards.

"Keep your eyes up too," Mallel warned.

"Ah, Tara, you put me through so much pain. I will return the favour, don't you worry. And Thomas, I thought we were friends. But you do seem to kill friends often though, don't you?"

"Enough with the mind games, Rella," Thomas shouted. "It's time we grew up and settled this like men ... well, like beings."

"If you insist." Rella dropped from the ceiling down the hall, on the other side of the hole from the New Symbicate.

They set themselves into a staggered formation, arraying against him.

"You didn't fare too well in that blast, did you?" Tara laughed. "And neither did your allies. Perhaps we shall have our fun with you?"

Rella hobbled forward, most of his body charred—more so than from the Light Wizards' barrage back on the beach—using his umbrella as a cane while his frayed moustache sizzled like a caricature of misfortune. His top hat was blown open at the top, and his fine clothes were in rags.

"As perceptive as ever, Tara. That's why it was you who turned the Symbicate's device against me and not the tinkerer's son, hah! But not perceptive enough. Before me are ..." he counted them with a mangled index finger, "Thomas's Blink, Eleanor's sword-shield, and Billie's grapple hooks and goggles. That's four symbioids I can easily take over. I can make your friends tear you apart, Tara." He noticed Thomas shift in front of Eleanor and chuckled. "I could make you tear your lover apart, Thomas. Would that be a step up from killing a friend?"

Thomas's grip tightened into white knuckles around his blade hilt.

"And you, Mallel ..." Rella continued. "It is a bit more difficult for me to infect a non-woven. I'd have to weave a fragment of myself into you, which takes a bit more effort. But imagine if I sent you, and you alone, to infect your whole world all over again? Now your mind might die before you get there, like the poor butler's did before he had a chance for his revenge against Thomas. But that is a die I am willing to cast if it means I have a chance to inflict pain onto you!"

"So cast it already, and rid us of your inane chattering," Tara said, squaring up. "I'm ready for a fight."

Thomas blinked away.

The New Symbicate and Rella looked around for him to appear in combat, but he didn't show.

"Your fearless leader wasn't even ready for a fight." Rella laughed. "But very well." Rella dropped his umbrella and flung his limbs out.

The first tendril to fly from his arm sailed for Eleanor's sword-shield. It twitched and fell from her hands, clattering down the hole to the levels far below as Rella's influence took over it. Eleanor fell back in shock with Mallel as the next tendril shot for Billie.

Without hesitation, Tara dove in front of her.

The tendril embedded deep into her chest, and she grunted.

"Ah, the luck symbioid," Rella said. "What a treat, I thought it slinked away in Masonville when you killed its previous owner; it must have slinked into you. How do you kill a man with all the luck in the world, Tara? How did you do that and still manage to end up in a predicament such as this?"

Tara writhed as the tendrils spread throughout her body, the luck symbioid twisting and succumbing within minutes, and confusion turned to realisation as she pieced her life together. She had told the symbioid not to weave with her back in Masonville, she turned from it, and it seemed to disappear ... it must have disregarded her advice.

Every folly she made since then, stumbling through the battle at the Establishment in Quartrant, fumbling through the fight with the Needle Gang and the Body Changers, surviving Crankod by bumbling into Regen, then Frogman and happening upon the Heroes as they were heading where she *needed* to go.

All the stupid clumsiness and bumbling that caused that arrow, or that bullet to miss her by the barest of margins.

She'd had luck on her side this entire time, accompanied by that friendly tingling in her spine to prompt her actions.

And now it was being stripped from her.

"Now you will REALLY be a monster, Tara!" Rella screamed in glee.

His weeding influence defiled her throughout her whole body. She writhed in revulsion and pain as his tendrils made for her spine and shot up her brain stem. She waited for the influence to take her mind as well, but it met something, some odd resistance, and Rella stumbled back in fright.

The tingling returned in force, meeting Rella's tendrils and pushing them back. This time the tingling felt almost smug.

"No!" Rella screamed, high pitched and panicking. "It's not possible! I destroyed it! You can't have that symbioid too!"

With excruciating pain he ripped his tendrils from her, and she screamed as he retreated from every fibre of her body, her muscles, bones, and nerves. He retreated from the symbioid she didn't even know was woven into her being. She collapsed onto her knees, scratching at her skin, as she could still feel his presence inside her. She screamed and wailed.

Rella recoiled and readied himself to attack.

"I'll kill you before you can use that *thing* on me!" He charged forward.

Mallel, Eleanor, and Billie readied to fight him off when Thomas blinked before them all, staff in hand.

"Staff!" he cried foolishly.

Rella squealed and recoiled again. He fled, diving through the hole in the building before them.

Thomas turned with the sheepish grin on his face disappearing. "I thought I saw this fly past me ... Tara?"

"Dammit! Cogrust! Dammit!" Tara struck the ground. "He was inside me! Twisting it against me! I told that luck symbioid I wasn't worthy of it! Why did it weave with me? It got Regen killed! He wouldn't be there at Crankod unless it was of lucky benefit to me!" Tara shot up to her feet.

"There was something else," Mallel said, his pistol levelled at Tara's face. "He said there was something else, something he feared. He ..." he lowered his pistol. "It stopped him from even trying to possess you."

"It's because I'm the thing you should have feared in this world, Captain." Tara stood over the hole, gazing down to the black nothingness levels and levels below, the tingling rising in her spine. "And I am going to finish this. I'm the only one he can't infect, for whatever reason. It has to be me."

"Tara, you don't know what's down there," Thomas said.

"I know that luck is on my side. I know that if you fight alongside me, you are more likely to die than I. I will fight him myself."

"I won't let you go alone," Mallel said, surprising even himself.

Tara turned on him. "Mallel, this is all my fault. The luck symbioid wove with me, unknown to me. Everyone who has died while I lived, died because the luck symbioid deemed it so. Regen ... if I didn't have luck on my side, he wouldn't have even been in Crankod to save me; he would still be alive. It's my fault. I didn't even try to control it because I was too stubborn to realise something was up. Every lucky encounter, every near miss, it was all me, at the detriment to others!"

"But Tara ..." Billie said.

"Fret not, sister." She turned from them and looked down the drop. "I am no one; I have no name to fall back on like you. You are the ones worth protecting, not me. I am a trained killer, a monster. And it takes a monster to kill a monster." She snatched the staff from Thomas's hands and leaped down the hole, fearless in the knowledge that she would land safely.

The voices of her companions calling out after her vanished as she fell from them. The floors strobed past her, buffeting her with currents of wind and the cacophony of embroiled battles raging across the building until she plunged through the ground floors and into the sewers below.

Her lucky tingling spiked, and she landed softly, splashing into a churning whirl of water which slowed her descent.

The chilling waters engulfed her, revitalising her as she touched off the bottom and pushed up for a gasp of air. She prepared herself for the horrid stench of sewage but found none. The blast from Scrond's staff had broken open a water main and was now flooding the area; she was swimming in clean water.

She climbed up the clumping debris by the edge of the waterway and found herself in a maze of tunnels and canals reminiscent of the Buttress Quarter in Masonville. She trusted the tingling down her spine and walked down a gas lamp-lit hallway through the tunnels, finally entering a wide, open space below the streets with grates up above, casting the cool light from the day into the redbrick depths below.

She knew this place well, one of the many pathways through the city so that the assassins could traverse it undetected. She had been discovered by the assassins down here, a lone orphan, shivering and seeking shelter. They took her in, and now she was back to fight the ultimate evil.

"How did you find me here, girl?" Rella emerged from the shadows on the far side, limping and brimming with rage.

"I'm lucky." She grinned coolly.

Rella shuffled from foot to foot.

"Are you … nervous?" she asked, bewildered.

"You have more than the luck symbioid woven into you. When you clamped the Symbicate's device onto me in Masonville—your first unwitting use of luck—a portion of the symbioid that powered the device must have woven into you. When the butler freed me, I stamped it out. I did think it seemed lesser than it should. I cannot possess you, as the symbioid will contort and drive me out. But you don't seem to know how to consciously use it. So I am safe from you whittling me down. I can still kill you the old-fashioned way," Rella said.

Rella's tendril shot out and struck a gas main, and the gas lamp lights of the tunnel flickered out. Then a horde of the husks ambled over the grating above, darkening the area entirely. Tara could just make out Rella's form, his monocle glinting as he took it off his face and clipped it to his ruined top hat to be out of the way.

"So what are you waiting for?" Tara asked. "Have your thousands of abominations tear me to shreds—vengeance like you promised." She hefted the staff. "Are you waiting because I will destroy you all regardless?"

Rella laughed. "You need light for that to work, and my minions are busy tearing your companions apart, or drowning out the light above. No, sweet Tara, I will kill you myself."

Tara glanced at the staff in her hands—her eyes adjusting in the dimness—shivering as she clamped down on the ignition switch with numb fingers. The prism in the top of the staff pulsed wanly, and the mechanisms around it whirred but failed to spin completely. She tried and failed to fire the weapon again, and again.

Rella's cackling filled the room. "Now, Tara, I will release you from your pained life." He leaped high and arched over to her position.

Out of reflex, she dropped a smoke bomb and rolled back away from his strike. His foot came down hard and cracked the brick floor where she had been standing. In riposte she lunged forward and wielded the light staff—the sacred, most advanced weapon of an alien civilisation—like a club, and clobbered Rella in the face. He fell back and she advanced through the smoke, clobbering him again, spinning to hook-kick him in the jaw; then she leaped herself and fly-kicked him in the face.

He hit the ground hard and extended sinewy tendrils from his legs. They wrapped around Tara's legs, and he wrenched her across the room, throwing her against the far wall. The impact knocked her senseless as she collapsed like a sack of bricks.

The husks above the grating were wailing as if cheering on the fight. Tara clenched her hands against the ground and coughed—winded—and attempted to rise. She took her first full breath of air, which she choked on.

A tingling travelled down her spine.

She hoisted herself up, using the piping on the wall as support, and coughed again, harder this time. *That isn't from being winded.* The tingling intensified at the thought. She inspected the wall-mounted pipe she was grasping for support, the damaged gas pipe that Rella punctured to starve the lights of fuel.

The tingling of the luck symbioid made sense to her, and now she knew how to act on it.

Where is the staff?

Rella shoulder-charged her into the wall. Her head banged against the busted pipe with a dull, hollow tone. He slashed at her back with hands which were sprouting tongues of barbed sinew. They ripped through her coat straight to her skin and bone. She cried in pain and kicked back. Rella grabbed her leg and struck down at her knee.

At the last second she pivoted her leg so the back of her knee faced the blow, and it bent with the impact. The force of the blow was so immense her tendons burned with tears despite her quick defensive reaction, but the knee held firm. The jolt brought her closer to him, and she slashed at Rella's eyes with a throwing knife. He recoiled and she pressed her advantage, raking at the burned flesh on his face.

With a snarl he struck back with a savage backhand—sending the knife flying from her grip—and grabbed her by the throat. He lifted her from the ground with one hand and struck her twice in the gut as he tightened his grip around her windpipe. He slammed her against the wall, once, twice, and then threw her across the open space to skitter across the ground like a rag doll.

She found herself struggling to breathe again, rasping a squeak through an inflamed, bruised throat and triply winded organs. The cheering wail of the husks grew in her ears as she crawled and tried to stand.

"It seems that the luck symbioid does not favour you as much; perhaps it knows that you really are a monster," Rella boasted, striding forward.

Tara tripped over something and tumbled all over again.

Rella stopped and laughed. "The bumbling assassin, the dull knife in the night. Not even with all the gifts this sun well has to offer can you even stand on your own two feet. You may as well give up. You don't deserve to win, you don't deserve to live. You should know by now that good things don't last, if you ever had anything good worth fighting for to begin with. Everyone you strive to protect will die. They will all perish."

"Good things may not last. I may not last." Tara gasped through pain and stood again, gripping what had tripped her up—the staff—and turned to face Rella. She pulled down Eric's scarf from her face and spat blood on the floor. "But my new family is beyond good, and the New Symbicate will last."

"Are you going to clobber me with that again, assassin?" Rella teased.

"No." Tara pulled out her last throwing knife and lobbed it at Rella.

He dodged it easily, laughing again. "Is that the best you can really do?"

"I wanted to miss." Tara smiled with bloodied teeth as the throwing knife struck the broken gas pipe behind Rella.

She braced, and the gas that was filling the room ignited with the spark of knife against iron. She planted the staff in the ground, gripping the activation mechanism. And she laughed, she laughed at Rella's bewildered face in the explosion, at his sudden realisation of terror as he was engulfed by the bright fire and the warm light it cast about the room.

The mechanism around the prism whirred, cogs turned, and the prism pulsed as the explosion dimmed. The light siphoned into the staff.

Rella tore through the dulling blast wave, the dimming fire and the smoke, reaching for Tara even as he was burned. He was a finger's breadth away from her—screaming, inflamed, and in panic—when she released the massed wave-form energy, powered by the light from the explosion.

A cube that was blacker than darkness flung from the tip of the staff and struck Rella in the chest at point-blank range.

There was a blinding white light, and Tara was flung back as her ears went deaf from the sound of a titanic impact. *Near infinite denseness*, she remembered the wizards saying. *Enough momentum in one small cube to break the moon*, she remembered Thomas saying, as she drifted into unconsciousness.

* * *

She didn't know how much time had passed when she opened her eyes. The ground was littered with scattered cubes, thousands of them. They ranged all the colours of the rainbow, from indigo so pale it looked white to an amber so dark it was black. The fortune of the world, condensed into this little sewer arena.

The roof of the sewer was a large crater in the city, and the snow drifted on gentle winds to caress her face. There were husks everywhere, most burned and dead—the ones caught in the blast wave. But many still lived and milled around the edges of the crater, shuffling uselessly without purpose.

She tried to get up, but struggled to even raise her head.

She still tried to look around though. The broken-open tunnels of the under city were honeycombed around her, and

249

buildings sat at the edge of the crater and swayed dubiously over disaster. The gentle wind blew a tattered umbrella across the chaos, followed by a blown-out top hat, with a monocle clipped to it, scraping along the ground.

That's probably a good sign, Tara thought, slumping back down.

A large, blurred object drifted into view over her, a black mass in the pale sky. A beam of sunlight refracted off it which hurt her eyes and made it hard to focus ... then there was someone next to her, someone friendly. *Had he just appeared there?*

Thomas.

She drifted into unconsciousness again as he lifted her into his arms and blinked somewhere else, somewhere safe and warm. It was something she was sure she did not deserve, but she had no energy to resist.

CHAPTER 20

Tara Night

Tara woke to the horrid taste of dry bile in her mouth, a throbbing headache to accompany her stiff, aching muscles, and a strange, sterile smell. She groaned and tried to rise.

"Hold up," a soothing voice said, and someone wiped at her brow with a damp cloth. "You took quite a bit of ouch from the blast."

"Bit of ouch?" Tara mumbled. She pushed the medic's hand away and swung her legs off the cot, her feet touching the hard ground, which meant—horribly—that she now had to follow through with her stubbornness and stand up.

With a grunt she hefted herself up, and her blurred vision swam with dancing colours.

After a moment of swaying and nausea, her vision cleared enough to make out a concerned bronze face before her, an older Prismath wizard lady with a wrinkled brow and greying hair.

"You are a stubborn one. I hadn't believed the Cap'n when he warned me about you," she said.

"Stubborn and concerned for my friends, Doc," Tara said. "Are they alive?"

The medic sighed, solemnity setting on her face as she straightened herself. "There were quite a few deaths in that battle, from our kind and yours."

"Who?"

"I don't know your people's names, I'm afraid, young dear."

Tara scanned the room, a quaint but lavish cabin with crystalline decorations on the walls and a red carpet over the chrome flooring. There was a large wooden desk pushed into a nook, full of scientific equipment and more of those strange monitor-windows.

"Where are the other wounded?" Tara asked.

"We have a field hospital set up in the cargo hold. Cap'n gave you Scrond's cabin, seeing as you wielded the staff."

Tara expected the High Wizard's room to be packed with scrolls and books and vials and potions. Perhaps that little monitor-window contained all of them? But she knew better— these people were not magical, only advanced.

"I've got to check on my friends." Tara pushed past the medic and exited the cabin into the chrome hallways of the *Motebeam*.

She scratched at the bandages all over her body as she painstakingly pulled on her brown jacket, wrapped Eric's yellow scarf around her neck, and hobbled down the hallway. There had been fighting inside; previously undamaged decor was scarred and stained with a different mix of blue and red blood and flecks of dismembered sinew. She quickened her pace despite the pain and headed for the cargo hold.

It was a buzz of activity; medical cots not only lined the space wall to wall, but spilled out the rampart and onto a park clearing in Copper Cobble. Wounded warriors, constables, and civilians were being tended to by the able *Motebeam* crew with odd, handheld, holo-scanning devices and clear sacks of suspended liquids dripping through tubing into their arms.

Thomas was sitting on one cot, his arm around Eleanor as she wept and a gash on his temple was dressed. Eleanor was clutching at the sword-shield in her lap. It was bloodied and battered and looked different to her own sword-shield.

"You're alive." Billie sidled up to Tara and clicked up her goggles with a flick of her head. "And so are we, thanks to you."

"Billie ..." Tara's eyes welled up. "The doc said we lost people." But Thomas and Eleanor and Billie were alive, and that made her glad ... and that made her hate herself.

Billie nodded sadly, peeling the eye patch from her scarred eye to dab away a stream of tears. "We lost most of the lobby team."

"Boss?"

Billie nodded solemnly. "Frogman survived, said Boss gave a valiant account of himself. Eleanor's brother died ... one of the Baul Islanders who stood with him gave her his sword-shield; they said they would search the lower levels for hers." Billie took a deep breath. "The day has taken its toll."

"Captain Mallel?" Tara asked.

Billie raised an eyebrow. "He leads the relief effort." Billie gestured across the cargo hold. "The husks were nulled by Rella's death. They just started milling around. We have teams making quick work of them as they search for survivors, but we will need to organise a militia to purge them properly. One of the constables I came up with said they received word that the Weznin regulars are even on their way from the lowlands to 'save' us." She laughed. "As soon as there was word of *two* world's supplies of cubes, they actually got their act together."

"What happened to the cubes?" Tara asked.

"Mallel did something with the staff to remove an egregious amount of them. He felt bad destabilising the economy after his people wiped out the moon," Billie said.

Tara nodded, looking across the devastated and the wounded; many were shell shocked and distant. She went to Thomas and Eleanor with Billie on her heels and embraced them. The four cried, holding each other tightly, sharing Eleanor's grief and the elation that they had survived at the same time.

Sometime later, after regaling tales of the battle with each other over broth in the mess—after Snipes and Frogman joined them with the Hired Heroes, the Baul Islanders, and the Quartrant constables who survived—the doors slid open and Mallel walked in with the staff in hand. Votly and two wizard marines flanked him. Bromean—the other wizard technician— lingered in the doorway, scowling in at the meeting.

The table went silent, and Mallel stared them all down, his sweeping gaze pausing on Tara. "Are we enemies?" he finally asked.

Silence ...

"No," Tara finally said, rising. "No we aren't. But there are people on this world who will never forgive you for what you did to Crankod, for what your people did to the moon. I might be one of them."

Mallel nodded. "This is a burden I will bear like all the rest."

"One we will all bear," Votly said. Her airy, squeaky voice was barely a whisper.

"You did kill a fair number of us before the truce was called," Bromean said, stepping in from the doorway.

Mallel glared at him and Bromean recoiled a step. The two marines flanking Mallel exchanged glances.

"We did burn a whole city of theirs to the ground," Mallel growled. "We are going to have to move past their retaliation, as difficult as it is. We would have responded the same way."

Bromean nodded. "Cap'n."

Tara regarded the exchange with churning doubts. "So, what now?"

"Our chief medical officer scanned you, and you are clear of Rella's influence," Mallel said, turning his steely gaze back to her. "Whatever secret symbioid you wove with saved you, saved all of us. And even though there are still hundreds of husks within this city, their nerve centre is gone. The Rel's influence has been expelled from this sun well." Behind him, Votly breathed a sigh of relief. "But the war is not yet over. Other enemies in this fight spread well beyond our shared sun. There are other people out there, other worlds who are in danger from these enemies. The primary task of the *Motebeam* is to seek out these threats and destroy them, before they make their way to our world ... our worlds, again."

Tara bit her lip, and her spine tingled. "And I will go with you."

After a moment of stunned silence, Snipes rose to stand with her. "Me too."

* * *

It was a clear afternoon by the Cliff Bunker at Tinrod. The sky was layered by the red glow of an approaching sunset, the wisps of the shattered moon were on the cusp of shining through the gathering night, and the seas were calm, lapping gently against the grey shore.

The New Symbicate stood before the loading ramp of the *Motebeam*. Over the past few weeks, the wizards—the Prismath—had split their time between providing aid to Copper Cobble, the Island of Bauttuon, and Crankod, and repairing their ship.

Now it was brimming with power. The rusty-hued sails coursed with amber energy that channelled down into the chrome vessel as it hovered above the beach at Tinrod. It was as good as new. Thomas's steam engine had been removed, but they had a version of his taser-rigged caging fitted to the bottom of the hull, being this close to the waters ... just in case.

The loading ramp was embedded in the rocky sand. Eleanor, Thomas, and Billie stood before it as Tara and Snipes readied to depart.

"Say your goodbyes now," Mallel said. "It'll take us weeks to reach the edge of the sun well, but years will pass here on your world. We only left Prismath a month ago, but it has progressed decades from their perspective."

Thomas furrowed his brow at this. The Prismath had explained the science of their wave-form space travel, but it still escaped his understanding. He had bigger things to dwell on right now, however.

Tara looked back from the loading ramp with tears in her eyes and hugged Thomas and Eleanor. "What will you do without me?" she said to them with a sorrowful laugh.

"I am going to set up a tinkering tea shop," Thomas said with a smirk.

"And I'm going to run it with him." Eleanor laced her arms through his, resting her head on his shoulder, her two sword-shields resting on the boulder behind her. "I can hang up my sword-shield now, give Alex's to Mother. My war is done. You take care, Tara." Eleanor leaned in and kissed Tara on the forehead, Thomas did the same.

"I will." Tara squeezed them tight, then moved to stand before Billie. "Besides Thomas, you were the first person I considered true family."

"I know," Billie said, she rushed in and hugged Tara. "And I feel the same about you. Out there you will see and do wondrous things—for good, yet you still berate yourself. Change that story, Tara, face that demon, and allow yourself to become who you were meant to be."

"She's right, Tara. You do have a name besides Night," Thomas said.

Tara chuckled, releasing Billie. "Tara Symbicate doesn't quite roll off the tongue."

They all laughed, but then Thomas answered seriously, "No, you moon rock moron. You thought you were only the Night; you feared that you had no other name to fall back on, like Billie. But you aren't the Night, Tara, you are visible because of the night, in spite of it. You're the light in the darkness. We all faced the horrors of the world, and among all of that you shine out, because you're a star, Tara. No matter how dark it gets, nothing will change what you are. You will always have a family here with us, but you're free to go out there among the celestial lights where you belong and find where you truly shine."

Tara bit back a sob. "Star ..." she tested the name out, "Tara Star."

"It's a fitting name." Billie smiled. Even her blinded eye seemed to sparkle with it. "You were destined for it."

"Thank you, Thomas, for my name." Tara embraced him again and squeezed hard. "And what will you do?" She turned back to Billie.

"There are several power vacuums to fill here. The Night Assassins are gone, the Hired Heroes have been devastated, and with these two retiring," she gestured to Thomas and Billie, "the Symbicate will need to be rebuilt, again. I will reorganise what is left. I will take the Symbicate and create a worldwide organisation. The Hired Heroes will follow me, I can push Frogman to get the Rent-A-Saviours to sign up, and I now have contacts with constables in two municipalities." She laughed. "I'll be just fine, Tara. You go do what you do best."

Sniffling, Tara stood back and waved to the three, and ascended the ramp with Mallel, stopping at the top to turn and wait for Snipes.

Snipes stood by his gun case, watching her go, then turned and held his hand out to Thomas. "Finally we part as friends," he said.

"Well," Thomas took his hand and shook it, "maybe just allies?" They laughed. "Look after Tara for us, please."

"I swear, I'll look out for her." Snipes then bid Eleanor farewell and hugged Billie. "You take care, Goggles."

"You keep your eyes open, David," she said. "Are you sure about this? I could use your help with the Heroes."

"This is my way to take control, Billie, to try and atone to the universe. What better way is there to do that than to go out there and fight evil? Besides, I hear you and Sally, our receptionist, got on swimmingly. She was the real leader behind Hired Heroes." Snipes chuckled. "And this idiot," he gestured to Thomas, "and Eleanor will still be around to help when you need. So long." He pulled back from Billie and followed Tara up the ramp.

The ramp cranked upwards, and Tara, Billie, Thomas, and Eleanor watched each other with tear-filled eyes until it was finally closed. The *Motebeam* rose into the sky as the setting red sun reflected off the chrome hull.

Within minutes it was sailing out of the atmosphere, passing through the shattered moon, gliding through the pale-green luminescence of the celestial dust tendrils, and jettisoning out into the deep, dark void.

"Wave-form acceleration will begin shortly, Captain," Votly informed them as he entered the bridge with Tara and Snipes in tow. "We have confirmed the strange readings at the edge of the sun well are not due to instrument failure, and by your orders we have plotted a course to investigate." She handed Mallel two cards.

Mallel took the cards and turned to hand them to Tara and Snipes. "Scrond was always better at this," he paused, "with people ... but we now officially welcome you to the *Motebeam*." His serious, deep voice broke with mirth for just a moment. "Or as our esteemed Votly here calls it, the *Dustmote*." Behind him, Votly blushed and looked back to her displays. "These are key cards to your quarters, David McGreck, Tara Night. If there is anything you need before we engage the wave-form engine, just let me know."

"Just call me Snipes," Snipes insisted.

"Star," Tara said. "My name is Tara Star."

"Snipes." Mallel nodded, and gazed at Tara. "Miss Star."

"Wave-form engaging, Captain," Bromean grumbled from his console.

"Now what?" Tara asked as the ship's humming intensified and the walls started to shimmer with cascading, rainbow light.

"Now," Mallel smiled, "we sail across space."

A note from the author

Thanks for reading The Symbicate 2!

Your review would make my day! An honest review on Amazon or Goodreads helps other readers find this story, and keeps me writing books for amazing readers like you.

Want more?

Continue the story in "The Symbicate 3: The Beast In The Void" available now!

This is a finished four book series.

Visit <u>SEANMTS.COM</u> to:

Get a free eBook (and audio stories) when
you join the community newsletter
Read free short stories and articles
Discover more books you might love

Stay in contact on Instagram: @seanmtshanahan
Email: sean@seanmts.com
If you enjoyed this series, you will love my other books. You can find an up to date list on my site.

Thanks again.
Take care,
Sean

About the Author

Sean M. T. Shanahan is a Science Fiction and Fantasy author from Sydney, Australia. He is known for writing emotionally gripping, high-stakes stories that blend dynamic characters with intriguing concepts and take you through darkness into the light.

He has a lifelong passion for storytelling, and since publishing his first book in 2021 has produced multiple books that span Fantasy, Steampunk, Sci-Fi, and children's fiction.

Drawing inspiration from history, science, mythology, and adventure, he weaves immersive tales that will pull you in from the start and leave you wanting more.

Besides reading and writing, Sean enjoys nature, gaming, parkour, endurance sports, and making terrible jokes.